DARK STRANGER
REVEALED

THE CHILDREN OF THE GODS BOOK 2

I. T. LUCAS

ALSO BY I. T. LUCAS

THE CHILDREN OF THE GODS ORIGINS

1: GODDESS'S CHOICE

2: GODDESS'S HOPE

THE CHILDREN OF THE GODS

DARK STRANGER

1: DARK STRANGER THE DREAM

2: DARK STRANGER REVEALED

3: DARK STRANGER IMMORTAL

DARK ENEMY

4: DARK ENEMY TAKEN

5: DARK ENEMY CAPTIVE

6: DARK ENEMY REDEEMED

KRI & MICHAEL'S STORY

6.5: MY DARK AMAZON

DARK WARRIOR

7: DARK WARRIOR MINE

8: DARK WARRIOR'S PROMISE

9: DARK WARRIOR'S DESTINY

10: DARK WARRIOR'S LEGACY

DARK GUARDIAN

11: DARK GUARDIAN FOUND

12: DARK GUARDIAN CRAVED

13: DARK GUARDIAN'S MATE

DARK ANGEL

14: Dark Angel's Obsession

15: Dark Angel's Seduction

16: Dark Angel's Surrender

Dark Operative

17: Dark Operative: A Shadow of Death

18: Dark Operative: A Glimmer of Hope

19: Dark Operative: The Dawn of Love

Dark Survivor

20: Dark Survivor Awakened

21: Dark Survivor Echoes of Love

22: Dark Survivor Reunited

Dark Widow

23: Dark Widow's Secret

24: Dark Widow's Curse

25: Dark Widow's Blessing

Dark Dream

26: Dark Dream's Temptation

27: Dark Dream's Unraveling

28: Dark Dream's Trap

Dark Prince

29: Dark Prince's Enigma

30: Dark Prince's Dilemma

31: Dark Prince's Agenda

Dark Queen

32: Dark Queen's Quest

33: Dark Queen's Knight

34: Dark Queen's Army

Dark Spy

35: Dark Spy Conscripted

36: Dark Spy's Mission

37: Dark Spy's Resolution

DARK OVERLORD

38: Dark Overlord New Horizon

39: Dark Overlord's Wife

PERFECT MATCH

Perfect Match 1: Vampire's Consort

Perfect Match 2: King's Chosen

Perfect Match 3: Captain's Conquest

SETS

The Children of the Gods books 1-3: Dark Stranger trilogy —Includes a bonus short story: **The Fates take a Vacation**

The Children of the Gods: Books 1-6—includes character lists

The Children of the Gods: Books 6.5-10—includes character lists

TRY THE CHILDREN OF THE GODS SERIES ON

AUDIBLE

2 FREE audiobooks with your new Audible subscription!

———————

NOTE FROM THE AUTHOR:

This is a work of fiction!

Names, characters, places and incidents are products of the author's
imagination or are used fictitiously and are not to be construed as real.
Any similarity to actual persons, organizations and/or events is purely
coincidental.

SYSSI

"*Wow*, that was one hell of a kiss," Syssi breathed. More like a total meltdown.

She was grateful for the call that had interrupted what might have ended in Kian's bedroom. It had broken the spell. If not for the emergency that had required Kian's immediate attention, she would've let him take her to his bed and would've regretted it dearly.

Even though she was no longer mad at him, Syssi still refused to become another notch on his belt. She held herself to higher standards.

Oh, God, she wished she didn't.

Relinquishing her outdated standards for a morning of passion with Kian would've been worth the sacrifice. The fire he'd ignited in her was like nothing she'd ever experienced before and she craved more, wanted to explore it and find out where it led.

Still hot and bothered, she wondered how long he'd be gone. It depended on what kind of emergency it was. Must've been something major to bother the CEO on a

Sunday morning. Unless he'd used it as an excuse to leave and cool down.

For some reason, Kian was fighting his attraction to her.

Did he deem her beneath him?

It wasn't as if he was some kind of an aristocrat while she was a pleb. The only things that defined social strata in the United States were money and political connections. Granted, she had none, but Kian didn't strike her as a snob. Maybe it had something to do with her working for his sister. He might have regarded a relationship between them inappropriate because of his financial connections to the lab. According to Amanda, her research was funded by one of the corporations owned by their family.

Syssi shook her head and gathered the dirty dishes left over from their brunch. Guessing would bring her nothing other than a headache. She would have to grow a set and ask Kian what was his deal.

God, what a big mess her simple life had become.

As she carried the dishes to the kitchen and got busy at the sink, Syssi reflected on the recent upheaval in her orderly routine. In the span of less than twenty-four hours, she had been chased by a group of dangerous zealots, spellbound by her boss's gorgeous brother, and hypnotized by him to forget all about it, including meeting him, only to have Kian star in her most erotic dreams ever.

In the light of day, however, the real Kian was better than any dream, and to be wanted by a man like him was one hell of a heady feeling.

If she was wanted, that is.

The man was a puzzle she couldn't decipher, a mystery. Not a problem she'd encountered often. Most people were transparent to her, their motives clear.

2

That fact in itself was cause for alarm, and then there was her insane response to Kian.

Syssi didn't know what to make of that. Yes, he was gorgeous, intelligent and successful, but that shouldn't have been enough to induce such a profound transformation in her.

The woman who had thought of herself as not all that sexual had been turned into a mindless puddle of need. And even more shockingly, it seemed that her newfound passion had a somewhat kinky twist to it.

Who would have thought?

Embarrassed, Syssi felt her face heating and attacked the dishes with renewed vigor, soaping and scrubbing the already clean plates.

"Please, mistress, let me." Gently but firmly, the butler took the plate she was washing out of her hands, then led her away from the sink.

"I'm sorry, I just thought to make myself useful." The poor guy probably thinks I'm after his job. "I'm not the kind of guest who needs to be waited on. I like to help."

"Oh, but madame, it is my distinct pleasure to serve you. You would not wish to deprive an old man of his pride and joy now, would you?" He smiled his weird mannequin smile.

Manipulative butler.

"Well, of course not..." And although it was hard to tell, she hazarded a guess that he was in his early forties—hardly an old man. "But please, call me Syssi."

Okidu squared his shoulders. "I certainly will not." He affected indignation with a heavy British accent. "Let me show you the guest rooms, madame." He dipped his head, and extending his arm motioned for her to precede him down the corridor.

There were four luxurious bedroom suites in addition to Kian's and the butler's, each decorated in its own unique color scheme and style.

Syssi chose the smallest of the four, snorting as she was reminded of Goldilocks in the Three Bears' House.

"May I unpack your luggage, mistress?" Okidu asked as he brought her duffle bag inside the walk-in closet.

"No, thank you. I'll do it myself."

"As you wish, madame." He bowed, then eased out of the room, gently closing the door behind him.

Syssi emptied her bag, fitting the few things she had brought with her all on one shelf, then moved on to the bathroom to deposit the Ziplock bag containing her toiletries and makeup on the vanity.

Eyeing the large jacuzzi tub nestled within an intimate enclave, with a big window overlooking the cityscape, she was tempted to try it out. Which reminded her that there was a lovely lap pool out on the terrace, and it would be a damn shame if she didn't take advantage of it while staying at Kian's amazing penthouse. The tub could wait for later.

Problem was, she didn't bring a swimming suit. Syssi was about to give up on the idea when a simple solution popped in her mind. In a pinch, a solid black bra and matching undies could pass for a bikini.

Still, on the remote chance that Okidu was more astute than most men and would guess it was underwear, Syssi wrapped a large towel around her makeshift swim attire.

The sun was warm on her skin as she stepped onto the terrace. Hopefully, the pool was heated and the water was warm as well. Dipping her toes, she was happy to discover that it was and jumped in. The pool felt heavenly, soothing away the remaining vestiges of her anxiety as she swam slow, lazy laps then rolled over onto her back and floated.

Sweeping her hands in circles to keep herself afloat, Syssi closed her eyes in bliss. It was like vacationing in some luxury resort, and to make the experience complete, Okidu even served her a piña colada smoothie, poolside.

Perfect.

Well, almost. Kian wasn't there, and she missed him.

A warm feeling suffused her. She really liked the big, arrogant oaf. He'd blundered badly, behaving like an ass, but any guy that was man enough to apologize and take responsibility for his mishaps, as well and as sincerely as Kian had done, was okay in her book. And anyway, the way the man got her heart pumping, she wasn't sure she wouldn't have forgiven him even if he had not.

Yep, I'm definitely turning into a horny, brainless floozy, she chided herself as she finished the last of the smoothie with a loud slurp.

Leaving the empty goblet by her towel, she glided into the center of the pool, turned on her back again, and paddled leisurely with her eyes closed.

"Hi, gorgeous!" Amanda startled her.

Splattering and splashing to right herself, Syssi soaked Amanda, who was squatting by the side of the pool and smiling like a Cheshire cat. Served Amanda right for sneaking up on her like that. "Hi, yourself, I completely forgot you're next door." Syssi wiped her eyes. "Wait a minute, you told me you have a condo in Santa Monica. When did you move here?" she asked, twisting her hair to wring it out.

Amanda brushed water droplets off her jean-clad legs and got up. "Oh no, this is just temporary. I definitely did not move in here, although Kian keeps nagging me to. I love him, but living right under his nose would be a really bad idea. Anyhow, he keeps it ready for me in case I change my mind, and with those crazy fanatics on the loose, I decided to humor him." She winked.

"Kian told me what happened at the lab. I would've called you, but he threw away my cell phone, and I didn't remember your number. How are you holding up?" She could've asked Kian, but it hadn't even crossed her mind. She'd forgotten all about Amanda. Apparently, with him around, her hormone level skyrocketed, affecting her brain's ability to function properly.

"I'm fine. The whole thing will blow over in a few days, and by then the lab will be as good as new. I've already arranged for cleanup and for new equipment to be delivered. The only task remaining is repainting the walls and maintenance is on it."

"Have you given any thought to how we're going to continue the research until the lab is ready? I think you're overly optimistic assuming all of this can be done so quickly. I'd give it at least two weeks, if not longer." Syssi got out and wrapped herself in the large towel.

"We can do some of the work from here, going over the data we already have, maybe even start a new paper. Don't worry, I'll make sure you earn your pay. It won't be all swimming and lazing around... Just most of it." Amanda snorted as she plopped down on one of the lounges.

"What about Hannah and David, are you planning on bringing them here as well?" Wrapping the towel tighter against the cool breeze, Syssi sat down next to Amanda.

"Heavens, no! I called Professor Goodbow and explained the situation. He promised he'd find them something to do until this mess is cleared. And anyway, Kian doesn't allow strangers up here. Top floors are for family only."

"I'm not family..."

"Yeah, but you're special. Besides being the lunatics' top target, I think my stubborn brother finally capitulated and went after you. Am I right? I hope I'm right. Tell me I'm right!"

Syssi's cheeks heated. What the hell had Amanda done? Had she been talking with Kian about her and he had not been interested? That would explain a lot. Like his reluctance to engage with her.

Damn.

"What do you mean—finally capitulated?"

"Yeah, I know. It's just that I wanted to get the two of you together for some time, but Kian being Kian refused all of my matchmaking efforts. So I didn't tell you anything because what was the point? Right? But now that the fool finally met you, he likes you, as I told him he would. I'm going to have such a blast saying 'I told you so.' You guys are perfect together." Amanda smirked, all smug satisfaction over the success of her yenta schemes, or perhaps over the prospect of endlessly needling Kian.

Amanda pushed up from the lounger and stretched her long body, the bottom of her T-shirt still damp and clinging to her skin. "I'm going back to my place across the hall. If you need anything, you know where to find me." She bent down and gave Syssi a warm hug. "I'm really glad you're here, Syssi. Kian needs someone to take care of him. And being the loving sister that I am, I found him the perfect someone." Amanda kissed Syssi's cheek.

Surprised and touched, Syssi hugged and kissed her back. Knowing Amanda liked her was one thing, but this was above and beyond. "Thank you. It really means a lot, you thinking so highly of me. But Kian and I have just met, and I don't know if anything will come of it. He is... well, you know... he is really handsome... obstinate... controlling... endearing..." Syssi laughed as Amanda rolled her eyes and made the go-on gesture with her hand. "And he seems to like me, but we don't really know each other, so don't plan the wedding just yet. Okay?" she said, meaning it as a joke.

"I've got a good feeling about this, girl, and I hate being disappointed." Amanda poked a warning finger at Syssi's chest before turning to go inside.

Syssi shook her head. Bossy family.

Lying down on the lounger Amanda had vacated, she turned on her stomach and cradled her face in her arms. Tired from the day's excitement, the sun pleasantly warm on her back, she grew drowsy and closed her eyes.

"Mistress," Okidu said. "I brought you supper in case you were peckish."

Slowly, Syssi opened her eyes. There was a thick robe draped over her back, which explained why she felt so warm and toasty even though it was getting late.

It was so nice of the butler to cover her. With the two of them alone in the place, it couldn't have been anyone other than Okidu. "Thank you for the robe. It was very kind of you."

She slipped her arms into the overlong sleeves and looped the belt twice around her waist, then brought the lapels closer to her cheeks. Kian's scent was all over the thing. Combined with the warmth of the thick terry fabric, it cocooned her in what felt like home—safe, hers. Syssi closed her eyes. She missed him, and his absence felt as if there was a hole in her heart.

Which was nuts.

"You are welcome, mistress. It was getting chilly, and I

did not want to wake you. You looked so peaceful. But it is late, and the master would not have been happy if I failed to provide you with nourishment. Would you like to dine outside? Or should I take the tray inside?"

By now, it was indeed a little cold out on the terrace, but recalling yesterday's sunset, she wanted to watch it again. "Here would be great, thank you."

Syssi ate her dinner at the small bistro table, watching the clouds turn all shades of orange, red, and purple until they faded into darkness by the time she was done.

She couldn't help feeling a bit disappointed that Kian had not returned in time to join her for dinner, and as she carried the tray to the kitchen, she wondered what was keeping him. He had been gone for hours. But then, he obviously couldn't just drop everything to be with her. Hopefully, he wasn't staying away because he didn't want her company.

A disturbing thought. But she couldn't allow herself to think like that.

Amanda had told her about Kian's insane workload and long hours, and so had he. Evidently they had not been exaggerating.

The little Syssi knew about Kian she had learned from Amanda's complaints about how difficult it was to get him to come see her teach because he was always working, busy running the family business. He'd mentioned real estate and a military grade drone factory that he was in the process of buying—two completely unrelated businesses. Supposedly, Kian was running an international conglomerate, which meant that there were many more.

She should Google it. Maybe she could find out more about their financial empire. One thing was clear, though, big money was involved, on a scale that was hard for her to grasp even though she'd minored in business. Later, she could ask Kian about it. It was a safe topic, far removed from carnal thoughts.

But right now, a Jacuzzi tub with her name on it was waiting.

DALHU

*D*alhu paced the length of the mansion's opulent home office, contemplating his newfound knowledge. The professor's little red notebook had been an eye-opener on so many levels.

With a light knock, the old cook pushed the door open. "Your tea, sir," she said and shuffled in, holding a tray in her trembling hands. On her first day, Dalhu had thought the tremor was caused by fear. After all, cooking for twelve large warriors wasn't something the woman was used to. But after she'd served them three meals that day, with her old gnarled hands trembling no more and no less, he'd realized it was just age.

Dalhu took the tray from her, afraid she would spill the hot tea on her large bosom. The last thing he needed was a trip to the hospital. The woman was in her seventies—there was no way any of his men could produce venom to heal her with a bite. "Thank you, Miriam."

"Would you like something to eat, sir?" she asked. "I can make a special treat just for you." At least once a day, she would offer to pamper him with something special, and each time he would refuse. For someone her age, she already worked too hard.

"No, thank you. That will be all, Miriam." She looked disappointed, but he wasn't particular about his food and was fine eating whatever she made for the men.

When she left, he closed the door behind her and resumed his pacing.

It had taken him a while to decipher the professor's illegible handwriting and cryptic references, but eventually an interesting picture had emerged.

First and foremost, he had discovered that the enemy still adhered to the old taboos against procreating between members of the same matrilineal descent. Second, and not less important, that they had no Dormants of other lines.

He had always assumed that they were a cowardly bunch—the kind who preferred running and hiding to honorably facing their enemies in battle. But as the real reason for their tactics became glaringly obvious—that there just weren't enough of them to offer a fight—he was grudgingly compelled to grant them respect.

How the hell had they managed to achieve so much—stolen knowledge notwithstanding—when there couldn't have been more than a few hundred of them?

Making tracks in the luxurious Persian rug, his mind went back to the issue of Dormants. Apparently, the professor believed that finding mortals with special abilities of the paranormal kind would lead her to potential Dormants.

Why?

None of his brethren had any of the various traits she had mentioned in her notebook. And certainly none of the Dormants he had encountered as a child had exhibited anything out of the ordinary—not his mother, his sister, nor any of the other women in Navuh's "special harem."

Navuh's powers were to be expected, after all he was the son of a god, and so were his sons' formidable abilities.

The rest of the men could thrall most mortals to some extent, but not all—the weaker the mind, the less it resisted manipulation—but that was it.

As to Dormants, they were a rare and precious commodity, guarded fiercely by Navuh for obvious reasons. And apparently, the despot was the only one to possess any.

Dalhu closed his eyes as his thoughts drifted back to his mother and sister. His mother had been a whore, as had all the other Dormant women in Navuh's special harem. And the same fate had been awaiting his sister. He just hadn't been around to witness it.

After all this time, he had trouble remembering their features. The only clear memory that he still managed to hold on to was his mother's voice. Some nights, he still heard her singing to him in his dreams.

Dalhu had been taken away to the training camp and turned at thirteen, never to see his small family again. He hadn't been allowed. The one time he'd tried, he'd gotten off easy with a severe beating as punishment, only because he'd been so young. An older male would've been beheaded.

The group of Dormant women were Navuh's secret broodmares. Selling their bodies to serve wealthy mortals provided him with a source of income and male children for his army of near-immortal mercenaries.

The sons were activated and became soldiers, the daughters were not and were relegated to prostitution like their mothers before them. Neither was given a choice.

Once the boys were turned, they were never allowed near the Dormants again. Fornicating with one carried the death penalty for both.

The Dormants were to serve mortals only.

In the past, Dalhu, like the rest of the soldiers, had assumed that the women weren't turned because according to the teachings of Mortdh they were deemed inferior. It had taken him centuries to piece together the real reason behind the segregation. If turned by an immortal male's venom, an immortal female's chances of conceiving dropped to nearly nonexistent. And Navuh needed the women to bear as many children as possible, which they had, providing over the millennia thousands of warriors for his army.

The *special harem* had always been heavily guarded— nowadays even more so as a fenced-off enclave of *Passion Island.*

A selective breeding program was pairing Dormants with clients believed to possess the traits valuable to Navuh—mainly physical size and strength, with socio-pathic tendencies a close second.

Navuh needed his soldiers to be strong and ruthless— nothing more.

Dalhu sat back at the desk and pulled out a quarter from his pocket. He tossed it up in the air and slammed it onto the desk when it came down. Repeating his experiment twenty times, he was assured of having no special precognition ability.

As expected, his predictions came true roughly half of the time.

"Edward!" he called his second.

The soldier came rushing in. "Yes, sir."

"Take this coin and flip it ten times. I want to see how many you can guess correctly."

Edward looked puzzled, but he did as he was told with no questions asked. He guessed right four out the ten.

"That will be all," Dalhu dismissed him.

Returning the quarter back to his pocket, he wondered if these abilities could be somehow developed, learned. He wouldn't have put it past Navuh to conceal this kind of information from his troops. As power hungry as Navuh was, the despot would not have wanted his divine status undermined by his lowly soldiers exhibiting even a fraction of his abilities.

Dalhu lifted the professor's small red notebook off the desk and leaned back in the heavy executive swivel chair. Flipping through the pages, he reached the one containing the list of paranormal subjects.

Interesting stuff really. Telepathy, both sending and receiving, or only one-way transmission; remote viewing, past viewing, precognition, influencing—emotional and otherwise; the ability to cast illusions. Communication with the dearly departed.

Most of the test subjects exhibited dismal talent. Except two.

Syssi, the professor's assistant, was the sole recipient of the score of ten—the highest. Her talent was precognition. How ironic that he'd met the girl and hadn't realized what a priceless treasure she was—a seer. What a powerful tool she could be. Dalhu wondered what kind of predictions she could make.

The other interesting subject was a guy named Michael, a student on the same campus. His talent was telepathy of the receiving kind, and his ranking was eight. Not bad. Being able to read other people's minds could be a great asset too, probably a more useful tool than that of the female's.

Soon, Dalhu would have both to do with as he pleased.

The woman's address had been easy to find in the university's Human Resources database. The hacker he had hired hadn't had much difficulty retrieving her record, especially with that weird spelling of her given name. He could've sent one of the men to the HR office for that, but hacking worked faster.

The telepath posed a greater challenge, but it was nothing money couldn't overcome. His cell phone number was listed on his parents' account in Minnesota, so the phone bill was useless for finding his address. And there were five students named Michael Gross living on campus. He had to be located by his phone's signal.

The guy Dalhu had found to do it had been expensive but worth it. Unfortunately, he encountered some trouble, and had gotten the job done only late this evening, pinpointing the boy's location to a popular student hangout, a club not far from the dorms, which was currently teeming with people.

Dalhu had men in position at both locations.

The team at the woman's house was poised to snatch her as soon as she came home. Though if she didn't show up soon, he planned to fork out the money for the guy to track her cellphone as well.

The other team, dispatched to bring the telepath, was watching the entrance to the club. Without a picture to identify him by, they would wait for the boy to get out and separate from his friends. Regrettably, the acuity of the tracking device was limited to pinpointing the place, but not one individual out of a tightly packed crowd.

It wouldn't be much longer.

Soon, Dalhu's phone would be buzzing with the confirmations of their capture.

This wasn't what excited him, though. Catching the two potential Dormants was almost inconsequential in comparison to getting his hands on the beautiful, immortal professor.

Dalhu pulled out the auto repair shop's estimate he'd found tucked between the journal's pages. Apparently, the professor's Porsche was undergoing repairs at a Beverly Hills collision center specializing in luxury European automobiles, and it would be ready for pickup next Thursday. Luckily, the estimate included the car's license plate number.

This time, he wasn't going to send any of his underlings. Dalhu was going to be there himself, waiting all day until someone came to pick it up. If it was the professor, he would snatch her from there. But even if someone else showed up in her place or the shop delivered the car, he would just follow the Porsche to the professor's actual residence.

Next Thursday, the lovely Dr. Amanda Dokani would be his.

KIAN

"Finally, it's done." Kian put down the phone and leaned back in Shai's chair. The deal had almost gone up in smoke. Several times he'd been tempted to let it go to hell, but Onegus had kept things going. His chief Guardian and negotiator was in Spain, ironing out the last details on the beach property Kian was trying to snatch before it even went on the market. But, as often happened, a competitor had also learned of the deal and offered a better price.

Kian wondered who'd tipped them off. Perhaps his sniffer had double dipped, selling the information twice.

Who else could've known that the owner of the shabby hotel had just lost his wife to heart failure and wished to get rid of the place they had run together for years? The guy had told his son, who had told his girlfriend, who had met the sniffer at a coffee shop and had told him about it during a random conversation.

Unless the guy had also sold the information to Kian's rival, no one could've known the place was on the market.

With the bidding war getting out of hand, Kian had

been about to give the thing up when the competitor bowed out. Not that he could blame the guy. With what he'd ended up agreeing to pay for the place, it would take much longer to realize profits, but Kian and the clan were in no hurry.

Time was on their side.

"You want to drink to that?" Shai opened his mini fridge and pulled out two Snake Venom beers—the world's strongest at almost seventy percent alcohol by volume, and the only beer immortals could get drunk on.

"Sure, why not." Kian accepted the bottle.

He needed something to take the edge off. Not an easy-going guy on a good day, which this one certainly wasn't, Kian was nearing his melting point. It had started with Amanda's ultimatum, then continued with a deal that turned out to be not as sweet as he'd hoped, and now he had no more excuses and needed to decide what to do about Syssi.

"It's not such a bad deal. We'll still make good money." Shai mistook his grimace.

Kian wasn't going to correct him. Let the guy think he was disappointed with the numbers, not with his sister and her cavalier attitude, and not with himself and his crumbling resistance.

"Good job, Shai." He clapped his secretary on the back. "Let's call it a day. I'm out of here."

"Thanks. But I'm just the pencil pusher. You and Onegus have done all the work."

Yeah, right. That was Shai's favorite expression, when in fact he was indispensable. The guy could've taken on more, but he didn't want to. He was comfortable with his position and didn't strive for anything more. Something Kian couldn't for the life of him relate to. He always

19

pushed himself to the limit, expected more of himself than others, and was incapable of giving up.

Except, it seemed that he was capable of giving in.

As he mulled over the situation in between the phone calls and the e-mails and the general hysteria that erupted around this fucking deal, he realized that he was being a hypocrite.

He hadn't forbidden Amanda from using another male to try to activate Syssi. Did he count himself above the other males of his clan? Was it okay for another to act immorally while Kian prided himself on taking the higher ground?

The answer was obviously no. But the last straw that had done it for him was thinking of some other male touching his Syssi. As soon as Amanda realized he was not going to do it no matter what, she would rope another male in. None of the others would refuse her, not unless Kian issued an order prohibiting it.

He could still do it, but Amanda must have anticipated this move before he'd even thought of it and had threatened him with involving their mother. There was no doubt in his mind that Annani would side with Amanda. The future of her clan was at stake, and she had no problem bending the rules when it suited her.

They had him cornered, which was a huge relief. Having no choice felt a lot better than admitting he couldn't control his craving for the girl.

Except, when he finally made it back to the penthouse, ready to pick up where he had left things off with Syssi, she wasn't there.

Searching, he poked his head into every room, even checking the terrace, but she was nowhere to be found.

Where the hell can she be?

He pulled out his phone and rang Amanda. "Is Syssi with you?" he asked without preamble.

"No, did you manage to scare her off already?" Amanda taunted.

With a grunt, he ended the call and shoved the phone back in his pocket.

The obvious conclusion was that she had left. Though, how she had managed to do that without a thumbprint access to the elevators, or security letting him know, baffled him.

Maybe Okidu had helped her, taking her down in the elevator. With that main obstacle out of the way, there would have been nothing preventing her from waltzing away.

And as the guys in security were more concerned with people coming into the building than leaving it, they would have thought nothing of her casually strolling out the front door.

With a vile curse, Kian kicked a planter, wincing as the thing toppled.

He had no one to blame but himself.

After all, he hadn't specifically forbidden her to leave, or informed security to detain her if she tried.

Walking back inside, Kian pulled out his phone, ready to call Okidu, when he heard a distant hum.

Jets.

Whirlpool tub's jets.

So that's where she is...

Relieved, he shoved the phone back into his pocket and followed the sound.

When he reached the room she was in, Kian shook his head. Syssi had chosen the smallest, most plainly furnished suite in the penthouse. It was so like her.

Though how he knew that about her puzzled him. He just did.

With a sigh, he kicked off his boots and plopped down on the bed. It seemed that despite the long hours it had taken him to get back to her, his wait wasn't over yet.

Closing his eyes, Kian made a go at some shut-eye, but it was no use. Problem was, he kept imagining Syssi's gorgeous body soaking naked in that tub, the tips of her perfect breasts peeking above the soapy water...

Oh, hell. With that scenario doing all kinds of things to his male anatomy, he itched to barge in there and...

Yeah, as if that would end well...

"Not!" he muttered as he reached inside his pants, adjusting himself. But his damned cock was so distended that it jutted above his waistband.

Cursing, he covered it with his shirttails.

With all that had been going on lately, he hadn't had the time or the inclination to go prowling for sex. And the long stretch of abstinence was taking its toll.

His biology was demanding its pound of flesh.

Except, the thought of slaking his need with some cheapie he picked up at a bar suddenly felt repugnant to him.

He craved Syssi. Her fresh, sweet innocence was calling to his tainted soul.

Soon.

She would get out of that bathroom and find him waiting for her like some creepy stalker, and realize that her time was up.

What the hell is taking her so damn long?

Kian was losing his patience. Now that the decision had been made, he could wait no longer.

As the tub began draining, his pulse sped up. Any moment now, she'd get out…

No such luck.

He growled deep in his throat. Then he heard her applying lotion. And more lotion. And just as his agitation was gaining critical velocity, he heard what sounded suspiciously like a moan.

What the hell?

Had the little minx rebuffed him just to go ahead and pleasure herself without him?

Oh, no, she didn't!

With a surge, Kian shot out of bed and was about to barge in on her, when he heard the hairdryer turn on. His palm a fraction of an inch away from the door handle, he barely managed to stop in time.

His body bursting with barely contained aggression, he plopped back down on the bed, crossed his arms over his chest, and ordered himself to calm the fuck down!

One deep breath after another, he kept talking himself down from the high tree branch onto which he had climbed.

Take it easy, moron. She has no idea you're lying in wait for her like a fucking perv.

He kept telling himself he needed to be patient, romantic, go slow…

Except, how the hell would he manage that when he was strung up tighter than a bow string?

Exasperated, Kian banged his head against the headboard.

SYSSI

*S*yssi's fingertips were starting to prune.

As fun as the spa was, it was time to get out. Turning the whirlpool off, she stepped out of the tub and wrapped herself in one of the plush towels stacked by its side.

All during her soak, Kian's words from earlier had been playing over and over in her mind, providing a background soundtrack to the vivid images they were painting.

On one hand, all these new and intense sensations electrified her. It was like discovering a whole new world of pleasure she had never known existed. It was exhilarating. On the other hand, she was afraid that once she had gotten a taste for how it could be, she would do just about anything to get more of it.

Before, she had never understood what drove people to indulge in careless sex, despite the potential utter devastation it entailed. Unwelcome pregnancies, ruined marriages, family feuds, wars... Literature painted an abundance of catastrophic scenarios Syssi had used to believe were mostly fictional. After all, what was so difficult about keeping your pants on?

But now, as need gnawed at her like a hungry beast, she understood.

Standing on the cold marble and looking out the window at the dark sky, she grew nervous. Kian would be back soon. And then what? Was she strong enough to say no to him, or at least not yet? Or was she going to surrender to her longing and have reckless sex with a man she barely knew but wanted desperately?

Toweling the moisture off with the excessive vigor of her rising frustration, she questioned her indecision. What was really the point of delaying the inevitable? If not tonight, then the next, or the one after that. If Kian still wanted her, that is. He might have concluded that she was too much trouble, and go for the easy and available.

Everyone around her was talking about hookups and booty calls, instead of dates and relationships. People treated sex as casually as going to the movies or out for a drink. In this uninspiring, emotionally disconnected landscape, the pursuit of sexual gratification was the norm, and the rare relationship an exception. An oddity.

Still, she wondered if all these people were deluding themselves into accepting this sorry state of affairs as gratifying. Perhaps they were just desperately reaching out for any kind of connection, hoping something real would sprout from all that carnality.

She couldn't see herself living that way. Maybe she was old-fashioned, or just naive, but she needed at least the illusion of a relationship, if not the real thing, to get all hot and sweaty with a guy.

Oh, but Kian...

He was like an addiction, an obsession, calling to her,

drawing her in like a moth to a flame. She knew she was going to burn, but at this point she didn't care.

She was going to do it, had to...

Catching her panicky reflection staring back at her from the mist-covered mirror, her hand flew to her chest.

Oh, God! She wasn't ready!

It had been so long since her last time, Syssi felt like a virgin all over again; nervous, insecure, frightened. So okay, it probably wasn't going to hurt like the first time had—thank heavens for small favors—but she felt anxious nonetheless.

What if she fell short of Kian's expectations, what if he found her unexciting... lacking...

What if, what if... stop it! She ordered the self-disparaging internal monolog to cease.

Rubbing lotion onto her hands, she decided a whole body rub would help with her jitters. Squirting a generous dollop of the stuff, she slathered it all over, watching her skin turn slick and soft.

She took a little longer than necessary to work it into the soft skin of her breasts, running her thumbs over her sensitive nipples and tweaking them lightly till they tightened into hard little knobs. It felt nice, but didn't come close to the kind of fire Kian's touch had ignited in her dream.

Would reality be as amazing as that fantasy? How would his hands feel? His lips? She closed her eyes, imagining, and as the slow simmer of arousal flared into searing heat, a quiet moan escaped her throat.

What am I doing? Syssi sneaked an embarrassed glance at the mirror as if catching herself red handed. Grimacing, she shook her head; how pathetic was it for someone her age to be so reserved. After all, she was by herself with no one to judge her one way or the other, but she still felt uncomfortable touching herself with the lights on and in the vicinity of a mirror.

With a sigh, she wiped her moist hands on the towel and began blow-drying her hair. Once she was done, she was ready to head out when a faint bang sounded from behind the closed door.

Cautiously, she opened it a crack.

It was dark, and coming from the brightly illuminated bathroom, it took a moment for her pupils to dilate enough to make out the large shape lying on her bed. As her eyes fully adjusted to the dim light, Kian's handsome but brooding features became clear.

He looks like the big bad wolf about to devour Little Red Riding Hood... Me. Syssi chuckled. Apparently, today was a fairy-tale day. First Goldilocks and the Three Bears, then Little Red Riding Hood, what next? Cinderella, or Beauty and the Beast?

Syssi leaned toward the second one. As gorgeous as Kian was, she had a feeling that he was more of a beast than a prince.

"Oh, my! What a big, strong body you have, Grandma!" Purring seductively, she sauntered into the room. But as Kian's expression turned from brooding to menacing, she chickened out, and cursing her inability to put a muzzle on her stupid mischievous streak, she turned to flee into the walk-in closet.

"All the better to pounce on you, my dear!" Kian took to the role play with gusto, and leaping off the bed with the swiftness and grace of a jungle cat caught her from behind before she managed to reach the closet. Holding her back against his chest, he lifted her up.

She jackknifed, kicking her legs and trying to get away

while laughing nervously and clawing at the strong fingers clutching hers on the towel.

It was futile.

In one swift move he swung and tossed her on the bed, then pounced, looming above her as he caged her between his thighs and outstretched arms. Still panting from the laughter and exertion of her failed escape attempt, she couldn't fill her lungs.

Or maybe her shortness of breath had nothing to do with exertion and everything to do with Kian. The long strands of his wavy hair falling around his angular features, he was insanely beautiful...

And terrifying.

There was no humor in that hard beauty, only hunger.

Caught in the intense glow of Kian's eyes, she felt trapped like a deer in the headlights of an oncoming car. Fear trickled down her spine in liquid drops of fire that pooled at her core, wetting the insides of her naked thighs.

He caressed her cheek, then kissed the hollow of her neck, gently soothing her before bringing his palm to rest over her fisted hand. "Let go of the towel, Syssi," he whispered. Except, coming through his clenched teeth, his words sounded hissed, rough and demanding.

Not ready to let go yet, Syssi shook her head.

He kept at it, stroking her straining knuckles with his thumb, until gently, one at a time, she let him pry her fingers open.

Gazing into his hungry eyes, she was still apprehensive but didn't resist when he entwined their fingers and stretched her arms over her head, holding them there as he brought his face down to shower her with featherlight kisses.

He kissed her eyelids, her eyebrows, her cheeks, her

nose, the hollows at the sides of her neck. He kept kissing her like that until she began to relax, her body growing slack. Only then, he released his hold on her hands and leaned back on his haunches to stare hungrily at her body.

Under Kian's searing gaze, laid out like a bounty before him, Syssi stretched out ready to be unveiled. There were no more thoughts, no more hesitation, only a burning desire.

Slowly, carefully, as if unwrapping a precious gift, Kian peeled away one side of the towel and then the other.

"Damn! Just look at you... perfection." He swallowed, gazing at her with an expression full of awe, as if he'd never seen a woman as beautiful as her. No one had ever looked at her like that. She basked, for the first time in her life feeling truly desired. And not just by any man, by Kian. The nearest male approximation of a god.

As his eyes lingered on her breasts, watching them heave with her shallow, panting breaths, Syssi felt her nipples stiffen. And when his tongue darted to his lip, her breath caught as she imagined him licking, sucking. Instead, he continued his tour of her body, his eyes traveling down until coming to a halt at her bare mound.

"Beautiful. All of you." He cupped her center.

With a strangled moan, her lids dropped over her eyes.

"Perfect," he whispered, bending to lightly kiss one turgid peak. "Magnificent." He kissed the other, then waited until she opened her eyes and looked at him.

"I want you so badly, I'm going to go up in flames if you won't have me," he breathed. Running his hands along her outstretched arms, he reached her hands and entangled their fingers. His face a scant inch from hers, he searched her wide open eyes.

Gazing up at his beautiful face, she saw her own raging

need reflected in his eyes. "I want you, Kian, so much that it hurts," she whispered.

It was a terrifying thing to admit, and the only reason she'd mustered enough courage to speak the truth, was the way he was looking at her. There was no way he was faking it. Kian's soul was shining through his eyes, and he was baring himself to her just as much as she was baring herself to him.

He closed his eyes in relief, but only for a brief moment. Then with a measuring look, he asked again. "Are you sure?"

She must've seemed shell-shocked to him, lying underneath his big body with her eyes opened wide, panting.

And in truth, she was.

Still, she needed this like she needed to take her next breath.

"I need you," she whispered.

The change in his expression was lightning fast. Sure of his welcome, Kian's last vestiges of restraint shattered, and he descended upon her like a hungry beast; smashing her lips with his mouth, thrusting his tongue in and out, and growling as he nipped at her lips.

Swept in the torrent of his ferocity, Syssi arched her back, aching to feel the length of his body pressed against hers—to feel his weight on top of her.

Except, he remained propped on his shins, his bowed arms supporting the weight of his chest, their bodies barely touching.

But with her mouth under attack and her arms pinned, there was little she could do about it besides moan and whimper.

Kian's mouth trailed south, kissing and nipping every

spot along her jawline and down her neck to her collarbone, then licking and kissing the small hurts away.

Syssi panted in breathless anticipation, her painfully stiff nipples desperate for his hands, his lips...

"Please...," she whispered, her need stronger than her pride.

He lifted his head, the hunger in his eyes belying his teasing mouth. "Tell me what you need, beautiful." He let go of one of her hands to caress her cheek, extending his thumb to rub over her swollen lips before pressing it into her mouth.

She sucked it in, swirling her tongue around it until he pulled it out to rub the moisture over her dry lips.

With the hand he had freed, she cupped Kian's lightly stubbled cheek, letting the last of her shields drop and allowing him to see in her unguarded expression all of the desire and adoration she felt for him.

He leaned into her tender touch. "My sweet, precious girl," he whispered, covering her hand with his own.

Holding her palm to his lips, he kissed its center before returning it to where it was before. "I like the way you look with your arms outstretched, surrendering to me, trusting me with your pleasure."

Hooded with desire, his eyes were pleading with her to give him that, promising only pleasure if she did.

Syssi felt powerless to deny him anything. Without a word she complied, stretching her arms and grabbing onto the headboard's metal frame.

How did he do that, she wondered, setting her body on fire—knowing what she needed better than she did herself.

To hell with precaution and consequences, she was done being careful. No more almosts, no more only ifs, no more maybe-next-times, this was it.

With Kian, she had finally glimpsed the path to the elusive bliss. And the only way she could traverse that road was with him in the driver seat. She needed to cede control to him. And to do that, she needed to trust him... which was scary.

It wasn't that she feared he'd hurt her physically, she knew he wouldn't. But to trust that he would not exploit the tremendous emotional vulnerability she was about to expose; that took real courage.

Or stupidity.

Still, she knew it was her one and only chance to take the plunge because there was no doubt in her mind that she would never even consider this with anyone but Kian.

Releasing a shuddering breath, she gazed into his eyes, and the way he looked at her, waiting breathlessly for her acquiescence, provided the final push.

She took the plunge.

"I don't know why I feel this way with you, trusting you to take control of my pleasure, but I do. I crave it," Syssi whispered, a rush of pure lust sweeping through her with the admission.

5

KIAN

*K*ian groaned. "Do you have any idea how perfect you are? How much your trust means to me?" He dipped his head, pouring his gratitude and appreciation into a tender kiss.

Well aware that lovely, sweet Syssi was nothing like what he was accustomed to, and the set of rules she played by was different than his, he had to make sure she understood the rules of this new game he was introducing her to. But now that she had given him the green light, he was in serious trouble because there was nothing holding him back, and his damned instincts were screaming for him to rip off his pants, plunge all the way into her, and sink his fangs into her neck while he was at it.

Not going to happen. Kian took a deep breath and closed his eyes, forcing the beast to back the hell off.

First, he would make sure to take care of her pleasure.

Kissing and licking the column of her throat, he needed at least a moment between her thighs, even if only to feel her through the fabric of his pants. Pushing her knees apart, he aligned his erection with her sex, careful not to scrape her with his zipper as he rubbed against her.

Fuck, it feels good.

With a groan, he slid farther down her body until his face was level with her stiff peaks. For a moment, he just looked at their sculpted perfection, watching them heave with each of her breaths. Until he heard her whimper.

Only then, he took one tip between his lips. He pulled on it gently, twirling his tongue round and round, while lightly pinching its twin between his thumb and forefinger and tugging on it in sync with his suckling.

As he kept alternating between the sensitive nubs, suckling them harder and grazing them lightly with his teeth, Syssi's moans and whimpers were getting louder and more desperate.

She was loving it. Her hips circling under the weight of him, she held on to the headboard with a white-knuckled grip.

Kian eased up, giving her a small reprieve. "Ask me to make you come, baby," he breathed around her wet nipple, lifting his eyes to her sweat-misted face.

"Please…," she whimpered.

"That's not good enough. You can do better than that."

Syssi arched her back, and as she turned her desperate eyes up to her tight grip on the headboard, he felt an outpour of wetness slide down her thigh.

"Oh, God! Yes! Please… Please make me come… Kian."

As his blunt front teeth carefully closed around one nipple, and his fingers around the other, Syssi erupted. And as he kept increasing the pressure, turning the slight ache into what must've been an almost unbearable hurt, her climax continued rippling through her—her beautiful body quaking with the aftershocks as she wailed until her voice turned hoarse.

That was it for him.

Unable to hold it off anymore, he came hard, erupting spasmodically inside his pants. Except, it did nothing to soften his erection, he was still as hard as before.

Releasing some of the pressure took the edge off, though. Now, with the wild beast raging inside him contained for a little longer, he could watch Syssi climax again and again.

He would never tire of seeing her like that. Her dazed, blissed out expression suffusing him with tenderness.

My beautiful, passionate girl.

Cupping her breasts with his palms, he soothed her tender nubs, waiting for them to soften under the warmth of his touch.

As her ragged breathing slowed down, Syssi mouthed, "Wow!" her cheeks flaming.

Kian smiled, peering at her from between the hands he had cupped over her ample breasts.

Releasing her hold on the metal frame, she took his cheeks between her palms and pulled him up for a kiss.

"Did I give you permission to bring your arms down, sweet girl?" he said before sealing his lips over hers. He then traced the line of her jaw with kisses and nibbles, all the way up to her earlobe, catching the soft tissue between his teeth.

Syssi squirmed. "No," she said in a small voice, caressing his stubble with her thumbs. "My hands have a mind of their own. I just had to touch you." She pouted, pretending contrition.

"Be a good girl and put your hands back up, or I'll have to flip you over and spank that sweet little bottom of yours." He tweaked her nipple and smirked, watching her eyelids flutter as a shiver of desire swept through her.

"Is that a promise?" Syssi taunted, whispering breathlessly as she lifted and tightened the aforementioned body part and pressed her pelvis up to his belly. Still, she hastened to obey his command, and stretching her arms, returned her hands to the headboard.

The hint of trepidation in her eyes hadn't been lost on him. Syssi wasn't sure if he was just teasing or intended to make good on that threat.

"Could you be any more perfect for me?" Kian said, shaking his head. "My little minx has some naughty fantasies I would be more than happy to fulfill. I promise. If you ask really nicely... or behave really badly, you can bet your sweet bottom on it." He winked, and with a surge, dived down and pressed an open-mouthed kiss to her wet folds.

Syssi squeaked, lifting and pulling away from him, but Kian gripped her hips and pulled her back down. Sliding both hands under her bottom, he lifted her pelvis up to his mouth and licked her wet slit from top to bottom and then back up, growling like a beast.

At first, she stiffened. But Kian kept at it even though he knew she felt scandalized. This was such an intimate act, demanding a level of trust and familiarity that must've been difficult for her. After all, he had her spread out naked, her sex soaking wet from her earlier climax, licking and feasting on it while he was still fully dressed.

He was pushing her, testing her limits, thrilled that despite her initial reluctance she was letting him have his way.

He loved that ceding control to him turned her on. The more he demanded, the more he pushed, the more she responded with wild abandon, rewarding him with her moans and whimpers and more of her sweet nectar pouring onto his greedy tongue.

He could go on like that for hours, savoring and exulting in the pleasure he was wringing out of her.

It wasn't about him being a selfless giving lover, not entirely. Having his pants on and not allowing her to touch him was the only way he could stay in control. His hunger for sex, for her, was so intense, he was afraid of what he'd do to her otherwise.

The beast in him wanted to impale her sex with his cock and sink his fangs into her neck in one brutal move. And then go on fucking her for hours, biting her and coming inside her over and over again. Rutting on her like the animal it was.

Traumatizing her.

It was true that she would climax every time he sunk his fangs into her neck... or her breast... or the juncture of her thigh. The aphrodisiac in his venom would make sure of that. And yes, her pain and bruising would fade from its healing properties. And after he was done, he could easily thrall the nasty memory away.

Except, he was neither a sadist nor a mindless beast... well... not entirely, and not as long as he remained in control.

He cared too much for this girl to let go—even a little.

Before he slaked his need, he would make sure she was properly pleasured, sated, and soaking wet from multiple orgasms. And even then, he couldn't let loose the monster lurking inside him.

6

SYSSI

he man is wicked.
Drawing lazy circles around her nether lips and scooping her juices with his tongue, Kian groaned with the pleasure of literally eating her up.

He'd been doing it for so long, keeping her at a slow simmer, skirting the spot where she needed him most, that she had to bite on her bottom lip to stifle the sounds she was making. Her needy groans sounded like angry growls.

"Please, I can't take it anymore!" she finally hissed.

Kian lifted his head. "Tell me what you need, baby." He smirked, licking her juices from his glistening lips.

Hanging on the precipice, she was beyond shame or reserve. "You... I need you inside me! Please..." She groaned—panting from parted lips as he pulled his hands from under her butt and lowered her back to the mattress. Eyes trained on her face, he tightened his grip on her hip, anchoring her down, and slid one long finger inside her slick core.

Her channel tightened, clutching and spasming around

the thrusting and retreating digit. It felt so good. Syssi moaned, closing her eyes and letting her head drop back.

"Look at me!" Kian growled.

With an effort, she lifted her head and looked at him with hooded eyes, her lower lip pulsing, swollen from where she had bitten on it before.

Holding her gaze, he pulled out his finger and pushed back with two. She inhaled sharply at the amplified pleasure. A slight burn started, reminding her how long it had been for her, and for a moment she got scared. But then as he lowered his chin and slowly, deliberately, flicked his tongue at her most erogenous spot, a flood of moisture coated his fingers, turning the intrusion from slightly painful to blissfully pleasurable.

His fingers pumping in and out of her, in that slow, maddening way, Syssi was hanging by a thread—straining on the edge of the orgasm bearing down on her. She needed him to move just a little faster, or pinch her nipple with the powerful fingers of his other hand, and she would've gone flying.

But Kian had other ideas. Joining a third finger, he stretched her even wider. Again, there was a slight burn, but she couldn't care less.

Let it hurt, just let me dive over that edge.

She kept her eyes on his face, watching him as a wicked gleam sparkled in his eyes, just a split moment before he closed his lips around the tiny bundle of nerves at the apex of her sex and sucked it in.

"Kiannnnn!" Syssi erupted, mewling and thrashing as the climax came at her violently, jerking her body off the bed. Kian didn't let go, pumping his fingers and suckling on her, he prolonged it, squeezing every last drop of pleasure out of her.

A moment later, or perhaps it had been longer than that, she came down from floating in that semiconscious, postorgasmic space and opened her eyes. A gasp escaped her throat. Kian was suspended above her—gloriously naked. Giving her no time to ponder the how and when he had shucked off his clothes, or to admire his beautifully muscled body, he speared into her with a grunt.

Syssi cried out.

It hurt. Boy did it hurt, and not in a good way. Not an erotic pain. Just pain, hot and searing.

As her channel stretched and burned, struggling to accommodate Kian's girth, Syssi wanted to push him off; memories of her first time intruding on and marring what was supposed to be something wonderful—casting an unpleasant shadow over the bliss that he had brought her before.

Tears streaking from the corners of her eyes, she panted, waiting for the pain to subside.

"I'm sorry," Kian whispered, kissing her teary eyes, as he tried to pull out.

"No, just give me a moment." She clutched him to her. This wasn't going to end like that, no way.

He didn't move, not even a twitch. With muscles strained and eyes blazing in his hard face, he looked at her, holding his breath as he waited for her body to adjust to his invasion. Only when the pain started to ebb and she began to moan and undulate—her lust and her pleasure overriding her pain—did he begin thrusting, carefully, gently, until she gasped again.

This time, in pleasure.

For what seemed like a long time, he moved inside her with infinite care, his thrusts slow and shallow, and eventually even the memory of pain was gone, there was only pleasure.

Syssi brought her palms to Kian's cheeks and pulled him down, kissing him softly. She was falling in love with this man, and there was little she could do about it. Right now she was overwhelmed with feelings of gratitude, for his patience, for his care. Kian was putting her pleasure first.

"I'm okay now. You can let go," she whispered against his lips.

His thrusts got a little deeper, but he kept going slow for a few moments, gauging her response. When she closed her eyes and moaned deep in her throat, he increased the tempo and force, gradually going deeper and faster until the powerful pounding rattled the bed, banging it against the wall and driving them both toward the headboard.

Kian braced himself by grabbing the metal frame above where she was holding on, his biceps bulging with the strain and sweat dripping down the center of his muscular chest.

As Syssi climbed toward another climax, Kian's grunts and her moans were accompanied by the sounds of the bed's feet sliding and screeching on the hardwood floor, and the headboard banging against the wall. A carnal soundtrack to the drama of their fierce coupling.

Forcing her eyes to remain open, Syssi stared at Kian's handsome face, awed. Straining, he was covered in sweat, his lips pressed into a thin line. And his eyes, those hypnotic blue eyes of his, were glowing with an eerie luminance.

I'm delirious, she thought, marveling at the sight.

Shifting those amazing eyes down to her neck, he dipped his head to suck and lick at her fast pulsing vein;

strands of his soft hair caressing her cheek as he kept his relentless pounding.

On an impulse, Syssi turned her head sideways, startled to find herself silently pleading with him; *Bite me! Please...*

Oh, God!

The sharp pain of his fangs sinking into her flesh shocked her, the needlelike incisors clearly not human.

Fangs... He had fangs in my dream... was her last coherent thought as his seed jetted into her, and she fell apart, her climax erupting in waves of volcanic intensity.

The euphoria that followed left her boneless and exhausted. Unable to open her eyes, blissful and content, she sighed, surrendering to oblivion.

7

KIAN

*K*ian retracted his fangs and closed the small incision points with a couple of licks.

Stroking Syssi's damp hair away from her temples, he looked at her peaceful, sleeping face, then pressed a gentle kiss to her parted lips.

He had exhausted the poor girl.

When he had entered her, he had not expected her to be so tight, and the look of pain on her face had startled him. After climaxing twice, she had been so wet, it should've been a smooth glide.

If he hadn't known better, he would have thought her a virgin.

He'd wanted to withdraw immediately, but Syssi had stopped him. Apparently, she was made from tougher stuff than he'd suspected. Still, he'd held himself in check. With his superior physiology providing stamina to match, he could've kept going. Except the same couldn't have been said about her. What was slow and gentle for him, had been a rough ride for Syssi.

She looked drained.

Pulling out, careful not to wake her, Kian remained suspended over her for a moment, and as he looked at her beautiful face, he was gripped by an intense craving to cleave unto her and make her his.

Heavens! How he wanted to come clean and tell Syssi everything: about himself, who he was, what he was... needing her to accept it all, accept him...

To love him.

His chest tight, he reluctantly prepared to perpetuate the deception and with a heavy sigh reached into her mind, carefully extracting the memory of his bite.

It had to be done.

Out of respect for Syssi, he resisted the temptation to take a peek and see himself through her eyes. It was selfish, but he hoped she was falling in love with him, even if just a little, because he couldn't help falling for her.

It was futile, and tomorrow he was going to exorcise these dangerous feelings by any means available to him, but tonight he would allow himself to feel. Just this once.

With one more kiss to her sweet lips, he got up and walked over to the bathroom, bringing back a warm wash-cloth for his girl.

Syssi didn't stir. Not as he gently wiped away their combined issue, nor when he climbed into bed, not even when he turned her sideways so he could spoon behind her.

Reaching for the crumpled comforter at the foot of the bed, he pulled it up to cover them both.

"Sleep tight, precious," he whispered.

Too early for him to fall asleep, Kian closed his eyes and focused on the sensation of Syssi's soft curves curled against his body. Ever since Lavena, he hadn't spent a night with a woman. Frankly, he hadn't been so inclined. But he would have loved to have Syssi pressed against him every night. There was a sense of peace, of rightness in having her there that he hadn't expected.

He wondered if Syssi had known it would be like this between them. She was a seer, so it was possible she'd gotten a glimpse of them together.

When his phone went off on the nightstand, Kian grabbed it quickly before the ringing could wake her up.

"Yeah," he whispered.

Syssi didn't stir. Yep, exhausted.

"Why are you whispering?" Yamanu asked.

"Never mind that. Do you have news about the boy?"

He'd assigned Yamanu the job of retrieving Michael, the other talent on Amanda's list who was a potential target for the Doomers. But instead of having them pick him up right away, he had instructed Yamanu and his team follow the kid around to see if Doomers showed up. There had been a couple of problems with that. Michael and his football team had traveled out of town for a game, while his phone remained behind.

"He is back and he has his phone. Someone found it and brought it to lost-and-found, but the battery was dead."

"Is he in the dorms?"

"Was, until about an hour ago. He went with a couple of buddies to a club."

"Wait until he gets back and then you can pick him up the moment he's alone. We've wasted enough of your time already."

"Yeah, I figured you'd say that. But if the Doomers don't make a move now that he has his phone back, he might be safe. One more day and we'll know for sure."

Kian chuckled. Yamanu was disappointed that no Doomers had shown up and there was no fight. Ever since

Brundar and Anandur's report about the skirmish at the lab, he'd been eager to test his skills against some Doomers. The Guardian hoped he would still get his chance. "I'm giving you until tomorrow morning."

"Thanks, boss."

8

MICHAEL

"I'm never going to get wasted like this again," Michael groaned.

Getting buzzed had been fun, but the aftermath was a bitch. He shouldn't have fueled up on all that crappy vodka before going to the club. But given the outrageous prices the place charged for drinks, Eddie's idea to buy the stuff cheap at the supermarket had been genius.

And besides, not being twenty-one yet, and getting in with a friend's ID, buying drinks at the club would have been pushing his luck unnecessarily, stupid. The guy at the door never paid close attention to the pictures, but the bartender had been known to occasionally double-check if something looked fishy to him.

Then again, it wasn't like his unfortunate shortage of cash had nothing to do with it...

Given his pitiful allowance, and not being that big on drinking to begin with, most nights Michael had been the one to volunteer as their triad's designated driver. But tonight they had flipped for it, and Zack had gotten to do the honors.

He had to admit, though, that there was something to be said for hitting the snooze button on his inhibitions—easier to flirt. Not that he suffered from a lack of confidence, but still, sometimes a dude needed something extra to go after the hottest girls everyone was hitting on.

"So, Michael, did you get Gina's number, or is she still moping after that douchebag boyfriend of hers?" His friend Eddie was too loud, too close, his voice pounding in Michael's ears.

"Shh... Eddie, you are drilling holes in my head. Don't you have any other volume besides loud and extra loud?" Michael rubbed his temples and increased the length of his stride, trying to put some distance between himself and his friend's booming voice.

The night was chilly, the light breeze carrying a faint smell of freshly cut grass, and if Eddie would just shut up, the ten-minute walk from the parking lot to their dorms might help with the headache.

"I'm not loud. You're drunk, bro... And back to the subject of Gina-the-football-player-slayer. If she's not interested in you, I might want to give her a try... If it's okay with you, that is... I don't want to infringe on your turf or anything."

"She is all yours. Just shut up already. You are loud." Michael walked even faster, the brisk pace helping sober him up.

Gina was hot, but she was dumb as a brick. And although she had given him her number, Michael wasn't sure he was going to call.

"Nice..." He heard Eddie from some distance behind him, and then Zack's snort from even farther away.

Michael was about to come up with some clever shit to say when he got a weird feeling that they were being watched. He'd been getting these strange vibes ever since they had returned from the game, but until now he hadn't sensed any malice radiating from whomever was watching him. Hey, it might have been Gina, or some other girl with a crush on him.

Right.

The thing was, this felt very different from before. Looking around the deserted campus, he slowed down, then stopped as the sensation got stronger. The small hairs on the back of his neck prickled.

Crouching low with his elbows tucked at his sides, fists up, Michael scanned for the source of his alarm.

With his sudden halt, Eddie and Zack stopped themselves from knocking him over by throwing out their hands and bracing against his back. Being built like a truck, the force of the impact didn't budge him an inch.

"What the hell, man? What's wrong with you?" Zack growled.

"Shh... Shut up for a moment..." Michael raised his palm to signal for them to keep quiet. The feeling of being watched was just amplified by a hefty dose of a menacing threat when his receptive mind tuned into someone's nefarious, dark intentions.

The adrenaline rush sobering him instantly, he listened for the source.

As his friends finally caught on to his defensive stance and positioned themselves back-to-back with him, forming a triad, Michael wondered who might be dumb enough to jump three football players weighing in aggregate over seven hundred pounds.

Regrettably, he was pretty sure it wasn't the cheerleading team. He wouldn't have minded being ambushed by them.

The list of possible suspects included junkies, armed robbers, or members of a defeated team. Though, this time they had been the ones who'd lost, so it ruled that out.

Except, nothing stirred in the eerily quiet night.

Disturbed only by the remote hum of cars passing by, Michael had the impression that it was the quiet before the storm. He could feel the imminent attack down to his bones.

His nemesis, whoever he or they were, was about to attack.

"Get ready, boys. Shit is coming down," he whispered.

As the last word left his mouth, two groups of some of the biggest, scariest motherfuckers he had ever seen came running at them from opposite directions.

"We're history," Eddie whispered as they braced for impact.

Except, it never came.

The two groups collided... attacking each other.

Surprised and relieved, Michael watched as these titans fought hand to hand, performing the best martial arts moves he had ever seen, in fiction or elsewhere, their bodies so fast they blurred.

"Fucking hell, what is that?" Zack's eyes darted left to right trying to follow the moves.

"We should scram..." For once, Eddie was the voice of reason. "Whoever wins will come after us next."

Except none of them moved, mesmerized by the spectacular show of combat skills.

Michael had the passing thought that they had somehow stumbled upon a movie shoot. No way anyone fought like that for real. Unfortunately, it wasn't only that the battle looked and sounded authentic, but the emotions he was picking up were of such deep mutual hatred, not even method actors could fake them so well.

"A gang war?" Zack suggested.

"On campus? Not likely," Michael whispered even though there was no need. The combatants were too busy fighting to pay them any attention.

Eddie nodded like he knew the answer. "Aliens. These fuckers are not human. No one can move so fast."

Yeah, right. Eddie had watched too many sci-fi movies. The thing was, Michael had no better explanation. Their speed was inhuman.

Even though he found it hard to follow the moves, the sounds told the story just as well. The fleshy thuds of fists and boots finding their targets, the metallic clank of knives clashing, and the grunts of pain and exertion of the combatants completed the picture.

9

YAMANU

*F*ollowing Michael and his friends from the club, Yamanu had gotten pulled over. Damn kids had been speeding while inebriated, and the idiot cop had let them go. It had taken Yamanu exactly two seconds to thrall the guy, but he'd lost at least three minutes while waiting for the cop to amble up to his window.

"Don't worry," Bhathian said. "Nothing can happen to him in two minutes."

Yamanu shook his head. When he caught up to the boys, he was going to box Michael's ears even though he wasn't the driver. The guy behind the wheel was probably just as drunk, and Michael shouldn't have gotten in the car with him. That's what Uber was for.

With his damn luck throwing obstacles at him at every turn, when he skidded into the dorm's fucking parking lot, it was full. There was no time to drive around the damn place in circles, looking for a vacant spot. Instead, Yamanu jumped the curb and parked on the lawn, squeezing the car between two trees.

"Let's go." He threw his door open.

"What if we get towed?" Arwel slammed his door shut.

"I'll call a taxi to—" Yamanu tensed and lifted his palm, while beside him Arwel unsheathed his dagger. He had no problem picking up on the Doomers' presence, even though he wasn't as strong an empath as Arwel. Differentiating their pattern of aggression from the normal currents produced by the many students occupying the dorms around them, combined with the sudden wave of fear coming at him from the boys, he could trace the signals like a beacon pinpointing their location.

"Follow me!" Yamanu sprinted toward that beacon.

With Arwel and Bhathian running close behind him, they reached Michael and his friends at the same time the Doomers did.

Three Doomers against three boys and three Guardians.

The boys, though quite brawny for young humans, posed no challenge for the Doomers. But at the same time, the Doomers didn't pose a real challenge for the Guardians either.

Good odds.

He had to hand it to the young men, though. They did good, proving that they had brains on top of brawn by forming a triad to protect each other's backs. Obviously, they didn't stand a chance against the Doomers' strength, training and weapons. But, at least they wouldn't have gone down without a fight.

As it turned out, though, Yamanu had underestimated the Doomers, and he realized his mistake as soon as he and his fellow Guardians engaged the fighters. Brundar had been right; this new breed of Doomers was nothing like those he had encountered in the past. Not only were they better trained and stronger, but the bastards fought with what seemed like suicidal desperation.

Still, the Guardians were better. It took a little longer than it should've, but eventually the Doomers started losing their momentum and making mistakes.

At that point, Yamanu detangled himself from the melee, confident in his companions' ability to finish the job without him.

Three sets of eyes moved away from the skirmish to focus on him and got even wider.

Yamanu chuckled. Any moment now their eyeballs would fall out.

As he approached them, Michael and his friends tensed, lifting their fists and readying for a fight.

"Calm down, boys. I'm not here to harm you. I'm here to protect you against these brutes." Mild term for what he thought about the Doomers, but the boys didn't know what kind of evil he and his friends had just saved them from, and it was better it stayed that way.

"Come with me," he commanded, motioning for them to follow as he threw an illusion over the scene, making it disappear from sight.

The boys didn't budge, staring frozen and slack-jawed at the spot where only a moment ago they had witnessed a fierce fight.

Damn, would he have to carry them to safety?

"Come on, girls, move it!"

That got their attention, but it seemed their feet were refusing to obey. Yamanu shrugged. He'd hoped to avoid unnecessary thralls, but it seemed there was no other way.

MICHAEL

$\mathcal{M}$ ichael watched the surreal scene unfolding right before his eyes, unable to reconcile what he saw with reality. And if things hadn't been weird enough before, featuring the clash of the titans Jackie Chan style, now the bizarre scene disappeared as if it never existed, leaving behind a dude that looked like something from a shroom hallucination.

Standing at least six and a half feet tall, the man's long black hair reached down to his waist, and his pale blue eyes looked eerie on his dark, angular face.

"Come on, girls, move it!" the dude said, shoving at Michael and his friends and forcing them to start moving.

Herded like sheep, with the tall dude pushing and prodding them to keep going, they made their way through a narrow alley between two buildings. When they came out on the other side, the guy found a bench and pointed to it.

"Sit!" he commanded.

Michael found himself obeying even though he tried to resist.

What the hell? Suddenly Eddie's aliens theory seemed

like the best explanation of what was going on. They were being abducted by aliens who were going to do all kinds of weird shit to them, and he was helpless to do anything about it. The one in front of them was definitely using mind control.

"Look at me!" he commanded in a singsong cadence, compelling them to obey.

Michael closed his eyes, refusing to look into the guy's hypnotic ones. He was going to fight with everything he had. No alien motherfucker was going to mess with him.

He expected the guy to command him to open his eyes, or reach into his mind and compel him to do it, but it seemed that he was more interested in Eddie and Zack.

"What you've just witnessed was nothing. A bunch of drunk students got into a brawl. By tomorrow, you'll forget it ever happened. I want you boys to get up, go on to your rooms and go to sleep. Michael, you stay. I'm taking you to see your auntie. It's a family emergency."

How did the guy know his name? Did aliens perform background checks on their victims? But wait, he'd just sent Zack and Eddie to their rooms. Was Michael the only one the aliens were interested in? Why?

His friends rose to their feet and walked away without giving Michael a second glance; following the dude's command like a couple of zombies.

Carefully, afraid of what kind of alien shit he was going to find, Michael let his senses probe, checking on the guy's intentions. Amusement; the guy thought this was funny.

Fucking alien was scaring the crap out of him, and he thought it was amusing?

Anger fueling his nerves, Michael asked, "How do you know my name? And what auntie? And what family emergency?"

"Good evening, Michael, I'm Yamanu." The stranger smiled and offered Michael his hand, his perfectly straight teeth flashing white in his dark face.

"Hi, normally I would have said nice to meet you back, but I'm not sure it is." Michael shook the frying-pan-sized hand. "And you know my name, how?" Again, Michael reached to feel the guy's emotions. Surprisingly, what he found was respect. What he didn't find, though, were malevolent intentions, or anything that would indicate the guy was an alien.

Yamanu smirked. "You have some balls on you, son; most guys would be a tad more polite in your situation."

"And what situation is that exactly? If you'd be so kind as to enlighten me?" Now that he knew the guy meant him no harm, Michael gathered the courage to stare into the guy's unnerving eyes, forcing himself not to flinch.

Yamanu threw his head back and let out a guffaw, the laugh reverberating through his massive body as he plopped down on the bench next to Michael.

Shaking his head, he wrapped his arm around Michael's shoulders. "I like you, son. Really big balls—coconut size." He gestured with his other hand as if weighing the big fruit. "Not many have the guts to stare down these peepers of mine." He pinned Michael with a stare. "So, I'll tell you what, let's say there are some weirdos out to get you." Yamanu chuckled at Michael's arched brow. "It has to do with the strange things you can do up here." He tapped Michael's forehead. "You ask me how I know," he continued, nodding at Michael's surprised expression. "Dr. Amanda Dokani is a good friend of mine, and she asked my friends and me to protect you. So here we are."

As if on cue, the other two showed up, looking like roadkill; bloodied, their clothes torn and dirty.

"Had a nice time chatting, girls? While we were doing all the dirty work, and the cleanup?" The shorter one of the two sounded only partially amused as he dropped tiredly onto the bench, resting his arms on its back and stretching out his legs.

The other one hesitated for about two seconds before shrugging and doing the same on the other side of the bench.

"Michael, this is Arwel, and that is Bhathian." Yamanu introduced his friends.

They each gave a nod when Yamanu said their name, looking too wiped out to respond. For a moment, the four of them just sat there saying nothing.

"What did you do with the Doomers?" Yamanu broke the silence.

"Sleeping peacefully, loaded and ready to go," Arwel said.

"We'd better get a move on, then." Yamanu rose, giving a hand to Arwel, who stood up groaning.

The guy held his side, leaning into his bracing hand. "I think I have a broken rib."

"You should go see Bridget when we get home, make sure that rib heals right," Bhathian advised while limping along. "I think I'll come with you. Something is wrong with my foot."

Michael walked beside Yamanu, shell-shocked.

Who or what the hell are Doomers? And what did Arwel mean when he said they were sleeping peacefully, loaded and ready to go... Was he talking about the guys they fought off? Was sleeping a euphemism for dead?

Glancing at his companions, Michael let his senses probe freely, but all he felt coming from them was their confidence in their strength and their ability to protect.

They meant him no harm, and they were friends of Dr. Dokani, not aliens. Now that he wasn't as scared, the whole notion seemed ridiculous. Aliens, really. Still, who were the weirdos that were after him, and why the hell did Dr. Dokani have friends who looked and fought like elite commandos?

He was intrigued by the powerful men. Who were these guys? How did they know Dr. Dokani? Were they some secret government agents? Special Ops? With his imagination churning up one fascinating scenario after another, by the time they reached the car, his head was pounding worse than before.

Sitting in the back with Arwel, Michael suddenly felt exhausted. And when Yamanu twisted back and looked at him, he felt compelled to let his eyelids slide shut.

Fighting the urge, he forced his eyes to remain open, hoping to see where they were taking him. But a few minutes into the ride, he lost that battle and passed out.

11

SYSSI

*T*he bedroom was still dark when Syssi opened her eyes, with only a smidgen of light coming through the bathroom's cracked door.

Still, it sufficed.

Looking down at the muscular arm draped around her middle, she drew in a deep breath, making an effort to exhale it as quietly as possible so as not to wake Kian. Not yet.

She needed a few moments to think and process what had just happened.

Oh, God. It had been real this time. And the proof was curled behind her back, his big body warm, and his chest rising and falling with each of his slow, rhythmic breaths.

He wasn't a figment of her imagination. She hadn't dreamt this.

Not that she could've imagined any of it if she tried. Syssi couldn't remember ever passing out after sex. But then again, she never had mind-blowing orgasms that left her boneless, breathless, and floating, either.

If she had known sex could be like that, she wouldn't

have stayed celibate for two years. She seriously doubted, though, it could've been so good with anyone but Kian. He had been well worth the wait.

As memories of the experience replayed in her mind, she touched her hand to her neck, for some reason expecting it to feel bruised. But there was nothing there. No tenderness, no teeth marks, and her skin felt as smooth and as flawless as ever.

She must've dreamt the whole bite thing. What was she thinking? It was not as if something like that ever happened outside of fiction. That vampire romance novel had apparently left an impression.

But if that hadn't happened, what else hadn't been real?

Except, she remembered the rest vividly. Every delicious little thing—even that first painful thrust. It hadn't been pleasant, but what had followed had been. At the memory, her channel tightened with desire—the feel of him inside of her, moving slowly, rhythmically, smooth velvet over a hard core...

Bareback! No condom!

Oh. My. God!

She had had unprotected sex with a man she had just met—practically a stranger.

Pregnancy wasn't an issue, as she still had her IUD. But that wasn't the only thing to worry about, was it?

Well, there was nothing she could do about it now.

The good news was that she felt no foreboding, and with her special gift she would've known if there was a reason for worry; her cursed foresight never failed to predict impending disasters.

Still, not using protection had been incredibly stupid.

In her defense, it had been so long since she'd been with a guy, and even then it hadn't been an issue since

Greg had been her first, and they had stayed together for four years.

Except, she should have known better. He should've known better. Kian hadn't been living like a monk before taking her to his bed.

I'm an irresponsible floozy, she thought without any real conviction behind the self-reproach. But even though Kian was guilty of the same, it bothered her that he might think so. After all, she hadn't offered even a token resistance. And to think she had given him that speech about being presumptuous.

What a joke.

Still, as much as she tried, she couldn't feel guilty or even remorseful about the best sex of her life.

Stifling a chuckle, Syssi remembered her grandmother's old-fashioned advice, cautioning her to develop a friendship with a man before jumping into bed with him, or else he'd lose interest once he had his way.

Syssi didn't care.

Even if it had been a one-time deal and she never got to see Kian again, she would've had her way with him anyway. The only problem was that no other man would ever compare. Syssi had a feeling that Kian had ruined it for her with anyone else.

With a heavy sigh, she turned in his arms to look at his sleeping face.

Beautiful.

She couldn't think of a better word to describe him. Handsome just didn't do him justice. It was more than that, though, a lot more. There was so much strength and honor in him. Kian was a leader in the best sense of the word. He led because he considered it his duty, not because he was power hungry or greedy. The poor guy didn't have a life outside of work. And yet, he didn't complain. Giving it all he had, he was sacrificing himself, his health, and his emotional well-being for his family. What bothered her, though, was that it seemed they were taking it for granted. Even Amanda.

Kian needed more balance in his life. If he let her in, she would make sure of it.

Leaning into him, Syssi burrowed her nose under the long strands of his hair and sniffed at the crook of his neck.

His scent was intoxicating.

Warmed by the vapor coming off his skin, she lingered there for a moment, lulled by his scent and the rhythm of his steady pulse. But then as her fingers began tracing the ridges and valleys of his well-defined chest, she shifted to follow them with her eyes.

"Hi, gorgeous," Kian murmured as his hand began a leisurely descent of her back. Palming both of her butt cheeks with one large hand, he pulled her closer, pressing her against his erection.

Lifting her head, she looked at his sleepy face. "Back at you, handsome. I thought you were sleeping."

"Must've dozed off. I still have work to do tonight."

Poor guy. Working on a Sunday night was true slavery. "You know, even slaves get a day off."

"I'm a captive, which is worse."

She quirked a brow. "Whose?" It was impossible to envision anyone bossing Kian around.

"My own flawed character. I'm an obsessive compulsive workaholic." He smiled and bent his neck to cover her mouth in a tender kiss. "But not now. My time with you is the best I've had in ages. I'm not in a hurry to give it up and go back to the drudgery."

Palming the back of her head, he brought her closer so her cheek rested against his pectoral, then resumed his leisurely strokes.

With a contented sigh, Syssi closed her eyes, wishing she could stay like that forever. Because nothing had ever felt that good before.

Not that the sex hadn't been out of this world, but this peaceful closeness was priceless.

Unfortunately, forever turned out to be less than a minute long, as a quiet knock on the door was immediately followed by the butler's hesitant inquiry; "Master? Are you there, master?"

Jerking out of Kian's arms, Syssi pulled the comforter over her naked breasts, afraid that the butler would open the door and poke his head in, looking for his master.

"Shh… It's okay. Come back here." Kian pulled her back down into his embrace. "It's only Okidu. Don't worry—he knows better than to come in."

"Yes, Okidu, what is it?" Kian asked.

"So sorry to disturb you, master. But Yamanu wished for me to inform you that the guest you were expecting has indeed arrived, and he—that is—Yamanu, is inquiring as to what to do with the young man."

"What is he doing now?" Kian asked.

"He is sleeping down in the guest suite, master."

"Let him sleep. Tell Yamanu I'll deal with the boy later." Kian dismissed him.

"As you wish, master." Okidu acknowledged so politely, Syssi imagined him bowing to the closed door. And maybe he had because it took a few seconds before she heard his light footsteps going back down the hallway.

With a relieved sigh, she snaked her hand under the

comforter, seizing him and stroking him lazily. She asked, "Who is the guest you were expecting?"

Kian's hand closed on her butt and he gave it a light squeeze, then trailed his fingers down the valley between the cheeks, reaching her wet folds from behind. With a feather-light touch, he circled her opening in sync with her up and down strokes, getting her wetter by the second. "It's not important. Keep stroking me like that and I'll be buried inside you in a flash," he slurred.

Syssi pushed back against his stroking fingers and tightened her grip around his length. "Is that a threat or a promise?"

"Stop." Kian gripped her wrist, stilling her hand. "You must be sore from before, and I don't want to hurt you again." He winced.

She smiled at him sheepishly. "Would it offend you terribly if I said I wasn't sore?" Biting on her bottom lip, she looked at him from under her long lashes.

"To the contrary, I take pride in a job well done." Kian chuckled as he stretched himself on top of her, pinning her arms to her sides. "Are you sure?"

The confinement ratcheted her arousal, and she moaned deep in her throat. "I want you."

With his eyes locked on hers, Kian raised his hips and positioned himself at her opening. Nudging her entrance with just the tip of his shaft, he waited as she grew wetter before pushing in slowly.

This time, as he slowly eased into her tight sheath, stretching her, there was only pleasure, and she felt her inner muscles ripple along his length, pulling him in.

Kian closed his eyes, groaning as he rammed the rest of the way in.

Syssi gasped at the sudden invasion, more from the

suddenness of it than any discomfort. He felt perfect inside her, and she pushed her thighs even wider apart, drawing him impossibly deeper.

They were both breathing heavily, their chests heaving, each inhale and exhale eliciting corresponding tightening and expanding in their sexes.

Kian retracted just a fraction, then slowly pushed back, repeating the shallow movements a few more times before wrapping his arms around her and flipping them over, positioning her on top.

Syssi pushed up to her knees and straddled his hips, bracing her hands on his chest. With her fingers splayed over his pecs, she rocked her hips, lifting and lowering herself on his shaft.

"You're so beautiful," she whispered and leaned to kiss his lips. But as she tried to lick into his mouth, he stopped her. Just as he had done before.

With his fingers pulling at her long hair, he took over and thrust his tongue into her mouth. Wrapping his other arm tightly around her middle, he held her down against his body as he pounded up into her with increasing ferocity.

On the verge of climax, her core tightening and rippling, Syssi whimpered.

Her response spurring his aggression, he fisted more of her hair, pulling on the roots and inflicting pinpricks of pain. As he pounded his hips up into her faster, harder— his penetration was so deep, he was hitting the end of her channel with every thrust.

Syssi's orgasm erupted in powerful spasms, her core tightening its grip around his thickening erection.

Battering into her, he came with a snarl, flooding her with pulsing spurts of seed.

She collapsed on top of him, her muscles going lax.

As they waited for their breaths to even out, Kian's hands were warm and tender as he stroked her hair and caressed her back—reassuring. Now that the storm was over, his gentleness seemed in stark contrast to his former aggression.

Her chest heaving in sync with Kian's and her cheek on his pec, Syssi listened to his strong heartbeat as it gradually calmed down. Impossibly, he began hardening again inside her. "You're a machine. I can't believe you're up again so soon."

"With you around, I'm afraid I'll be suffering from a case of perpetual hard-on." Kian smirked, but then his expression morphed into one of concern. "Are you okay?"

It seemed he wasn't over her pained reaction to his initial invasion. Apparently, it had been just as traumatic for him as it had been for her. The thing was, she had all but forgotten about it while he was still obsessing. Part of his nature, Syssi supposed, he'd told her so himself. It was sweet, though, the way he kept making sure. It showed that he cared.

"I'm more than okay. A little sore... wink, wink... but in a good way." She smiled coyly, pursing her lips for a kiss.

Flipping them sideways, he kissed her gently. "I have no words, Syssi. I'm afraid anything I'll say wouldn't do justice to the way you make me feel."

She cupped his cheek, caressing it and watching his eyes close in pleasure at her soft touch. "You don't have to say anything. Your body and your eyes tell me all I need to know. For now. Later, when you find the words, you'll tell me." She kissed each eyelid softly. "Don't fall asleep. We both need a shower." She traced his lips with her fingers.

"I'm not sleeping." Kian opened his eyes. "I would love

to take a shower with you, but we better not. I wouldn't be able to keep my hands off of you, and you need time to recuperate." He kissed her fingers, then got out of bed and grabbed his clothes from the floor.

Syssi barely stopped herself from rolling her eyes. She was fine.

"I'll go shower in my room. There are a few things I need to do before I can turn in, but I'll come back and join you later... If it's okay with you?" He paused to look at her.

Syssi lay sprawled on the bed, unabashedly naked under his gaze. And why not? Kian made her feel sexy and desirable.

"You're so beautiful...," he breathed. "I'd better go before I jump you again." Belying his words, he remained rooted in place. With his clothes bundled under his arm, he gazed at her with longing.

Syssi smiled smugly, his praise infusing her with a rush of feminine power. "Just make sure you come back to me. I want to wake up in your arms."

"It's a promise." Kian winked, providing her with a perfect view of his sculpted ass and powerful thighs as he turned to leave.

Once he was out the door, Syssi lingered before getting out of bed. With the endorphins gone, she felt like a wreck; bone tired despite the little shut-eye she got after that first bout of sex with Kian. And it wasn't even eleven at night yet.

Her body protesting being moved, she winced as she shuffled to the bathroom and filled the tub with water—going for another soak to soothe her aching muscles and relieve the soreness she could no longer deny.

So strange that she hadn't been sore at all after the first time, when she should've been. There had been no pain, not even discomfort during the second time, Kian and she fit perfectly, and yet she was sore and achy all over.

Syssi shrugged. The simplest explanation was usually the correct one. After the first time, she probably had been so high on endorphins that she couldn't feel anything other than bliss.

12

KIAN

*B*racing his hands on the shower's marble wall, Kian let his head drop between his outstretched arms. With the hot water blasting him from multiple jets, he felt good, relaxed.

Syssi was a perfect fit for him. So much so that he doubted he would've been able to conceive of someone like her even if he tried. Without knowing her, experiencing her, he wouldn't have known what to ask for.

It was like she was made for him. And although he had just met her, he had yet to find even one thing he didn't like about her. But then, on some level he hoped he would. Some annoying habit, or a personality flaw that would make it easier to let her go.

It would be excruciating otherwise.

Just thinking about it brought on a tight, uncomfortable feeling in his gut, and he wished he could drop everything and get back in bed with her, even if only to hold her as she slept.

Except, the anticipated guest was the boy, Michael, and

he needed to check on him and get an update from Yamanu.

As it was, he felt a twinge of guilt for forgetting all about the young man while indulging in mind-blowing sex with Syssi...

Making love, he corrected himself. That definitely was making love.

Sweet Fates. All he wanted was to go back to her, wrap his arms around her, and lose himself in her.

Man! Was he in a shitload of trouble.

What had he done to annoy the vindictive Fates that they would deal him such cruelty? Giving him a taste of heaven, showing him how perfect his life could be with Syssi, and then forcing him to give her up?

He'd been a good son and a good brother, he'd always tried to do the right thing. Why couldn't he get a break?

Unless, he was wrong and Amanda was right and Syssi was indeed a Dormant. In that case he was being rewarded rather than punished.

A fleeting sense of hope banished some of the darkness that had descended on his soul, giving him the burst of energy he needed to keep going and do what needed to be done.

Finishing up quickly, Kian got dressed and headed for the basement.

The guest suites were on the same level as Bridget's clinic and the large commercial kitchen. Getting out of the elevator, he heard Arwel's and then Bhathian's voice coming from the clinic.

Damn, they must've encountered Doomers if they were being treated by the doctor.

"What's going on, guys?" he asked as he entered through the door that had been left open.

Bhathian treated him to one of his ogre frowns. "Doomers, obviously."

"Did the boy get hurt?" Kian hoped the answer was negative. He'd risked the boy's life for the chance of capturing Doomers.

"No, we got there in time. Though barely."

"How are you doing?" Kian was dismayed to see them so banged up.

"On the mend." Arwel pulled down his T-shirt over his bandaged torso.

"Broken rib?"

"Yup."

"How about you, Bhathian?" It was worrisome that the Doomers had managed to get close enough to the guy to cause damage. Bhathian was a powerful and skilled fighter.

"A wrong move, that's all. Busted my ankle, but now it's fine. I'll be as good as new by tomorrow."

No doubt, but that didn't mean that the pounding the men had taken by a bunch of fucking Doomers was not a cause for worry. Unless they had been outnumbered. "How many Doomers showed up?"

Arwel avoided Kian's eyes as he muttered, "Three."

"That's bad, guys. Three Guardians against three Doomers should've been child's play for you."

Bhathian shook his head. "The fuckers have improved a lot since the last time we had a chance to fight them."

"Obviously. Where is Yamanu?"

"Getting a beer in the kitchen."

Beer sounded like a great idea. "You guys want some?"

Bhathian shook his head again. "I'm going to bed. Doctor's orders." He glanced at Bridget.

She patted his wide back like he was a schoolboy with a

scraped knee. "To heal faster, they need to rest, and Bhathian needs to lie down with his leg up."

"Yeah, you're right. Go, get a good night's sleep and we'll discuss what happened out there tomorrow." Kian wanted all of his seven Guardians in top notch condition as soon as possible. Two down, even for one night, was worrisome.

He needed to talk to Yamanu. Kian found him in the kitchen, nursing a beer and demolishing a bag of potato chips.

"I heard you got your asses handed to you." Kian walked over to the fridge and pulled out a cold one for himself.

Yamanu smirked. "I wouldn't go that far, but it was a nasty surprise. They fought to the death."

Kian lifted a brow. "You killed all three?"

"No, they're in the crypt, together with the other two."

Kian popped the cap off the bottle and took a swig. "I wish you would've left one conscious for interrogation. We need to find out how many of them are here, and where they are staying. I'm so damn tired of being on the defensive. For once I would've loved to go after the fuckers. Get to them before they got to us." Kian took another swig.

Yamanu shook his head. "That was the plan. But the Doomers fought a suicidal battle, and I had to leave Arwel and Bhathian to it and go take care of Michael and his friends."

"That's not good."

"We had no choice."

Kian nodded. "What about the boy? You said his friends were involved?"

Yamanu waved with his beer. "It's all taken care of. I

thralled the other two and sent them to their rooms, then compelled Michael to sleep."

"Good."

"He is a fighter."

"Michael?"

"Yeah. His friends too, but they are human."

"So is Michael."

Yamanu nodded. "So you don't think Amanda is right about this?"

"No, I don't. But too much is at stake not to give it a try. We'll see how it goes."

"The kid has potential; courage, cool head, good instincts. Michael has all the makings of a good fighter. Guardian material."

"It's a little premature to talk about recruiting. First, we need to find out if he is one of us, which is doubtful."

"You're the boss." Yamanu saluted with the bottle.

Kian walked over to the suite adjacent to Michael and watched the kid sleep through the two-way mirror as he contemplated what to do with him. Pulling out his phone, he rang Amanda.

"What?" She sounded agitated. Well, tough, he needed her help.

"We have Michael. I thought you would like to know as soon as he got here."

"Is he okay?"

"He is fine, the Guardians not so much." He heard Amanda gasp and quickly added. "A little banged up, that's all. They had a run in with Doomers."

"Damn, I should come home."

"Where are you?"

This was an improvement; Amanda calling the keep "home."

"Same as every night, I'm on the prowl."

"When can you be back?"

"Half an hour."

"Come down to the basement. I'm in the room next to Michael's, the one with the two-way mirror."

"Fine." The line went dead.

Michael's *guest room* was nothing but a fancy jail cell; complete with an en-suite bathroom, a big flat-screen, a PlayStation, and an assortment of DVDs and video games.

Very comfortable accommodations designed to keep guests for as long as needed, willing or not.

Finally, when the door banged open, more than an hour later, Kian didn't bother to look—recognizing his sister's signature dramatic entrance. He rolled his eyes; Amanda couldn't do "subtle" if her life depended on it. And instead of hi-how're-ya, the first words out of her mouth were, "I see you got the poor kid thralled."

"What did you want me to do? Tell him bedtime stories until you showed up? You said half an hour!" Annoyed, Kian waved his hand in the air.

"Oh, excuse me. Unlike my high and mighty brother who has a sweet, little hottie waiting for him in bed, some of us still need to go prowling."

"Watch your tone, Amanda. You sound like a petulant teenager, and just as inappropriate."

"I know, right?" Amanda ran her fingers through her short hair and shivered. "It's just that I had a sucky night. The guy I picked up… Ugh… big mistake."

Kian tensed immediately, ready to storm out and do some damage. "Did he hurt you?"

"Oh, please…" Amanda rolled her eyes. "As if a mortal could. Let's just say that if not for your call, I would have gone looking for the next one to erase the memory of the first one… Never mind; it happens. Thankfully, not often."

Crossing over to the two-way mirror, Amanda braced her palms against the glass. "What a shame this cutie is too young, just look at that body…"

Kian smirked. "I didn't know you had an age limit."

"I draw the line at twenty-one. If they can't drink…"

Kian walked over to stand next to her, shoving his hands in his back pockets. "There is always Mexico. I think the drinking age is eighteen over there. You could go for a visit."

"Ouch!" he exclaimed when she kicked his shin. "What was that for?"

"For being an ass." She smirked. "So tell me, how did it go with Syssi?"

"You want the long or the short version?"

"I want all of it. Spill!"

"I like her."

"Oh, come on! That's all you're gonna give me?"

"Yep."

"You mean, mean, old goat… I hate you!" She slapped his back, slanting her eyes at the smug smile he was trying to suppress.

"What do you want to do with the kid? We can't hold him down here forever." Kian returned to the subject at hand.

Amanda shrugged, crossing her arms over her chest. "We can try turning him. He is as good a prospect as Syssi, and we've already got him here."

"It's not as simple as it is with Syssi… I can't believe I just said that… I'll rephrase… In some ways, it's even more complicated than it is with Syssi. He has to fight one of us aggressively enough for the guy fighting him to generate venom. How are we going to explain that?"

"Tell him the truth?"

"Are you out of your mind?"

"You can always thrall him later if it doesn't work."

"And what, keep him locked up down here while we beat the shit out of him on a daily basis?"

"Just look at him!" Amanda pointed at Michael. "He is a football player... this kind of challenge will appeal to his testosterone-impaired, guy-brain. He'll probably think it's all a great macho test and love every minute of it."

"I don't know..." Kian rubbed the back of his neck, still unconvinced.

"Let's go to sleep. We'll decide how to do it in the morning. I'm bushed."

Leaving, Amanda leaned and kissed Kian's cheek. "Good night. Sleep tight. Keep Syssi's neck safe from your bite...," she singsonged on her way out.

As the bed sunk under his weight, Kian cursed silently. But Syssi just sighed and turned around. Lifting the comforter, he carefully slid behind her warm, sleeping body.

Bummer. She wasn't naked. And under the long T-shirt she wore as a nightgown, she was wearing panties as well —and not the thong kind.

How disappointing.

"Hi, what time is it?" she whispered groggily and yawned.

"It's late. Go back to sleep, sweet girl," he whispered and kissed her exposed neck.

"Hmm... that felt nice." Syssi sighed.

Smiling contentedly, he relaxed behind her, cocooning her with his body.

Good night, sleep tight, don't let the immortal bite. Amanda's little rhyme played in his head as he drifted off.

DALHU

*D*alhu paced the mansion's long upstairs gallery, seething with impotent rage. To say he was disappointed was the understatement of the century.

The team he had assigned to lie in wait for the woman had given up at sunrise, requesting permission to abandon post when it had become clear she wasn't coming home. The team he had sent after the guy had never come back or reported at all.

Their phones were dead.

The men were dead.

As capture wasn't an option for Doomers, they would've kept fighting until dealt a mortal blow. If struck down by mere mortals, they would've been left for dead, only to regenerate later and come back to base. But as none of the three had, he had to assume they had been taken out by Guardians. Just like the first two.

The Guardians were proving to be a real pain in his ass. He was down to six men.

Fisting his hands, Dalhu gathered his resolve. With the

obvious presence of his enemy luring him like a vulture to the smell of carrion, there was no way in hell he was going to give up. He would just have to regroup and reevaluate his strategy.

It had been monumentally stupid of his men to ransack the lab and alert the enemy to the fact that they'd gotten their hands on that notebook—allowing the Guardians to take preemptive measures.

Those two potential Dormants should've been free for the picking if not for the morons he had sent to the lab.

It should have been a stealth operation.

Lucky for them, those men were already dead. Taken out by the Guardians that had been protecting the telepath. Otherwise, he would have slaughtered them himself. Slowly.

Nevertheless, it was nothing but another setback.

He needed to come up with a plan. And to do so he had to make a list of all that he knew about the enemy; their strengths and weaknesses, patterns of behavior, how and where the few other immortal hits the Brotherhood had scored over the centuries had been accomplished. Only then could he figure out the right approach.

The next order of business would be to ask for rein-forcements, which would be tricky. He would have to come up with a way to make the request without revealing the losses he had incurred. Reporting casualties, in the absence of results substantial enough to justify the losses, could have dire consequences for him.

Failure was not tolerated in Navuh's camp. Men lost their heads for less.

In the meantime, though, he had to boost morale among his remaining men. Not to mention his own.

The hookers he had reserved for tonight, or call girls as they preferred to be called, would be a step in the right direction.

Nothing like a night of debauchery to make everyone happy.

14

KIAN

"Where are you going?" Syssi asked groggily.

"Go back to sleep, sweet girl. I'm going down to the gym. If I don't squeeze my workout in first thing in the morning, I'll never get to it later." Kian kissed her warm, smooth cheek.

She turned, peering at him from under heavy lids. "What time is it?"

"It's five in the morning. Way too early for you."

"You slept even less than I did!" she protested, pulling on his hand to get him back in bed.

"I don't need as much sleep as you do, and you definitely need the rest." Kian winked and leaned to kiss her mouth.

Syssi shook her head, pressing her lips tightly together. "Morning breath," she mumbled through clenched teeth.

Kian cocked an eyebrow. "Mine or yours?" He smiled and kissed the corner of her mouth anyway.

Grabbing a pillow, she hid her face under it to escape his kisses.

Not discouraged by her antics, Kian leaned down to her

other end, kissing the little bit of butt cheek protruding from her panties. Her skin there was so soft and her scent so sweet, he couldn't help himself and nipped a little.

"Stop that!" Syssi tugged on her nightshirt to cover her cute little butt.

"I can't help it. You're too tasty..." He pulled her shirt back up, and after another quick nip to her bottom, rushed out, dodging the pillow she threw at him.

———

Down at the gym, the activity was already going full swing when Kian walked in.

"Boss man! Over here!" Yamanu called from his station next to the racks of barbells, curling his bulging bicep.

Kian lifted a barbell as well and started his reps. "I'm surprised everyone is here so early. What's going on?"

"Finally seeing some action got everybody excited. There's nothing like the prospect of kicking some Doomer ass to motivate the guys to get back in top shape."

"And here I thought all of this time you were training hard to be ready for battle, when all along you were only doing it to look good for the ladies." Kian shot Yamanu a mocking grin.

The guy arched his brows and flipped Kian the bird before getting serious. "The SOBs are strong fighters. Last night, they managed to inflict some serious damage on us. That never happened in the old times. It shouldn't have been that difficult to subdue the motherfuckers. And regardless of whether they've gotten better or we've gotten weaker, we cannot afford to leave it at that." Yamanu paused as he switched hands. "We've been slacking off lately. It's time to get back in the game."

"It's good that you guys got some fire under your lazy asses, but I don't anticipate any more skirmishes." Kian switched sides as well. "As it is, we already have five undead in our crypt. At this rate, collecting more of their worthless carcasses will necessitate an expansion." Kian chuckled, taking a small rest before starting over on his left side.

Yamanu switched hands again, continuing the reps without rest. "What do you plan to do with them?"

Kian shrugged. "I don't know. It's not like we need to feed them. They just take up space. If it was up to me... well, you know my opinion on the subject. But Annani doesn't want them dead."

Kian had learned long ago that there was no point in trying to change his mother's mind once she made her decision. And as the head of their clan her word was final. Besides, more often than not, she had proven to be right in the end.

He had to wonder, though. Did she plan to keep the Doomers frozen like that indefinitely? Or did she delude herself that they could be redeemed; made to realize the evil of their ways and see the light.

She should know better than that.

Centuries of brainwashing and hatred couldn't be undone. Wishing it would not make it so.

Kian shrugged. "How is the boy doing, still asleep?"

"I didn't wake him, so he'll keep sleeping until I do. What's the deal with him? Do we keep him?" Yamanu shifted the barbell and began working on his triceps.

"Amanda wants to try turning him. I'm going to give him the option of giving it a try or having his memory scrubbed. Then we will need to figure out where to hide him so the Doomers can't find him, and what story to plant in his head so he can tell his parents he is alive. I don't want to ruin the kid's life. It's a messy situation."

"What about the other one? The girl?"

Damn. Anandur and his big mouth. He had probably told every occupant of the keep about Syssi. Not the way Kian wanted to play this.

"I don't know what I'm going to do with her. In the meantime, she stays with me. So hands off." The last thing he needed was for the Guardians to start sniffing around his woman. A potential Dormant was a huge deal, something every immortal male coveted; a beautiful potential Dormant was a cause for riots. Besides, he would rather not have to kill any of his nephews because they'd made a move on Syssi.

The way to solve it would have been to declare her his officially, but he couldn't do it, not before he told her everything and she accepted him as hers. The thing was, he couldn't tell her anything yet.

Yamanu flashed Kian his perfect smile. "Nice... Let me guess... You are in charge of turning the girl. You lucky bastard!"

Kian ignored Yamanu's big grin, doing like the three wise monkeys, and switched subjects back to Michael. "When you're done here, go wake the kid up. I'll get Amanda and we'll talk to him."

Kian replaced the barbell on the rack and walked over to the row of treadmills. Switching one on, he began pounding away at a clip pace.

15

MICHAEL

"*T*ime to get up, kid!"

Startled by a hand shaking his shoulder, Michael surged up. "What? Where?"

He had no idea where he was, but he recognized the tall, dark man staring at him with a pair of eerie pale blue eyes.

Yamanu—the dude from last night.

"Where am I?" Michael rubbed at his temples as he swung his legs down the bed's side, then looked at his socked feet. Someone had taken his Converses off. Luckily, his socks were relatively clean and free of holes. Getting dressed for the club last night, he realized that he had run out of clean ones and had pulled the least dirty pair out of his overflowing laundry bin.

With a quick glance around, he saw his brand-spanking-new Converse shoes lined up against the wall with their toes pointing in like two misbehaving brats sent there to serve penance.

"You're enjoying Dr. Dokani's hospitality. Five-star accommodations, including a change of clothes, a new toothbrush, and a razor. It's all in the bathroom. And when you're done there, your complimentary breakfast is waiting right here." Yamanu pointed to the covered tray on the coffee table.

As the appetizing smells registered in his sluggish brain, Michael salivated, suddenly feeling hungry as hell. No big surprise there. He always woke up hungry. But for once, there was something more pressing than food.

"When is Dr. Dokani going to see me? I really need someone to clue me in as to what kind of shit I'm in, and how deep."

"Go get cleaned. And better be quick about it, she'll be here shortly…" Yamanu scrunched his nose in distaste. "You stink."

Lifting his arm, Michael sniffed at his armpit. It wasn't that bad… "I don't know what you're talking about, dude. You're worse than my mom."

Yamanu shook his head as he turned to leave. "Just trust me on that."

Trust him… like he had a choice.

Taking off his clothes, Michael looked around the bathroom for a place to dump his dirty stuff, but there was nothing that looked like a laundry basket. And unlike his bathroom at the dorms, this one was nice and clean and smelled good. So instead of dropping them on the floor like he usually would, he folded them on top of the counter next to the new clothes Yamanu had left for him.

First, he used the razor to shave off his stubble. Some guys looked awesome with a little growth, but not him. Michael's square jaw was too big and too pronounced already to add anything to it. A shame, because he hated shaving every morning.

Next, he got into the shower and used the soap liberally, especially on his armpits. If Yamanu could smell him, so would Dr. Dokani, and he couldn't allow that. The professor wasn't the kind of woman any guy dared approach in a less than perfect state of grooming.

Not that he thought he had a chance with her, or anything ridiculous like that. The woman intimidated the hell out of him.

He actually preferred to come for testing when the professor wasn't there. Syssi was much more approachable, and he felt comfortable with her, enough to even flirt a little. He had no chance with her either, but at least she was nice about it, letting him get away with way more than anyone in her position would. It was a shame she was older. Not that he had a problem with that, but she obviously did.

After the shower, Michael got dressed quickly and headed back to the suite's small living room where his breakfast was waiting. Hopefully it was still warm.

When the knock came, Michael was about to inhale the last pastry on his plate. Stuffing it into his mouth and chewing quickly, he walked over to the door.

Opening the thing from the other side, Dr. Dokani walked in with an enviably good-looking dude.

Figures, Michael thought, *for a chick like her to have a boyfriend that looks like that.*

"Good morning, Michael, I hope you had a pleasant and restful sleep," she said.

Michael shook the hand she offered.

"This is Kian, my brother." She motioned to the guy.

He shook the dude's hand as well.

A brother then, not a boyfriend... As if it matters... Like I had a chance in hell, Michael thought while fronting like he was cool—confident.

"Let's have a seat, shall we?" She pointed to the couch and sat across from him on the chair. She was wearing a skirt. It wasn't short, but it must've ridden up a little as she sat down, because part of her thigh was showing and it was very shapely. In fact, it was so shapely that he had trouble looking away.

The brother cleared his throat, and Michael had no choice but to tear his eyes away from the professor's legs. The stern stare he encountered was enough to chill his overheating blood.

His butt dropped onto the sofa as if he'd been physically pushed. Sitting on the very edge, Michael planted his elbows on his knees and clasped his hands in front of him. Leaning toward the professor, he purposefully kept his eyes level with hers. "Dr. Dokani, what's going on?"

"Amanda... please call me Amanda. We are all friends here. Kian?" She turned to her brother who was still standing. "Would you like to be the one to explain?"

"No, sister mine. You do the honors, I insist." The dude pinned her with a hard stare.

Not fair, she mouthed at him.

He is your talent, he mouthed back.

"Guys? How about you clue me in? You're freaking me out."

What the fuck?

How bad could it be, for these two to argue about who would deliver the grim news?

"Okay, I'll start." Amanda sighed and recrossed her long legs. Michael prided himself on keeping his eyes on her face and not taking a peek to see if her skirt had ridden even higher. And it had nothing to do with the intimidating brother who had sat down next to her in the other chair, facing Michael as well. Nothing at all.

"What I'm about to tell you will sound unbelievable, fantastic, and though I'm sure you'll have many questions, I ask that you just listen until I'm done."

Michael swiped two fingers over his lips in a zipping motion.

"Okay, then," Amanda said.

"Thousands of years ago, a species of nearly immortal people lived among humans, who believed them to be gods. Their bodies neither aged nor contracted disease. And as they healed and regenerated from most injuries quickly, they were almost impossible to kill. They also possessed special abilities, like the ability to create powerful illusions. These powers, along with their immortality, made them seem divine to the primitive people.

"They took mates from among the humans and many mixed children were born, possessing some of the powers as well. But as in any society, there were internal struggles for power, which eventually resulted in a nuclear catastrophe that wiped out the gods and a huge chunk of the mortal population.

"One lone goddess escaped the cataclysm, taking with her the advanced knowledge of her people. She had made it her mission to trickle this knowledge to humanity, and over the millennia guided it to become a more advanced, better society. But she had enemies.

"The scions of her nemesis survived the nuclear disaster and embarked on a road of destruction, vowing to eliminate her, her progeny, and any progress humanity achieved through her help.

"We, as her descendants, are helping her achieve her goals. Unfortunately, there are not many of us. We believe, though, that there are Dormant mortals, people carrying our genetic code that we can activate. To date, all our attempts at identifying Dormants have failed. I started my research on a hunch, believing some Dormants might exhibit paranormal abilities. Among all my test subjects, you and my assistant Syssi were the only ones talented enough to be considered potential candidates."

Amanda paused to take a breath. "Our enemies of old, the Doom Brotherhood or Doomers as we call them, got hold of parts of my research that contained information about Syssi and you. Being identified as potential Dormants, you became highly coveted targets for them. Luckily, we were able to get to you before they did. Now we face a dilemma. I'll let Kian explain."

Michael looked first at Amanda's serious face then Kian's, then back at Amanda's, waiting for them to crack and tell him they were pulling his leg. But as they held on to their serious expressions, gradually his mouth morphed into a smile. Clapping his hands and laughing he looked at the ceiling and the two-way mirror.

"I knew it. I've been punked! You have a camera crew behind that mirror. Damn!... For a moment, you got me there... unbelievable.... Okay, guys, you can come out now... you had your fun..." Michael looked at the door, waiting for it to burst open.

"Guys?" He looked at Amanda and Kian. "Oh, come on, how long are you going to drag it out? I'm on to you..."

"I think Michael needs a demonstration." Amanda turned to her brother.

"It would be my pleasure." Kian's evil smile should've warned Michael something other than a joke was up. Though later, when he would think about it, nothing could've prepared him for what came next.

Right in front of his eyes, Kian began morphing into a creature straight out of a nightmare. Somehow he was becoming larger—like in huge—his skin turning red, and black horns sprouted on top of his head. His eyes, which had been blue a moment ago, turned completely black, and long, sharp fangs protruded from that cruel mouth that was still smiling that evil smile.

But now it was absolutely terrifying.

"What the hell?!" With no way to escape other than going through that demon, Michael scrambled back and climbed the sofa's back, screeching like a chick.

The demon disappeared in a flash, and in its place Kian was back, with the same god-awful smile plastered on his smug puss. "Need some more convincing? I can do Bigfoot, King Kong… Ask me. It's the only time I'll take requests, so don't be shy," the jerk taunted.

"You put something in my food, drugged me, I know it…" Michael's heart was pounding in his chest louder than it did when he had faced those titans last night. He got so scared, his hands were shaking.

His hands had never done that before. Ever.

This must be what a bad trip feels like, he thought as he wiped his sweaty palms on his jeans. Zack had one, after trying some weird stuff the guys from the chemistry department had cooked, and he had sworn never to touch hallucinogenics ever again. Now Michael understood why.

"There was nothing in your food and you know it. You're just trying to rationalize the unbelievable, choosing to believe in something even more outlandish instead. Does that make sense to you?" Kian sounded like he was losing his patience.

Michael rubbed his chest as he tried to force his brain to stop misfiring so he could think for a moment. The demon from hell had appeared right after Kian had promised a demonstration. From the little he knew about how hallucinogenic drugs worked, it didn't make sense that the effect could have been so well timed.

But Amanda's story was just too out there.

Except, why would they go to all this trouble to deceive him? He was a nobody. What would they gain by messing with him?

"I'm listening…," Michael capitulated, figuring he had nothing to lose by hearing the rest of the story: incredibly scary guy getting pissed, notwithstanding.

"Good, so here is the dilemma. In order to activate your dormant genes, one of us has to inject you with venom… Yeah, venom. You heard me right." Kian raised his palm to stop Michael's what-the-hell?

"The males of our species have fangs that produce venom in two situations." Kian lifted his hand, two fingers up. "During sex or when aggressing on other males. This venom is what facilitates the activation. We know this because that's how we activate our boys when they reach puberty. We treat it as a right of passage ritual. An older boy is chosen to fight the Dormant, who only has to fight well enough to generate the level of aggression needed for the older boy to produce venom and bite him. For a thir-teen-year-old, in most cases one time is enough. In an adult male your size, we have no clue. We've never done it before. This means that you'll have to go through gladiator style matches every day until you turn or give up. If you turn, you gain immortality and become one of us. If you don't, we erase your memory of our existence."

"So what's the dilemma?" Michael asked. "It seems you've already decided what you want to do with me."

"First of all, no, it's up to you. You decide you don't want to get beaten bloody and pumped with venom every day—we erase your memory now. You choose to stay—I already explained what happens then. The problem is that out there Doomers are waiting to snatch you, either to kill you or somehow use you. You cannot go back to school or to your parents' home.

"We'll take care of you, of course; provide resources for relocation, new name, new school, whatever you need. Plant new memories in your mind, giving you some plausible explanation for the whole mess. But you need to make up your mind and decide if you're willing to give it a shot. I will not sugarcoat it for you. I don't think it will work. Amanda believes there is a chance and I'm willing to give it a try, but I don't want to give you false hope."

The room went quiet as Michael took a moment to think it through, which wasn't easy with Amanda and Kian staring at him. He felt like the poor schmuck on a game show, standing on a podium and sweating for the answer as the annoying music played in the background.

Michael suppressed a snort as it crossed his mind that Amanda and her jerk brother were certainly pretty enough to play as hosts on this freaky gameshow from hell.

"I'll do it." He broke the silence. "The way I see it, I'm screwed anyway. I can go into your version of a witness protection program now or later, it doesn't really matter. But on the remote chance that I can gain immortality, I'll say it's worth my while to stay here for a few weeks and give you guys a run for your money."

Kian nodded. "There is one more complication you need to consider. The longer you stay, the more memories we'll need to replace, and it may mess with your head. Besides the large chunk of missing time you will not be able to account for, you might remember bits and pieces of events, not knowing if you lived through them or dreamt them, and that's if you get away with no permanent brain damage. I want you to make an informed decision." Kian watched Michael, waiting for him to acknowledge that he understood.

"Yeah, well… I made up my mind. We'll need to come up with a good story to tell my parents, though. I don't want them freaking out when they can't find me at school."

"You come up with the story, we'll help with the details. One last thing; as long as we are running our little experiment, you will have to remain locked up down here. I can't have you wandering around with the knowledge of our existence and our location. I'm sure you can understand the necessity."

"I guess," Michael said in a small voice.

This was the hardest part of the deal for him. He liked being around people. Solitary confinement, even in a sweet dig like this, would be tough.

16

SYSSI

*S*yssi had been disappointed when Kian had left her alone earlier in the morning. The bed felt cold and lonely without him. But she'd gone back to sleep and woke up a few hours later feeling wonderful. In fact, she stayed in bed long after waking, trapped by the tactile pleasure of the duvet's soft fabric and the thick fluffy down comforter it covered.

What a night, she sighed.

In her wildest dreams, she had never imagined she could be like that. Wanton, uninhibited, and what's more, with someone she had just met.

It defied how she defined herself.

Cautious, reserved, shy, risk-averse, was how she thought of herself. Well, she'd have to adopt some new adjectives. Not to replace the old ones, those still applied, but in addition or rather as qualifiers.

She could begin with wanton, though only with Kian… and that was true for uninhibited and a little kinky as well.

Still, it was a good start.

Stretching her arms and toes, she felt good, which

considering the vigorous activities of last night was surprising. And it wasn't just the sense of physical well-being and vitality.

She felt content.

Such a simple and unassuming word—content.

Except, before experiencing it, she hadn't been aware of its lack. It took the absence of the uneasy hum always simmering below the surface of her awareness for her to realize it had even been there.

Syssi wondered how long this I-am-at-peace-with-the-universe sensation would last. Better not to dwell on it, though, lest she hasten the hum's return.

There were more pleasant things to contemplate. Like how comfortable she felt letting go with Kian, or how he seemed to enjoy everything about her.

He'd spent time with her, even though he was so incredibly busy. He'd listened to her talk as if she was fascinating. He'd made love to her, teaching her things about herself she hadn't known. He'd told her over and over again how much he loved the way she yielded to him, ensuring she felt good about it. There had been no artifice in any of it. He had no need. And yet he'd taken the time, showing that he cared.

Kian made her feel secure that way.

Except, was he like this only with her? Or was he making all of his partners feel special?

How many?

The sudden flare of jealousy blew away any remaining vestiges of her peaceful happiness; its shattered pieces lying like boulders on her chest, constricting her ability to draw breath.

She felt queasy imagining the line of gorgeous women coming and going through Kian's home.

His bed.

With that disturbing thought, Syssi was out of bed and in the bathroom in seconds.

Splashing cold water on her face helped. And as she attacked her teeth with the toothbrush, brushing so vigorously that her gums ached, she made up her mind to find out more about Kian.

The best candidate to pump for information was obviously Amanda. Except, protecting her brother, she might not cooperate. And anyway, it would be too awkward.

Okidu, on the other hand, was a different story. Syssi remembered reading somewhere that it was impossible to keep any secrets from the household staff. And if that was true, the butler must know everything that was going on.

With her mind made up, Syssi headed for the kitchen. She was going to have a little chat with the guy.

"Good morning, mistress," Okidu greeted her. "May I offer breakfast? I brewed a fresh pot of coffee and kept some of my famous waffles in the warming drawer for you." He was again smiling that fake-looking smile she had noticed before.

"Thank you, I would love some." Syssi pulled out a stool and sat at the counter.

"Is Kian coming back for breakfast?" She began her casual interrogation.

"No, mistress, he might not be back until lunch. Very busy man, the master. Lots of work to do. Sometimes he even asks me to bring him a sandwich to the office." Okidu placed the steaming mug of coffee in front of her.

"Is his office in the building?" Syssi sipped on her coffee as she observed the butler, trying to glean more information from his expressions and body language.

Nada. Zip. There was nothing there.

Usually, she was very good at reading people; noting the slight changes in their expressions, the way they held their bodies, what they did with their hands—combining all these clues to form a more complete picture than what their words alone provided.

But the butler gave nothing away.

"Yes, indeed it is," Okidu answered, serving her a plate of waffles that smelled divine, covered with fruit and topped with whipped cream.

"In that case he should be back already. I'm sure his workout is not as long."

Okidu smiled again. "Mr. Shai has an office down in the basement, and the master often works from there."

"Who is Mr. Shai?"

"The master's assistant, of course."

Well, at least the assistant was a guy and not some gorgeous secretary in high heels and a miniskirt.

"I guess he doesn't get out much; working as hard as he does, and his office being right here in the building." Feigning nonchalance, Syssi dug into the waffles.

"I would not say that." The butler turned toward the coffeemaker and picked up the carafe to refill her mug.

So, he knows how to be evasive.

Syssi contemplated the best way to phrase her next question to corner him into a yes or no answer. "Do you get to entertain a lot of ladies up here? Besides myself and family members, that is?" She tacked on the last part to close any loopholes. Concentrating on his face, she gave her perception another go. Maybe this time, she'd discern some minute changes in his expression.

"No, mistress, besides you, only family comes up here, and the master begrudges me entertaining even them. They usually come uninvited."

With that fake plastic smile plastered on his wide face, Okidu's demeanor revealed nothing. Still, she didn't think he was lying.

It was a tremendous relief, knowing that Kian had made an exception in her case. The tightness in her chest eased. She was the only woman he had ever brought home. Well, this home, the butler had said nothing about prior residences.

Still, for some reason it placated her. Even if Kian went out every night and had sex with God only knew how many women, he had treated her differently.

She must've meant more to him.

She was special.

DALHU

*D*alhu stared at the empty yellow pad in front of him.

What did he really know about the enemy? Most of his information had come from the Brotherhood's propaganda; admittedly, not the most reliable of sources. And his own experience dealing with the clan had been limited.

To make informed decisions and avoid mistakes, he had to stick to the facts. Things he knew to be true for certain.

That list was frustratingly short.

Starting with what he had learned recently, he filled the first half of the lined page.

First, there couldn't have been more than a few hundred of them, as they were all the descendants of one female and adhered to the old taboos against mating within the same matrilineal line. Which made them desperate enough to search for Dormants descending from other lines among mortals with special abilities.

Second, there was a concentration of them in Los Angeles, the presence of a Guardian Force indicating that there was someone of vital importance here for them to protect. Maybe even their Matriarch...

And wouldn't that make him one lucky SOB.

As he imagined the glory of being the one to lead the final battle over the control of humanity and taking down that abominable female, his chest expanded and he straightened, squaring his shoulders.

Unfortunately, her being here was a speculation and not a fact. Sighing, he slumped back in his chair and looked down at the yellow pad.

Thinking back to what he knew for sure, or at least could make an educated guess about, he flipped to a new page and started a second list.

Most of them weren't fighters; academics, scientists, writers—they didn't pose much of a physical challenge. And in addition to the males who lacked any kind of combat skills, he could completely discount the female half of their small population as well.

The force of Guardians, though, was something to reckon with. These warriors were legendary among the Brotherhood. Part of what had created his impression that the clan was larger than it actually was were the myths surrounding them, making them seem like a large and fierce force.

Dalhu wondered how many Guardians the clan actually had. Not that it made a difference, he seethed. Even if their numbers were small, they had still decimated almost half of his men with ease.

But then, he had no intentions of seeking out Guardians. He definitely didn't need any more proof to convince him that he stood no chance against them—not with the inferior fighters at his disposal.

The rest of the clan was up for grabs, and he didn't

need to catch a Guardian to lead him to their nest. A civilian would do. He just needed to figure out where the rest of them hung out.

There were things all near-immortals had in common; sharper senses and reflexes, stronger bodies that required only a few hours of sleep, and most notably—one hell of a sex drive. Lacking suitable partners in their community, the clan males, just like Navuh's troops, had to rely on mortals to satiate their ferocious appetites.

His brethren, himself included, used hookers, and so had the enemy in days past. Stumbling upon a near-immortal in a whorehouse accounted for the few kills the Brotherhood had scored.

But nowadays, living in the West, women were available to them everywhere. The males were probably prowling the nightclubs and bars, looking for hookups. The corrupt western females, the willing and easy sluts, made themselves available like whores in those places without even asking to be paid for their services.

Dalhu reclined in his chair and smiled as an idea began forming in his head. Nightclubs and bars; that's where he'd find his targets.

Except, the obvious hitch in his brilliant plan was the fact that there were probably hundreds, if not thousands, of those in a city this size.

18

KIAN

"What do you think?" Ingrid asked as Kian followed her into his new informal conference room.

"I'm impressed."

Ingrid's tense shoulders relaxed. "I'm glad. You didn't give me much time."

"I have to hand it to you and William. You've done a spectacular job without my input or interference."

She beamed, straightening her back, suddenly looking a couple of inches taller. "I don't think you complimented me like that even after I did your penthouse, or any of the other spaces I've decorated for this building. I remember you grunting 'good job' and shooing me out."

Kian scratched his stubble. Had he been so callous? He didn't remember what he'd said to Ingrid, but he didn't doubt her words. He wasn't normally generous with praise. If it meant so much to his people, maybe he should make an effort. The thing was, it didn't come naturally to him. He expected top notch performance from everyone around him and took it for granted when things were done to his satisfaction.

"When I'm not happy about something, you'll know it. So when I say nothing it means you've done a great job."

Ingrid grimaced. "I'll remember it for the next time I walk out with tears in my eyes."

"If you don't want this to be the last time you hear a compliment from me, don't try to guilt me into it. I have a mother and three sisters, I'm immune to female manipulation."

She smirked. "If you say so."

Was he that easy to read? Her words had managed to penetrate his thick skin, bringing on an uneasy feeling. He'd kept his expression neutral by going on the offense. She was right, he was an ass.

"I like the clean contemporary lines of the furniture. Are they made of wood? Or is it some composite material?" A useful trick he'd learned to use with the other females in his life—change the subject and have them talk about something they were passionate about.

Worked every time.

"It's not fake. They are made from several varieties of highly polished woods. Cost a fortune, but I saved on the art. How do you like it? I wasn't sure about the black and white, but I thought it would be less distracting for a business environment."

Kian glanced at the large still-life photographs adorning the walls, their unobtrusive lack of color providing some interest without calling too much attention to themselves.

"Good call."

"Thank you." Ingrid bowed her head a little. "I could stay longer and wait for more of your rare words of praise, but I'm sure you have work to do, and so do I. I'm still up to my eyeballs in the other project you assigned to me. Furnishing apartments for all the people coming down from the Bay area is one hell of a task. But it came in handy for getting this office done so quickly. I dangled the huge order in front of my supplier to have him deliver your stuff as soon as possible. He must've given us someone else's order and made them wait instead."

Kian shrugged. Throw enough money at a problem and things happened the way you wanted. "Do you need help? I can assign you an assistant." For a moment, he considered giving the job to Syssi. Decorating wasn't architecture, but it was closer to her field of study than working at Amanda's lab. Except, he had to remind himself that she wasn't staying, and the more memories he would have to scrub, the more damage her brain would sustain. During Syssi's brief stay at the keep, it would be better to keep her as isolated as possible.

Ingrid shook her head. "Thank you, but I'm managing just fine. A little less sleep at night, but it's not like this madness will not end soon."

"For you, yes." For him, not so much. He was stuck in the insane rat race with no exit in sight.

Ingrid nodded. "I'd better get to it. See you later, Kian. Enjoy your new office."

"Thanks."

He waited for her to close the double French doors behind her, and walked over to the massive desk facing them. It was already set up with a desktop and a laptop, no doubt hooked up and ready to go. Behind it a credenza, just as massive, was topped by a huge screen that took up half of the wall above it. The screen would be useful for presentations. That way everyone would be able to watch in comfort instead of cramming together around a laptop.

His favorite was the long conference table with a top made from some beautiful, exotic wood. With six large chairs on each side and one at each end, it could accommodate the smaller meetings of either the Guardians or the council members or both.

He wasn't sure, however, that the fully stocked bar on one side and the serving buffet on the other were such a hot idea. With food and drinks being served, the meetings might drag on forever.

Nonetheless, he liked it.

Sitting behind the desk, Kian smoothed his palms over the glossy surface, contemplating doing his work from down here instead of his home office upstairs.

It was true that he would miss the magnificent view he had from his penthouse. But, on the other hand, it would solve the problem of Guardians intruding on his privacy and barging in on him at all hours of the day. And what's more, with Syssi there, he really didn't like the idea of the men sniffing around his woman.

No, wait, she wasn't his... Couldn't be.

Propping his elbows on the desk, he let his head drop onto his fists. What was he going to do with her? Should he offer her the same deal he'd offered Michael? Somehow that seemed inappropriate. Cruel.

Hey, honey, I'll be fucking and biting you for the next couple of weeks or months. But if you don't turn, I'm going to erase that memory and send you on your way.

Except, what other options did he have? To keep thralling her daily was just as cruel—as well as deceitful. And harmful.

The only decent thing to do was to let her go. Yet, he knew he wouldn't do that.

Couldn't.

She was too important to the clan...

Hell, who was he kidding? She was too important to him.

But what could he offer her that would make it okay? Ease his guilt?

And what about her family? They would be in danger as well.

Sighing, he leaned back in the chair and let his head go lax on the padded headrest behind him. Kian wanted the lie off his chest. But that too was selfish of him.

On the other hand, he'd believed he had been protecting Lavena when he had concealed who he was from her. And look how well that had turned out...

Fuck! Kian banged his head against the headrest. He had completely forgotten about the addiction. They all had— that little ditty of their fucked-up biology being irrelevant to their revolving-door style of sex partners.

The bloody venom was addictive—ensuring mated couples stayed faithful to each other.

At least in theory.

He hadn't known that when he had run away to be with Lavena. Enlightened by his mother upon his return, he'd learned that in addition to becoming a widow at eighteen, Lavena would also suffer from withdrawal.

Apparently, being repeatedly injected with the venom of the same sexual partner created an addiction in his mate. She would be physically repulsed by the sexual scent of other males and crave only him.

Supposedly, it took a long time for the addiction to set in, and just as long for it to wane.

Annani had laughed at his naive assumption that as a result mated couples in their society must've been very faithful to each other.

"To the contrary," she had said.

To avoid getting addicted to one person, some had made sure to be with several partners. Mixing it up. Being such a lustful species, monogamy hadn't been at the top of their highly valued morals. More like near the bottom.

The males hadn't escaped unscathed either; eventually, the addiction had gotten them as well. As the scent of the female had changed with her growing attachment, she had become as irresistible to her mate as he had been to her.

For some, it had happened sooner than for others, Annani and Khiann becoming attached within weeks. She claimed it had happened so fast because they had been so in love.

Kian wondered, though, what came first: the chicken or the egg. The love or the addiction.

Still, he had to consider the possibility that he and Syssi might be of the sooner variety. Which meant that if they were forced to part, in addition to the mental agony, they would suffer painful withdrawal.

Damn, the thought of taking other partners as a preemptive measure sickened him. Worse, the thought of Syssi doing the same enraged him to the point of turning homicidal.

19

SYSSI

"Is there anything else madame requires?" The butler bowed his head.

Someone to talk to, Syssi thought. She was bored out of her mind. "No, thank you."

"I have to leave, but there are plenty of snacks and various beverages in the refrigerator. Please, Madame, feel free to help yourself."

"I will."

The butler retreated with another slight dip of his head.

Great, now she was totally alone in the penthouse. Not that Okidu had been much company, but at least she'd known someone was there.

Having nothing better to do, Syssi poured herself another cup of coffee. She even hazarded reading the headlines of the *Los Angeles Times* that Okidu had left for her on the kitchen counter. Luckily, there had been no new disasters reported.

With the butler gone, all alone in the big, empty penthouse she felt even more restless and bored. Kian must've gone to work straight from the gym, and he hadn't even bothered to call.

Kind of disappointing. And disheartening. The night they had spent together had been monumental in the effect it had on her. That didn't necessitate, though, that it had been even remotely meaningful to Kian.

It made sense. She was young and inexperienced and being with Kian had been like a discovery—a perception-altering one. He, on the other hand, had most likely already experienced the full gamut of things. It had been nothing new for him.

With a sigh, she walked over to the couch, sat down and let her head drop on her fists. All that self-doubt was killing her, and it was made worse by the oppressing quiet of the apartment and having nothing to do to keep her busy. It wouldn't have been so bad if she at least had something to distract her like surfing the Internet.

Kian had left his tablet on the coffee table. Not really expecting it to work for her, Syssi reached for it and turned it on. But it was passcode protected just as she'd known it would be. So that was out. And to use her laptop she needed the access code to the internet, which, of course, she didn't have.

That left only the boring neuroscience papers Amanda wanted her to read. She had them downloaded already, but her brain felt too scattered to concentrate on such heavy reading.

She should call Andrew. In fact, she should've done it as soon as Kian had disposed of her cellphone. If her brother tried her at home or on her cell, not finding her would freak him out. He would think something had happened to her and might mobilize a taskforce to look for her. She'd better let him know that she was alive and staying with Amanda.

Well, she was… kind of.

Shit. She definitely wasn't expecting to find the kitchen phone blocked as well. Who did a thing like that? This was a private residence, not a public office. Had Kian thought that she would make long-distance calls?

The thought was ridiculous. The guy threw money around as if it grew on trees. Phone charges would be the last thing he would've been concerned with.

Maybe it was just the one in the kitchen.

With the coffee mug in hand, she walked down the hallway, checking the phones in every bedroom and finding each and every one blocked.

The last door to the right led to what must've been Kian's home office. And though it was neat and tidy, it didn't look like the kind a decorator stocked with shelves full of leather-bound books no one ever read—for the sake of appearances.

It was obvious Kian worked here.

A stack of correspondence was piled next to the keyboard, with colorful sticky notes peeping between the pages. Behind the desk, a large cabinet housed a multitude of name-tagged folders—their crumpled edges indicating that they were frequently used.

Curious, Syssi tilted her head to read some of the labels.

It was an interesting assortment of enterprises. The information the folders contained must've been on companies comprising an investment portfolio, as it didn't make sense that Kian's family business was that diversified.

Some of the names sounded like biotech companies, software firms, building projects, ore and coal mines. Others had been marked by acronyms that bore no meaning she could decipher. He'd told her about the real estate and the drone factory, but apparently Kian was investing heavily in other industries as well.

Taking a seat in his executive swivel chair, she checked the phone on his desk. It was blocked like the rest of them, and so was the desktop.

Seriously annoyed, she considered leaving.

As far as she knew, she wasn't a prisoner and could come and go as she pleased... unless the elevator was code blocked as well, and she'd have to take the emergency stairs to get down to the lobby. For a moment, she actually contemplated trudging the many floors to reach the street level.

Exasperated, Syssi returned to the living room and took to pacing it in circles. The longer she paced, the angrier she got at Kian.

The nerve of this man, leaving her without any means of communication. And where was the new cellphone he had promised her?

Evidently, he was just as thoughtless and clueless as the rest of his gender. Only, being gorgeous and sexy, he was more likely to get away with it.

As her next round brought her to the glass doors, she paused to look out, pining for the outdoors like a caged bird.

Well, she wasn't really caged... she was free to roam the terrace... Har-har, hardy-har-har.

With a strong shove, she sent the glass panels into their concrete hiding place and stepped out. The distant sound of the city hustle and bustle was a welcome intrusion after the solitude of the inside. Standing in the light breeze, she felt it waft across her face and carry some of her ire away.

Taking a calming breath, she walked over to where she

had eaten her solitary dinner last night, and sitting down, noticed Kian's forgotten pack of cigarettes.

It had been years since she had smoked as a rebellious teenager pushing at her boundaries, but here and there she still craved it. Especially when she got seriously pissed off. Like now.

What the heck, why not, she thought, it wasn't as if she was planning on making it a habit.

Pulling one out, she held it between her thumb and forefinger and moved to lie down on the lounger. Lighting up, she was careful not to inhale too much, letting most of the smoke out.

The point was to enjoy the little sinful pleasure without getting dizzy, which was what would happen if she inhaled too much too fast. She needed to ease into the tobacco's effects.

Still, as careful as she was, she got a little light-headed and closed her eyes.

Funny, how this forbidden pleasure made her feel naughty. Or how ridiculous it was that she felt grateful that there was no one around to witness her crime.

Most of her friends smoked pot, which she refused to touch, but they frowned on cigarettes. Kind of hypocritical. But whatever, people justified their own vices anyway they could, but they didn't extend the same courtesy to others.

Hannah claimed it was the smell that was offensive, but Syssi thought pot smelled way worse. Like mold and dirty socks. Ugh. How could anyone put it in their mouths?

She chuckled. They probably thought the same thing about tobacco.

Pulling small drags then exhaling them, she felt herself

relax, and with each pull her tight muscles released more of their tension.

It wasn't long before her mind wandered back to last night. Syssi felt changed by the experience. What was hidden and repressed even from her own psyche had gotten loose. And instead of being terrified, she found it liberating.

Whether there was a future for her with Kian or not, she'd be forever grateful to him for helping her get rid of her suffocating inhibitions.

Taking another drag on the cigarette, she let the carnal scenes replay in her mind. Embracing them, owning them, feeling empowered by them... getting aroused.

20

KRI

ood; someone was cooking something that smelled delicious. Kri stopped in her tracks as the appetizing smells hit her nose. The thing was, no one ever cooked in the basement. Curious and rather hungry, she followed her nose to the kitchen.

"What are you doing here?"

It wasn't every day that Kian's butler roamed the lower levels of the basement in general, or visited the big commercial kitchen that no one ever used for anything other than storing beer and dried goods in particular.

"I am cooking for our new guest, Madame," Okidu said.

"Could you stop calling me that? It gives me the creeps. The humans call old ladies Madame."

He quirked an eyebrow. "Would you prefer mademoiselle?"

"I would prefer Kri. That's my name."

"I cannot oblige you, Madame, or if you prefer, Mademoiselle."

Yeah, he probably couldn't. If it had been hardwired into his programming, nothing could change it.

"Fine, the other one. At least it doesn't sound like you're addressing an old lady."

He dipped his head. "As you wish, Mademoiselle."

Kri got closer and peeked to see what was in the pot. Some kind of stew that didn't look very appetizing but smelled divine. The good news was that there seemed to be enough in there to feed the entire Guardian force, including Anandur and Bhathian, which was saying a lot. Okidu was using one of the commercial sized pots.

"Is it ready?"

"It is, Mademoiselle."

"Can I have some?"

"Naturally. I cooked enough for twenty-seven people."

Kri chuckled. "Which means it's just enough to feed the Guardians."

"If you say so, Mademoiselle. The Guardians and Master Kian and his two guests and several others."

Right, she'd heard about Amanda's assistant staying at Kian's. Not something Kri appreciated at all. Even though there was no chance that there could ever be anything between Kian and her, she certainly didn't want to see another female sharing his penthouse. Too cruel.

Well, if Kian was entertaining one of the guests, she could entertain the other.

"Okidu, would you mind if I bring our guest his lunch?"

"Not at all, Mademoiselle. Let me prepare a tray for you."

"Thank you."

When it was ready, Kri hefted the thing and carried it down the corridor. Standing outside Michael's room and listening to the sounds coming from behind the closed door, Kri's lips curled in a knowing smile.

Machine-gun fire and exploding grenades accompanied by a litany of expletives could mean only one thing—the kid was putting the PlayStation to good use. And by the sound of it, he was playing Call of Duty—her favorite game.

Holding a tray with one hand and balancing it on her hip, she entered the numbers into the room's code-protected lock and pushed open the door.

"Room service!" she called out, snapping Michael's attention from the game.

"Oh, hi." He looked up from the couch, his eyes widening as they traveled up and down her body.

"I've got your lunch, kid, where do you want it?" She stifled a grin, glancing away from his blushing face to the coffee table, which was littered with open covers of DVDs and video games, a half-eaten bag of potato chips, and two empty beer bottles.

"Just give me a moment to clean up this mess." Michael got busy stuffing the games and movies back in their cases and putting them away, then threw the rest of the stuff into the trash container.

"Here we go!" He straightened to his full height and pointed to the table.

Nice. The kid was tall and built like a linebacker. And that cute, shy smile was... yum.

Shooting him her crooked smile, Kri lowered her butt to the couch and placed the tray on the table.

"Come, let's eat." She moved two plates off the tray, then patted the spot next to her. "I figured that being stuck here all by yourself you'd like some company. By the way, I'm Kri." She extended her hand, which he shook.

21

MICHAEL

"*N*ice to meet you… Thank you. That's really nice of you…" Michael sat down next to Kri.

Wow, that is one helluva woman.

He'd been surprised by the strength of her handshake. Hell, he'd been surprised by the whole package. It wasn't often that he met a girl who was almost as tall as he was, had more pronounced biceps than most guys, and looked like she could kick some serious ass.

Catching a glimpse of her impressive cleavage as she bent down to scoop rice onto her plate, his eyes got stuck staring, and he salivated a little.

She was so damn hot…

"Eyes up here, kid!" She pointed with two fingers at her clear blue eyes.

His ears heating up in embarrassment, he quickly lifted his eyes to her face.

Up close, Kri was very pretty.

Her smooth, creamy skin was clean of makeup, and the peach shade of her full lips was all her own. A few wayward strands escaped the thick braid of her wavy, light-brown hair, or dark blond, he wasn't sure what to call it, softening the tough impression of her tall, muscular build.

She was tough, but she didn't look any older than he was. So why the hell was she calling him "kid?" Maybe she thought he was younger than he actually was. Not that he could blame her for the misconception, not after the way he stared at her breasts. Like he was some stupid teenager who had never seen boobs before. Well, he hadn't, not like hers. Kri's belonged on a sculpture.

"Sorry, my bad." Michael looked down, busying himself with loading rice and stew onto his plate.

"Nah, it's okay. I get that reaction all the time. Apparently, guys do not expect such a lovely set of double Ds on an athletic female like me." She cupped the bottoms of her breasts, hefting them up for emphasis.

Michael almost choked on a mouthful of rice, spewing some of it out across the tray and spraying it all over their food. Some of it ended up going down the wrong pipe. He coughed, trying to get it out.

Kri's powerful pat on his back didn't help much with the coughing, sending his whole upper body in the same direction instead.

"Stop... please... I'm okay... really..." Michael coughed out the few remaining grains of rice. He'd made a mess of things, but that didn't mean that he deserved broken ribs. The girl was freakishly strong.

"I'm so sorry that I've ruined your lunch. I'm such a klutz..." He looked at the rice-sprinkled food. What the hell was he supposed to do now?

"Don't worry about it. I'm not some delicate, dainty doll. I'll eat it if you will." She took another forkful from her plate, chewing deliberately to make her point.

She certainly wasn't dainty... or girly... or like any other woman he had ever met. His first impression of her just got reinforced. She was a hot, strong, no-nonsense warrior chick.

"Are you married?" he asked, hoping she wasn't.

"Why would it be any of your damn business?"

"Because short of a husband, I don't care who I have to fight for you. You're amazing."

Now it was Kri's turn to do the whole choking, spewing, spraying routine, and Michael offered the back patting.

"You're joking, right?" she finally croaked. "You got me good for my boob stunt, didn't you?" She laughed, slapping his shoulder. Hard.

"Yeah, it was a joke... But no, it wasn't revenge. I meant it as a compliment. I like your style. You're a Guardian, right?"

"What do you know about Guardians?" She narrowed her eyes.

"Yamanu spent some of the morning keeping me company, then Arwel showed up with the beers and the chips. We watched some, played some, talked some. They told me some stuff. I know that they are Guardians, a kind of internal police for your people. Last night I got to see them in action, kicking some serious Doomer ass. It was fucking epic. If I turn, I definitely want in. Yamanu thinks I have what it takes, so does Arwel." Michael pushed out his chest and squared his shoulders, looking at Kri for affirmation.

Chuckling, she patted his shoulder, gently this time. "We'll see about that. First, you need to turn, and there is no guarantee you will. And then it takes years of training. It's not an easy path. Before deciding that you want to sign up for this kind of life, you need to be sure you want it above all else."

He shrugged. "If I have what it takes, then I want in. The way the guys talk about it, it's obvious that they love what they do."

"So, what did they tell you about me?" Her lips pressed into a thin line and she narrowed her eyes again, evidently expecting some snide comments from the guys.

"Nothing, they didn't mention you at all. It's just that you look like a soldier, move and talk like one too. A mighty Amazon warrior..." Michael demonstrated, flexing his biceps.

By the smug look of satisfaction on her face, Kri took it as the compliment he'd intended. "Good. Even though they are well aware of my amazing skills, they still treat me as if I'm a little girl they need to protect. I hate it."

"Maybe it's because you're the youngest recruit?" He understood her frustration, but he also understood the guys. He would've been protective of her as well, even though she seemed perfectly capable of taking care of herself. It was something that was hardwired into his psyche.

"That's part of it, but I'm sure the old timers still think that a girl can't do what a guy can."

Michael knew he was treading on thin ice, but for some reason he felt like he needed to explain the guys' reasoning. He didn't want her to be angry at them, because he didn't want her to be angry at him for thinking the same thing. "I'm sure you are stronger and more capable than most guys, and in a situation where it's you and some average Joe against some thugs, you'll do better. But faced with the same situation with a male Guardian by your side, who is at least as well trained as you are, he will do better for the simple reason of having more muscle power. So the same way you feel protective of those who are not as strong as you are, the guys are protective of you."

She pinned him with a hard stare. "I know. Doesn't mean I have to like it. Eat your lunch, kid, before it gets cold so you can grow up and become a big, strong, male Guardian." Kri sat down to polish off her plate.

Great, she was pissed.

Idiot, you should've kept your mouth shut.

KRI

*I*t wasn't his fault, and Kri shouldn't have felt angry, but it was a sore point with her. She trained harder than any of the guys, was faster than most of them and more flexible, which she believed compensated for her lesser muscle power.

She could hold her own.

The thing was, none of the men had ever gone at her the same way they'd gone at each other. So how the hell was she supposed to know if she could handle an opponent as strong as a Guardian if they never gave her a chance?

Couldn't they get it through their thick male skulls that they weren't doing her any favors? What would happen when she faced a Doomer? Would he take it easy on her as well? Not likely.

It might not have been Michael's fault, but she was going to take it out of his hide anyway.

"How about a game of Black Ops?"

He arched a brow. "You play?"

"You bet your ass, I do. And I'm going to show you how it's done."

Michael snorted. "Not likely. I beat all of my friends hands down."

"Prepare to lose, kid."

"Let's do it."

As she'd expected, he held back for a little while, probably thinking that he'd let her win a few rounds before he obliterated her, so she wouldn't feel too bad about it. But as she kept winning round after round, the kid began taking her seriously.

"Damn, you're good."

"Told you."

By the time she called the game over, there was a sheen of sweat on his forehead.

"It was fun." Kri patted Michael's shoulder. "You're good, kid. Just not good enough." She winked.

"Yeah, it was. Though next time, I'll be ready for you, and your ass will be mine... Sorry, it came out all wrong... You know what I meant... in the game."

"Aha, sure, whatever you say. I'll come back tomorrow. Be ready." She pointed a finger at him.

Pushing up to her feet, Kri picked up the tray of dirty dishes and headed for the door. Then caught him checking her ass as she turned to say goodbye.

Well, what do you know... Kri smirked. Walking out, she gave him a nice, exaggerated saunter to admire.

Cute. Obviously, he was into her. But was she into him?

Nah, he was still a pup; handsome, eager, but too young.

Maybe... She shrugged.

He was a nice kid.

Michael was young and fresh, and his eyes were still hopeful, innocent, still excited about life, so different from the jaded expressions of her companions—of Kian's. Old eyes that had known too much, had seen too much—the spark of excitement extinguished long ago.

Or perhaps, the only reason the boy had piqued her interest was because he was there? A male she was not related to?

She had been pining for Kian since she had been a little girl—long before she had reached the appropriate age for her mother to explain that clan members were forbidden to each other. But by then it had been too late. She had developed a crush and it wouldn't go away no matter how many hookups she tried to distract herself with. None of those guys interested her beyond what it took to seduce them. Once her lust was sated, she felt nothing.

But Michael had managed to stir something inside her.

Maybe… She smiled. It was a definite maybe.

23

SYSSI

*O*ut on the terrace, Syssi stubbed out her cigarette in the ashtray and seriously contemplated lighting another one. What she'd hoped would be a relaxing experience had unexpectedly turned into anything but.

The trouble with having a vivid full-color imagination was that it had hijacked her memories, turning them into a stream of X-rated scenes that had been no fun to watch by herself.

And as hard as she'd tried to think about something, anything else, it had been as effective as resisting the pull of a black hole.

Syssi ran a shaky hand over her prone body, wishing Kian would be back already, so she could bite his head off not only for abandoning her with no means of communication, but for turning her into a sex addict as well.

Yeah, it was that bad.

She needed a distraction.

With Okidu gone, she could commandeer his kitchen

and make lunch. If she prepared something complicated, it would keep her busy for at least an hour.

The butler would be mad as hell, but she could feign innocence and claim she didn't know kitchen access was restricted.

Her Nana's lasagna recipe was the only fancy dish Syssi knew off the top of her head. It was delicious, unique, and labor-intensive. She hardly ever made it because it involved too many pots and pans that she later needed to clean, and it took over an hour to make. Perfect.

Hopefully, Okidu kept his kitchen well stocked and had all the ingredients she needed.

As she stepped inside, Syssi turned to close the sliding door panels behind her, and it wasn't until she turned back that she realized she had company.

Sitting on the living room's couch, Anandur and Brundar were eyeing her with matching smug smirks.

Just peachy.

They must've witnessed her little adventure with the cigarette, and were now giving her their version of the hairy eyeball.

I'm being ridiculous... acting as if smoking was a criminal activity. Although as shunned and ostracized as it was, she probably wasn't the only one made to feel like a felon for lighting up.

"Hi, guys, I'm afraid Kian is not back yet." She smiled politely, though in truth she wanted them to leave, so she could run to the bathroom and get rid of the smelly evidence before Kian showed up.

A toothbrush and plenty of perfume were in order.

"And hello to you too, pretty lady." Pushing up to his feet, Anandur uncoiled his massive bulk from the couch and took hold of her hand, planting a kiss on the back of it.

In a perfunctory bow, Brundar lifted slightly off the sofa.

"We'll wait for him," Anandur whispered, looking both ways as if letting her in on a conspiracy. "You see, Syssi... we are here to mooch off Okidu's cooking. He'll be serving lunch soon... Shh..." He winked. "Don't tell anyone..."

If that were the real reason for them sitting uninvited in Kian's living room, she could get rid of them easily. "Okidu isn't here, and there is no lunch."

Anandur smirked. "Not yet, but there will be. I bet he will walk in any minute now, carrying a huge tray. There is no way Okidu wouldn't have lunch ready for Kian. At half past twelve, like clockwork. That's how we knew exactly when to show up."

"I see," she said. "And I guess Kian is not too happy about you guys joining him?"

"Nope, but we don't care. Okidu's cooking is worth the pain of Kian's ranting and raving."

"What if he kicks you out?"

"He hasn't yet—and my brother and I have been pulling this stunt for years."

Unfortunately, it seemed there was no getting rid of them. The good news was that Kian would be back soon for his lunch. Glancing at her watch, Syssi estimated she had another twenty minutes or so until lunch time, but there was a chance he would come home earlier, which meant she should hurry up and cover the cigarette stink.

"Okay then, I'll leave you boys here and go freshen up. I'll be back in a jiffy."

Feeling awkward, Syssi headed for her room. It had been on the tip of her tongue to offer them refreshments while they waited, but it had seemed inappropriate. She was even more of an interloper in Kian's home than they were, and it wasn't her place to offer them anything other than her company. Besides, if it weren't outright rude, she would've preferred to avoid entertaining them as well. Right now, the only company she wanted was Kian's. Though she wasn't sure what she wanted to do first—clobber him over the head with a frying pan, or jump his bones.

24

ANANDUR

"*D*id you smell that?" Putting on a lecherous smile, Anandur turned to Brundar as soon as he heard the door closing behind Syssi. "My favorite bouquet —a female in need of shagging."

Brundar shrugged, ignoring him, but Anandur knew his brother well enough to know he hadn't been unaffected. Hell, no male immortal could've remained indifferent to a powerful attractant like that.

"Which of us do you think it was for?"

"Neither, you dimwit. I smelled it as soon as she slid the doors open—before she even noticed we were here."

Anandur smirked. Brundar saying two whole sentences, or even bothering to answer his taunt in the first place, was a clear sign that he'd been right. His brother had been just as affected by the irresistible call of the female's arousal.

"So what, you think someone parachuted onto the terrace and turned the heat on? No one can come up here. Unless it was another Guardian."

"How the hell should I know? Maybe she was having phone sex with her boyfriend, or watching porn."

Man, this is going to be fun... "Did you see a phone anywhere on her? With those painted-on jeans, and a white, thin T-shirt I could see her bra through, she couldn't have been hiding a tube of lipstick. And she wasn't holding anything in her hands either."

"Maybe she left it outside. Could we please drop the subject? It makes me uncomfortable." Brundar wiggled, adjusting his pants.

"I still think it was for me." Anandur kept pushing.

"You think every female has the hots for you, you arrogant bastard."

Brundar's normally stoic face was getting red. One more push and he would snap.

"Because they do... son of my mother but not my father. And as you are well aware, we are all bastards in this big happy family. Some of us are just sexier than others, and you're jealous." Anandur ran his hands over his big body and began singing and undulating his hips to the tune of "I'm Sexy and I Know It..." Until the throw pillow that Brundar chucked at him smacked him in the face, shutting him up.

For a moment.

25

SYSSI

*B*ack from the bathroom, Syssi sat across from the brothers, fidgeting with her bracelet in the uncomfortable silence. For some unfathomable reason, the guys seemed antsy, with Anandur alternating between scratching his beard and the back of his head, and Brundar crossing and recrossing his feet at his ankles.

Both were regarding her as if they were waiting for her to do or say something.

"Did you leave your phone outside, Syssi?" Anandur finally spoke, his eyes darting for a split second to his brother.

"No, why?" she asked, puzzled.

"I thought I heard you talking to someone on the terrace, and as there was no phone in your hands when you came back in, I assumed you left it out there." Anandur wasn't even trying to conceal the smirking glance he shot at Brundar as if saying 'I told you so.' And when Brundar rolled his eyes in response, he confirmed her suspicion.

What the heck was all this about? Was it the cigarette?

Syssi got pissed. "Okay, so you caught me. I had a smoke outside. Big deal!"

"Must have been one hell of a cigarette. I wouldn't mind having one myself, love…" Anandur chuckled.

"I don't know what you mean, but be my guest. They are Kian's anyway. He left them there." She motioned toward the terrace.

"Kian's… I see… No, thank you, Syssi, I'm not into that brand." Anandur turned to Brundar, who nodded his head in agreement with a little knowing smile blooming on his austere face.

Why did she feel as if they were having two separate conversations? An overt one she was having with Anandur and a covert one between the brothers.

"What's going on, guys? Are we talking about the same thing here?"

"I don't know what you mean."

Anandur's feigned innocence didn't impress her at all. What's more, he was too… something she couldn't put her finger on. Too cocky? Too happy with himself?

Without Kian around to keep him in check, she had a feeling the guy would start flirting with her, which would put her in the uncomfortable situation of having to tell him no thank you. Anandur was a good looking guy, and she was sure he had no lack of female attention, but a rejection was a rejection and she hated causing anyone unnecessary hurt feelings. The best strategy was to avoid the situation in the first place.

"It seems Okidu is a no-show. I think I'll go to the kitchen and start working on the lasagna I'd been planning to make before you guys showed up." Syssi pushed up from her chair. She would pretend to be getting ready while waiting for Okidu or Kian to get back. In the meantime, she could munch on whatever Okidu had left in the fridge for her.

Pushing off the couch, Anandur got in her face and gripped her hands. "I'm sure Okidu wouldn't want you working in his kitchen. A beautiful woman such as yourself should be kept pampered and spoiled, and her delicate hands kept safely away from the hazards of hot pots and sharp cooking utensils." He lifted her hands and kissed the back of each one before letting her pull them out of his grip.

Shit, it was exactly what she'd been afraid of. Without Kian around, Anandur was allowing himself to get too friendly.

She was about to give him the 'only friends' speech when Kian's icy tone took them all by surprise.

"Oh, really? I wasn't aware that you had experience keeping beautiful women, your usual fare being more of the disposable kind."

Syssi had no idea where he had come from. They had been sitting in the living room this whole time, in full view of the front door. "Oh, hi, Kian, I'm so glad you're back. I told the guys you weren't home."

"Right." Kian lowered the tray he'd been carrying onto the counter and wiped his hands on a dish towel.

He hadn't smiled at her, hadn't even said hello. The guy was so mercurial. "Is there another entrance to the penthouse? I didn't see you come in."

"Obviously," he barked back.

What is his problem? Kian looked furious, his tone sarcastic and accusatory.

Anandur took a step back away from her. "Hi, Boss. We just got here. And we found the lovely lady waiting for you. She was really disappointed it was us, and not you. I told her we came for Okidu's cooking, nothing else."

Whatever Anandur was trying to hint at was falling on deaf ears. Kian wasn't paying attention to a word that left Anandur's mouth. Holding his fists tight by his sides, he looked like he was a breath away from pounding Anandur's face into a pulp.

Syssi held her breath, waiting for Kian to release the punch that would come smashing into Anandur's face. Kian's anger and barely contained aggression was frightening.

"Yeah, it's like he said. We got here, and here she was like that…" Brundar was obviously trying to communicate something to Kian and avert the brewing storm by backing his brother.

But why? What was he so angry about?

It must've had something to do with her; both brothers were acting as if Kian had caught them with their hands in the cookie jar, or rather the bone stash—cowering before the alpha dog and crawling on their bellies.

Was this about Anandur's flirting? That little thing?

It was ridiculous.

It was insulting.

It reminded her of Gregg.

Fits of ungrounded, irrational jealousy—she was well acquainted with those.

Any man glancing her way had been a suspect. Any guy she had happened to mention, regardless of the context, had been a suspect as well. It had been even worse than the constant complaining, because his accusations implied that on top of what he had perceived to be her many other flaws, he had also deemed her untrustworthy.

For Syssi, it was a deal breaker.

Overcome by bitter disappointment, she felt the bile rise up in her throat. Her Prince Charming, the man that had rocked her world only the night before, had just turned into a slimy toad.

Ugh!

Talk about naiveté…

"You boys go on playing your wolf-pack power games and growl at each other's throats to your hearts' content. I'm out of here."

Turning away and marching to her room without looking back, Syssi hoped she'd sounded as disgusted as she'd felt. In truth, though, she was fighting back tears.

The last thing she wanted was for Kian to see her cry and realize he had disappointed her. Because it would imply that she'd entertained unwarranted expectations. After all, for Kian she was probably nothing more than a convenient lay, and an easy one at that.

A woman he believed would jump on any attractive pair of pants that crossed her way.

26

BRUNDAR

*B*rundar cringed. Kian looked like he was hanging by a thread, and if he snapped… well… it was hard to tell who would have the upper hand in this fight. Though Brundar had a strong suspicion that it wouldn't be his brother.

Coming up in the service elevator with Okidu, Kian had been helping the butler bring lunch up from the basement kitchen. He must've smelled the girl's arousal as soon as its door opened. Her scent was sure potent enough to overpower even the strong aroma of the freshly cooked food. Then walking in on the big jerk flirting with Syssi, he surmised what had gotten her so aroused, or rather who.

"Get the hell out!" Kian barked at Anandur as he whipped around to follow Syssi.

"Don't be a jerk, Kian, it had nothing to do with us. She came in after smoking outside and that scent was already there…" Anandur tried to explain.

Turning his head with just a slight twist of his torso, Kian pointed his finger at Anandur, staring him down. "If I ever catch you flirting with her again or even looking at her with anything other than courtesy and respect, I'm going to pound the living daylights out of you. Are we clear?"

"Crystal!"

"Good! Now, get out of here before I change my mind and beat the hell out of you just to make sure you got it!"

"Yes, Boss!" Anandur dipped his head and headed for the front door.

Behind him, Brundar threw an apologetic glance at Kian before following his brother out.

It wasn't really Anandur's fault. How were they supposed to know Kian felt so possessive about Syssi? It wasn't as if he'd ever acted this way before. There was no way for them to recognize the signs.

Although thinking back, they should have.

The way he had been frantic to get to her before the Doomers had. The way he'd snapped at Anandur and him for checking her out. Staying at the hotel with her though keeping his distance. It had been more than a simple concern for a mere acquaintance that he happened to like.

Standing next to his brother as they waited for the elevator to come up, Brundar accused, "You really did it this time."

"What? You were just as surprised as I was that he called dibs on her."

"Yeah, but you kept on going even after we figured it out."

"I know... Just couldn't help myself. You know how I get." Anandur shrugged. "No big deal. He'll get over it. You know how Kian gets all worked up. And anyway, he couldn't have done any serious damage to me even if he tried." Anandur stretched to his full height and pushed his massive chest out.

"You're so full of crap." Brundar shook his head, doubting Anandur had it right. Kian wasn't as big and didn't seem as strong physically, but he was, after all, Annani's son.

A direct descendant of the gods.

27

KIAN

*R*ushing after Syssi, Kian reached her room in a few long strides. But then, standing in front of her door, he hesitated before knocking.

Not because he sensed she was angry, that would've been fine. He could've dealt with that. But because the dark scent reaching his nose was laced with disappointment and regret.

Fuck! Can you say overreact?

What had gotten into him?

When the elevator's door had opened, the scent of Syssi's arousal had hit him head-on, making him instantly hard. With a big grin spreading across his face, he'd marched toward the siren call of Syssi's aroma, passing through the kitchen with the tray he had been carrying. But then, hearing Anandur's come-on lines and thinking that's what had gotten Syssi so aroused, or rather who, he had been gripped by intense jealousy. He'd dropped the tray on the kitchen counter and turned around.

Blinded by fury, Kian had strained the limits of his hard-won self-control, keeping himself from leaping at

Anandur and ripping the jerk apart. Or maybe it had been the nagging feeling in the back of his mind that there was no way a girl like Syssi could've been attracted to Anandur.

Even if the guy was known as an irresistible female magnet.

If nothing else, the way she had stormed off had convinced him that he had gotten the situation all wrong.

Way to go, asshole… Kian felt like banging his head on the closed door.

He had to fix this somehow. The prospect of Syssi looking at him with anything other than her sweet, wide-eyed adoration was killing him.

Rapping his knuckles on the door, he probed, "May I come in?" hating that he sounded like a wayward child begging for forgiveness. But then, if it came down to that, he knew he would beg—on his knees if that was what it took. And it pissed him off that he found himself needing to apologize.

Again.

It wasn't something he found easy to do. Truth be told, even when an apology was in order, he rarely did. Maybe it was a personality flaw.

Fuck maybe!

It was a flaw.

Each time he had been forced to make amends, getting the words out had felt like chewing on shrapnel.

28

SYSSI

*A*s she stuffed her few possessions into her travel bag, Syssi's anger gave way to disappointment. She was forced to recognize her mistake for what it was.

She shouldn't have come here in the first place, and definitely shouldn't have stayed with Kian at his home. She knew next to nothing about him. And evidently, being great in bed did not equate to him being a nice guy. Trouble was, she had chosen to trust him when she should've been more careful and guarded.

It appeared that contrary to the way she saw herself, she was still naive.

Damn Kian for giving her a beautiful illusion and then shattering it. Except, she had only herself to blame.

Stupid! She was so bloody stupid!

Kian's rap on the door came too soon, and she wanted to tell him to go away.

She didn't want to face him, or the drama that was sure to follow when he'd see that she was packing to leave. But something in his voice tugged at her stupid soft heart, and she invited him in. "Sure, it's your home..." And anyway, she figured refusing to talk to him would only postpone the inevitable.

"Why are you packing?" Kian pointed at the bag the moment he stepped in, his angry face belying his apologetic tone from a moment before.

Well, surprise, surprise. That's what she got for being a softie...

"It was a bad idea for me to come here. I should've stayed at my brother's. I would be just as safe with him as I am here," she said in a flat tone that could've made Queen Amidala from *Star Wars* proud, while pretending to rearrange her bag so she wouldn't have to look at Kian.

It was all a front, though, and on the inside she was falling apart, struggling to keep breathing through the choking in her throat. Berating her own stupidity for making what was nothing more than a tryst into something meaningful, she was trying to reignite her anger in order to fortify her resolve.

I'm such a girl, she thought, *tearing and choking instead of lashing out and giving him a piece of my mind.*

But what would've been the point?

The disappointment would still be there, and venting her anger would not make that sour feeling go away.

He was who he was, and not who she wished him to be, and that didn't give her the right to penalize him. Only to walk away.

"I'm sorry." He surprised her. "Please don't go."

She lifted her head from where she was bending over the bed and turned to look at his pleading eyes.

He had gotten her attention.

Not making demands or pounding his chest with his protector routine, he had said the only thing that had any chance of changing her mind.

With a sigh, she sat on the messed up bed and faced him. "Do you even know what you're apologizing for? Or is it a blanket statement meant to absolve you of whatever I might find objectionable?"

It had crossed her mind that he might be clueless as to what had offended her, and she had no intention of making it easy for him.

"I don't know what came over me. I felt this insane surge of jealousy... It's never happened to me before, and I didn't know how to deal with it. I'm sorry if I acted like a jerk..." He pinched his forehead between two fingers. "And for being rude," he tacked on.

"Why?"

"Why was I rude? Because I'm an uncouth brute? What do you want me to say?"

Yep, clueless.

"Why were you jealous?"

"Isn't it obvious? Anandur was flirting with you, and the big oaf has a reputation as an irresistible ladies' man..." Kian rolled his eyes. "And you seemed to like him. A lot... That incredible smell you gave off—" He stopped mid-sentence.

Looking up at Kian, Syssi felt profound sadness. He had no idea that it wasn't his rude behavior that had hurt her, but his misguided belief that there was anything to be jealous about.

"What?" Seeing her resigned expression, he raised his hands in defeat.

"Don't you get it? How offensive and degrading it feels? Your lack of trust in me? Your belief that I might be tempted by any attractive man that passes my way? Like some floozy? Maybe you have some justification to feel this way, as it sure as hell didn't take you long to get me in

145

your bed. But rest assured it's not something I often do, or ever..." Unable to hold back the tears anymore, she felt them slide down her cheeks. It took all her willpower just to stifle the sobs that were stuck in her throat and pushing to get out.

"Oh, sweet girl..." Kian dropped to his knees in front of her and hugged her to him tightly. Stroking her hair, he pulled her head to rest in the crook of his neck. "I'm so sorry, baby. If it's any consolation... I wasn't thinking rationally at all. It was pure animal instinct. If I had stopped to think for a moment, I might've realized how stupid I was. Can you forgive me? Chuck it to 'the-clue-less-male-defense-plea'? Please?"

"I don't know...," she croaked, smiling behind the tears that were wetting his skin.

Shaking her head, she couldn't believe she was contemplating giving him another chance. But the feel of him, and dear God... his scent... were scrambling her brain.

"What's going on?" Amanda said from the doorway. "What did you do to the poor girl?"

Walking in, she sat on the bed next to Syssi and pushed Kian away. Then tugged on Syssi's shoulders to bring her into her own arms.

"What did this meanie do to you?" Amanda patted Syssi's hand while glaring daggers at Kian.

"Nothing, I just need some time to figure things out. I need to call Andrew. If he calls and does not get a hold of me, he is going to freak out."

Syssi looked at Amanda, beseeching her with her eyes to stop the questioning. They could have a girls' talk later. As it was, letting Kian glimpse her vulnerable underbelly, she was already feeling too exposed.

146

29

KIAN

*G*laring at Amanda, Kian was infuriated with her for poking her nose where it didn't belong. This intrusion on his privacy was becoming intolerable. "Go home, Amanda. Everything is under control," he dismissed her, trying to pull Syssi back. Amanda didn't let go, though, and the tug of war was becoming ridiculous.

"Yeah, I can definitely see that. Crying girl and all... Syssi, would you like to stay with me for a while? It's only across the hallway, but I promise you it's way more fun than here... We can do each other's nails and gossip about Kian... Play with makeup and trash talk Kian... You know, all the fun things we girls do."

He hated to admit it, but Amanda's attempts to cheer Syssi up were working. She chuckled and dried her tears with the comforter, thankfully ignoring his furious expression that had nothing to do with her and was directed at Amanda, who couldn't care less.

"Thanks, I would love to. I think the last time I had a sleepover at a girlfriend's house was in middle school."

Pretending to be excited by Amanda's invitation, Syssi

was putting on a good show. Except, he wasn't sure who she was trying to convince: them or herself. But he wasn't fooled. She looked as if she would do just about anything to get out of there as quickly as she could, and Amanda's offer just provided her with a convenient excuse.

As if to prove him right, she got off the bed and shoved whatever was still strewn about into her duffel bag. "I'm good to go. Packed and everything." She slung it over her shoulder and headed for the door.

He just couldn't let her go like that. Not without setting things right between them first. But as he reached for Syssi's arm to stop her, he felt Amanda's hand on his shoulder.

She shook her head at him. "Syssi needs some space. Let her go," she whispered so quietly only he heard her.

Nodding reluctantly, he let Syssi pass and followed them to the front door.

"I'll see you later." Syssi said her goodbye with a slight tilt of her head, without even looking at his face.

"Don't worry. I'll take good care of her," Amanda mouthed before shutting the door behind them.

Standing at the threshold of his apartment, Kian looked at Amanda's closed door. Just a few steps across the vestibule, it was so near, and yet as far as his welcome went it might have been in a different zip code.

Sighing, he stepped back inside and closed the door, then headed for the kitchen to eat his lunch by himself.

Alone, sitting at the counter, the irony of his situation was not lost on him. Finally, he got his wish and none of his relatives were there to bother him.

So why did he feel like shit?

30

SYSSI

*A*manda's place was a mirror image of Kian's. Same layout, same placement of furniture—the decor and colors a slight variation on the same theme. Clearly, both apartments were done by the same interior designer.

"Come on, sweetie, I'll show you to your room." Amanda led the way down the corridor and opened a door to the left. "Just drop your bag on the floor. Let's go and have something to eat. I can hear your belly rumbling from here." Throwing her arm around Syssi's shoulders, she turned on her heel and walked her toward the open terrace doors.

"Onidu, honey, we have a guest. Would you be a dear and serve us lunch on the terrace?" Amanda called out before stepping outside. "It's such a beautiful day. The sun is out but it's not too hot." She pulled out a chair for Syssi and sat down across from her.

"Onidu? Is he related to Okidu?" Syssi asked.

"Yes, my darling butler is the same as Kian's—a present from our mother."

Perplexed by Amanda's peculiar choice of words, Syssi asked, "Your mother gave you butlers as presents?"

Amanda smiled and waved her hand dismissively. "It didn't come out right. You see, the Odus were trusted members of her own staff for years, and she wanted her kids to be well taken care of by someone she could count on. So she assigned one to each of us. I grew up with Onidu as my companion, and when I left home, naturally, he had to come with me. Without him, I'd be a complete mess. He does everything for me. And he keeps me safe. Don't you, sweetheart?" She smiled at her butler as he arrived with the tray of food.

"Whatever you say, mistress." Onidu bowed before placing the tray on the glass table.

"Wow, they look like twins." Syssi glanced at Onidu's retreating back. Both men had similar height and build with just slightly different hair and eye color. "Are they brothers? And by the way, do you and Kian have more siblings? You said each one... sounded like more than just the two of you."

"We have two more sisters. And about the Odus... yeah, it's kind of obvious that they come from the same stock." Amanda lifted her sandwich with both hands and took a bite.

"Older? Younger?"

"Who? The Odus?"

"No, silly, your sisters. You never mentioned them before. I'm curious."

"Older, I'm the baby. Alena is the oldest, Kian is next, then Sari."

"And...?"

"And what?"

"Where are they? Where do they live? What do they do?"

"Alena stays with our mother, and Sari is in Europe, heading the family business over there."

"And your father? Is he still around?"

"No, he passed away a long time ago."

"I'm so sorry to hear that." Syssi lowered her eyes. She knew how hard it was to talk about a lost loved one. Sighing, she took a forkful of the delicious apple crumble Onidu had served for dessert.

"Nothing to be sorry about. I never met him, so I couldn't really feel sorrow at his passing." Amanda shrugged, a shadow darkening her expression.

"Did he die before you were born?" It was so unlike Syssi to be asking all these personal questions. Still, she felt compelled to keep it up and find out more about Kian and his family.

"No, but it wasn't the poor schmuck's fault either. He didn't even know I existed. Mother had never told him. And I never got to meet him."

"How about Kian and your other sisters' father, did your mother divorce him? Or did he pass away as well?" Syssi made the logical assumption that Amanda had been a love child, arriving later in her mother's life.

Amanda paused with her sandwich suspended in front of her face. A moment of contemplation later, she sighed and lowered the thing back to the plate. "Fathers, as in plural. We each have a different father, and not one was married to our mother or informed of becoming a father." Amanda picked up her sandwich and took another bite.

Uncomfortable, Syssi looked down at her hands. That was somewhat unorthodox, but who was she to judge someone else's choices in life?

To each her or his own.

Life's twists and turns made for different paths for different people. She wondered, however, what was the story behind this one. "It must have been hard for your mother to raise four kids on her own. Not financially, as it seems she didn't suffer for a lack of means, having a staff of servants and all. But why did she choose to do it this way. Didn't she love any of the men?"

Amanda wiped her hands on the napkin before dabbing it at her lips. "She was married once when she was very young and deeply in love. When her husband died, she vowed to remain faithful to him in her heart and never love another man again. But she wanted children, and she loved sex, so here we are."

Amanda smiled her radiant smile, but then her eyes narrowed with a wicked gleam. "Speaking of sex... You and Kian?" She arched one of her perfectly shaped brows in question. And yet, judging from her smug expression, she already knew the answer to that.

Syssi almost choked on a mouthful of cake, feeling a blush spread all the way up to the roots of her hair as she swallowed it. "He's your brother, for God's sake, how can you ask me that?"

"Oh, please. We are all adults here. If I can talk about my mother's sex life, you think Kian's is off limits?" Amanda laughed. "There is nothing to be bashful about. Remember who you're talking to—the self-proclaimed queen of sluts." She pointed at herself. "And proud of it."

"Yes... happy?" Syssi blurted and immediately dropped her eyes to her plate.

"Ecstatic!... But what did the stupid goat do to make you cry? And don't you dare try covering up for him." Amanda crossed her arms over her chest, waiting. "Well?"

Syssi sighed and folded her napkin, smoothing it next to her plate. "Anandur and Brundar showed up for lunch when Kian wasn't there, and when he came back and saw them with me, he went bonkers, threw a jealous tantrum and kicked them out." She shrugged as if the whole thing hadn't been a big deal.

"That's all? That's what got you so upset? I think it's sweet that he got jealous over you. That means he cares for you. What's wrong with that?"

"It's disrespectful to me, don't you think? Assuming I'd even show interest in another man after spending the night with Kian. He made me feel cheap, like he thought I was some kind of floozy." Cue the quivering chin.

"Oh, sweetie, I forgot how inexperienced you are with men. You assume that he was thinking and analyzing what was going on because women overthink everything. Men don't. He went ape-man territorial when he found another virile male sniffing around his female and felt threatened. If anything, it shows his own insecurities, not his opinion of you."

"Look who's covering for Kian now. I thought I was the one who was expected to do that." Syssi filled her cup from the steaming pot of coffee and stirred in the cream and sugar. "And the fact that I only had one boyfriend doesn't make me inexperienced. Well, maybe variety-wise it does… But be that as it may, Gregg and I were together for four years, during which I got my share of irrational, unfounded accusations. In the beginning, I dismissed them the same way you just did, feeling flattered. But believe me, after a while I got so sick of them, I felt like he was pounding another nail into the coffin of our relationship with each new onslaught. Kian's behavior today was a very unpleasant déjà vu. It made me want to throw up." Syssi pretended to gag, and sticking out her tongue, made a face like she was about to puke.

Amanda didn't respond for a while. Sipping on her coffee, she picked apple-crumble crumbs off her plate and placed the tiny bits on her tongue one at a time.

"Are you sure it's the same? Maybe you're just projecting your ex on Kian. Knowing Anandur's antics, he was probably flirting with you shamelessly, so the jealousy wasn't completely unfounded. Am I right?" she asked.

"So what if he was flirting. I wasn't responding to him or anything!"

A flash of understanding crossed Amanda's eyes. "Were you thinking naughty thoughts about Kian before the guys came in?" She looked pointedly at Syssi.

Her cheeks began burning again, and the heat was spreading all the way to her earlobes. "So what if I did? What does that have to do with anything?" How on earth could Amanda have known that?

With a wide grin spreading over her face, Amanda lifted her hands as if it was self-explanatory. "It has every-thing to do with it… I'll run by you the scenario from Kian's point of view. He walks in, sees you all flustered from your earlier carnal musings, while Anandur is putting his moves on you. Reaches the wrong conclusion, thinking your arousal is the other guy's doing, gets crazy jealous… Sounds plausible?"

"How would he know I was… you know…?"

"You have a very expressive face, and Kian is very perceptive."

Was he? Syssi didn't notice that about him. In fact, he was just as oblivious as the next guy. "Even if you're right, he still should have known better."

"Oh, really? Picture the same scenario with different

players. You walk in, Kian is in the company of two gorgeous women, one of them flirting with him unabashedly, and a hard-on is tenting his pants. Would you be all smiling and thinking rationally? Or would you want to strangle all three of them?"

"I wouldn't get physical… Just imagine it… Very, very, vividly…" Syssi chuckled. "Okay, you made your point. I forgive him. But I'm not going back to his place. You promised me a sleepover and I'm holding you to it."

"I wouldn't let you go even if you begged, you're all mine for tonight. We are going to go out, and we are going to party hard. I need to teach you how to live a little."

"Fine. But first I need to call Andrew and let him know I'm okay, and that I'm staying with you. Maybe he can even help us in some way. After all, he deals with these kinds of situations in his line of work. I told you he used to be Special Ops, didn't I?"

"No, you didn't. How fascinating… And now that you did, I want to meet him. Can you introduce us? I have a thing for dangerous boys… grr…" Amanda did her cougar imitation, growling and swiping the air with pretend claws.

Syssi laughed. "I wouldn't call him a boy. Andrew is pushing forty. But sure, I would love to introduce you guys." Then getting serious, she added, "I think tomorrow I'll go to his place. I should have done it from the start, instead of coming here. But everything happened so fast, and Kian kind of took control of everything and it was easy to just let him. He managed to convince me that I would be putting Andrew in danger if I go to stay with him, but the more I think about it the more ridiculous it sounds."

Amanda frowned. "I trust that Kian knows what he is

talking about. You shouldn't dismiss what he said. If he thinks it's not safe for you to stay with your brother then he is probably right."

Unless he is lying about it to keep me here.

"I think it would be better for everyone if I kept my distance. We got too close too fast. It cannot be healthy for a new relationship. If it is a relationship... Shit! I don't know what to think." Syssi ran her fingers through her hair.

"Is Andrew listed as your next of kin anywhere?" Amanda suddenly looked worried.

"No, because of his job I couldn't. I listed my parents. Why?"

"It's a remote chance, but if they can't get you they might decide to go after other family members. Special abilities sometimes run in families. Any other siblings?"

"No... my other brother died four years ago in a motorcycle accident." Syssi tried to swallow as her throat convulsed with the familiar choking sensation.

"I'm so sorry, sweetie. How about your parents? Still in Africa?"

"Yeah, still there."

"Good. I don't think the lunatics will venture that far."

Looking down at her plate, Syssi chased the scattered crumbs of cake with her fork, struggling to regain her composure. "What are the police doing about this mess, did you check with them?" she asked.

"They took pictures of the damage at the lab, but they're not taking the incident seriously. They're convinced it was a prank. Drunk students, maybe someone who got a bad grade. I don't think they are going to do anything about it."

"Did you tell them about the people chasing after us? They should investigate that group."

"Yeah... about that. First, I have no evidence, just my suspicions. Second, it's a shadow organization no one knows about. It's a dead end."

"So, what are we going to do? I can't keep hiding forever, and we need to resume our work. Besides, how do we know they even came looking for me? Maybe we over-reacted and they are already gone?"

"I wish. We didn't want to alarm you, but Michael Gross got jumped last night. He escaped and is fine, but I think that proves that we weren't paranoid. The goons really went after him."

A cold chill ran up Syssi's spine. "But if he was attacked, isn't it proof enough for the police to get serious about investigating these people?"

"He was attacked at night, outside a night club. They assume it was a drunken brawl." Amanda looked apologetic as if any of this was her fault. "Look, Kian had a surveillance camera installed at your place, and our security is moni-toring the activity there. If nothing suspicious happens over the next couple of days, you can go home. Deal?"

"I guess... I need to call Andrew, though. And by the way, why are all your phones code protected?"

"Mine are not. I don't know why Kian's would be." Amanda shrugged, though for some reason looked like she was still feeling guilty over something. Leaning with her elbows on the table, she kept fidgeting with her fork when she added, "Listen, when you call your brother, don't tell him exactly where you are and why. I know it sounds a bit strange, but we need to keep a low profile. Our family has enemies—vicious business competitors that will stop at nothing to bring us down. Okay? Can I count on you to keep us a secret?" She looked into Syssi's eyes.

"Of course." Syssi thought it was beyond strange; talk about paranoia. But whatever, if she was asked to keep a secret, she would.

"And I don't want to hear another word about you staying elsewhere. Did you forget that you are supposed to do some work for me while you're here?"

"If it's only a couple of days, then I'll stay."

"Good!"

31

SYSSI

"*Y*ou must be kidding, right? You dropped your phone in the sink?"

Syssi grimaced. Not surprisingly, Andrew sounded suspicious of the story she had concocted.

Damn, how she hated having to lie.

"Yeah, I answered a call while washing the dishes. It just slipped and fell right in. Died on the spot." Syssi looked at the ceiling, hoping he'd drop the subject. "Anyway, as I said, I'll be staying at Amanda's for a couple of days, just until they are done repainting the lab. We have a paper we need to rush and finish by the end of the month, so I will probably be staying here overnight until we are done. I'll call you as soon as I get my new phone."

"Are you calling from her place? The number is blocked."

"Yes."

"And where is that?"

Okay, that would be tough to wiggle out of... "It's somewhere downtown. Amanda was driving and I didn't pay attention, so I'm not sure exactly where. All I know is that it's a fancy penthouse apartment."

Well, it wasn't a complete lie... after all, she didn't know the exact address. Still, she had a feeling he wasn't buying any of it, or maybe it was just her guilty conscience talking. She wished she had never made that promise to Amanda.

The loud music suddenly blasting from the direction of the living room rescued her from having to make up any more lies.

"What's that racket?" Andrew asked, providing the opening she needed.

"It sounds like Amanda's idea of background music. I'd better go and tell her to turn it down before the neighbors complain. I'll call you later."

"You do that."

Hanging up, Syssi exhaled a relieved breath and got up.

The music got louder as she crossed the few feet separating the office from the living room, and what was worse, Amanda began singing along. Out of tune.

So there was something the woman was not good at... what a relief...

Well, if you can't beat them—join them. Syssi added her own voice to the cacophony.

Dancing and singing along with the hard rock blasting from the powerful speakers, Syssi had more fun than she remembered having in ages. From good old Van Halen and Led Zeppelin to Aerosmith and Metallica, the playlist kept going strong long after they had gotten tired of dancing and switched to painting each other's toenails on the living room's couch.

With Onidu pushing one margarita after the other at them, Syssi lost count of how many she had, although she was pretty sure Amanda had way more.

By the time it got dark outside, Syssi was hoarse from singing and very drunk. "Wow, Amanda, I forgot how wonderful it feels to do things just for the fun of it," she slurred and tried to lie down on the couch. Immediately, her head went spinning, and she sat back up, resting her neck against the upholstered back.

Oh, boy. Was she in trouble.

Every time she tried to close her eyes, the feeling of vertigo forced her to snap them open, but keeping them that way was a struggle. "I swear not to touch another margarita for as long as I live," She moaned, clutching her head.

"Onidu! No more margaritas!" Amanda called out and turned off the music with the remote.

Syssi sighed in relief. "Thank you!"

Sounding a little slurred herself, Amanda patted her shoulder. "Don't you worry, by the time we're ready to go, you'll be fine."

"I don't think I'm in any shape to go anywhere. What a bummer. I haven't been to a club since before Gregg."

"No worries. We're going to fix this." Amanda headed for the kitchen and beckoned Syssi to follow. "Onidu! We need food and coffee. You got us drunk, and now it's up to you to sober us up!"

Sitting at the kitchen counter, they gulped several cups of water before moving on to the coffee.

"I'm glad you enjoyed yourself. You've been all work and no play for far too long, and the night is still young. We have lots of partying left to do." Amanda's eyes sparkled mischievously.

"Are we going by ourselves?"

"Two is not enough for a girls' night out. We need rein-forcements. I'm going to call Kri, my cousin."

"What's she like?"

"Muscle…" Amanda snorted, the twirl of pasta on her fork shaking along with her body.

"Okay… that tells me a lot… not… What do you mean —muscle?"

"When you see her, you'll get it. She's the kind of gal you want to watch your back, in case some jerk gets too frisky, uninvited, that is. Some you'd actually want to get frisky with you." She winked. "That girl can inflict some serious damage, and that's just a bonus to being way cool and lots of fun to hang out with." Amanda stuffed the twirl of pasta into her mouth.

"All I have are two pairs of jeans, some T-shirts, and a semi-okay blouse… but I can wear my platforms to spruce up the look. You think that will do?"

"Don't be silly. You can borrow some of mine. Wait till you see what's in my closet. Poor Onidu schlepped half my wardrobe over here." Ignoring Syssi's panicked expression, Amanda rubbed her hands together in glee.

ANDREW

*A*s he drove home through the quiet residential streets of his middle-class neighborhood, Andrew thought back to his phone conversation with Syssi.

She was so full of crap.

Careful, cautious Syssi would never drop her cellphone in a sink full of water. She wouldn't even have the thing in the proximity of anything wet.

Who did she think she was fooling?

Lucky for her, he couldn't observe her through the phone—then there would've been no doubt—no one could lie to his face.

He wasn't sure how he did it, but he was better at detecting lies than the machine. The only caveat being that he had to be face to face with the person to be certain.

He was never wrong.

And the story of staying at Amanda's to finish a paper while the lab was being repainted? Right... At the least she should've thought of something more plausible.

Syssi was such a straight shooter. She couldn't lie convincingly if her life depended on it. Andrew smiled as he recalled the few times she had tried to put one over on him.

He'd have to coach her to become better at it.

Lying was an important skill that had saved his butt on several occasions. Being an open book the way she was, was a luxury for either those who had nothing to fear or those who had nothing to lose.

Neither applied to his baby sister.

Still, he wondered what the real story was. Did she finally meet a new guy? He certainly hoped so.

That douchebag Gregg had ruined her confidence, turning his vivacious sister into a pitiful hermit. Not for the first time, Andrew wished he could beat the shit out of the jerk, or at least make life really difficult for him.

His lips lifted in a sinister smile as he imagined the possibilities. A few incriminating items could find their way into Gregg's file, making finding a job or obtaining credit impossible. He could envision the asshole squirming, trying to figure out who was ruining his life.

It could've been so satisfying.

Unfortunately, guessing his intentions, Syssi had forbidden Andrew to touch the guy, physically or otherwise. He would have done it anyway, but the jerk still called her from time to time, and she would've found out and figured right away who was behind her ex's misfortune.

Damn it! Why did she have to be such a softie?

After easing his car into the garage, Andrew waited for the garage door to close before exiting, then walked in through the kitchen, disarmed the alarm, and turned the lights on. On his way to the spare bedroom that he had converted into a home office, he dropped his keys on the counter and grabbed a water bottle from the fridge.

Sitting at his desk, Andrew booted up his satellite laptop and brought up the sophisticated tracking software: courtesy of Uncle Sam. For his peace of mind, he needed to find where Syssi was staying.

Let's see where this mystery guy lives. Andrew took a long gulp from his water bottle as he waited for the program to pinpoint the signal.

Hopefully, she had kept her promise to always wear the pendant he had given her on her sixteenth birthday. The one with the tracking device he had installed.

It was a beautiful piece of jewelry, a small gold heart surrounded by diamonds that he had inscribed with *You're always in my heart.*

Syssi had vowed to never take it off. He made sure she made good on that promise whenever he saw her. It was always around her neck.

Andrew felt a twinge of guilt for deceiving Syssi for years, but he was glad he had done it nonetheless. At the time, he had felt compelled to do it because he hadn't been around anymore to keep her safe. And considering how spacey and self-centered their mom and dad were, he had wanted to be able to keep track of her.

Now that she was an adult, he still liked the idea of being able to find her.

With their parents always too busy with their careers, with each other, with their social circle—he had practically raised his two younger siblings.

God bless them, his parents were good people. Even before they had retired, they had routinely volunteered their time and resources to charities for children, doing it now full-time in Africa.

Funny, how they took care of so many but had neglected their own.

When he had confronted them about that, his mother's reply had been that the three of them were capable, intelligent people and didn't need their parents to hover over them.

"You'll be just fine taking care of yourselves and each other," she had said.

And they were. Fine.

There had been the nannies and the housekeeper and grandma and grandpa who had lived nearby. And yet, as much as he hated to fess up to any lingering resentment, he could've used some more help. The truth was that he had been the one in charge. Making the numerous day to day decisions that had been needed to run the household, he had been forced to become a part-time surrogate parent at fourteen.

Right. Water under the bridge and all that.

Thank God, the red dot showing the tracking device's location wasn't at Syssi's home, so he was reassured that she hadn't left the pendant behind. It was blinking over where she'd said she was staying, somewhere in downtown Los Angeles.

Zooming in on the building the signal was coming from, Andrew whistled as it came into focus and he recognized the lucrative address.

Nice. A wealthy boyfriend... Not bad, Syssi.

That was one fancy place. It was one of those new trendy residential towers, built for those who craved the Manhattan lifestyle and could afford it. But then, he had to wonder where his sister had met someone with that kind of money, given the way she was always hanging around campus.

Right, he shrugged. Probably a student or a teacher at the university who came from money.

Make it a lot of money. A penthouse in a building like that must cost a small fortune. Okay, next step. Let's see who owns the top floor residence.

Rubbing his hands gleefully, he pulled up the tax assessor records. Ah, the things he could learn from all the information his employer made available to him.

His job didn't pay enough to make him wealthy, but it sure as hell provided him with a wealth of information.

SYSSI

*A*manda hadn't been kidding about her closet, the contents of which could've made up the entire inventory of a high-end boutique. Or two.

Finally, after trying on at least a dozen outfits, none of which Amanda had deemed hot enough, they had compromised on a short, gray silk dress.

On Amanda, the dress probably bordered on indecent, barely covering her bottom; on Syssi it reached mid-thigh.

One hand on her hip, the other propping her chin, Amanda regarded the outfit critically. "I wish we had time to adjust the hemline. This dress is too long on you."

"It's perfect, and it even matches my shoes." Syssi twirled to demonstrate how well the dress hugged her curves, praying Amanda would let it go and wouldn't make her try any more outfits.

"I guess it'll have to do… Don't get me wrong—you look gorgeous. I just wanted you to look a bit more daring. But never fear, a little makeup and you're going to knock them dead anyway." With a wave of her hand, Amanda dismissed any further discussion and moved to examine her own reflection in the mirror.

Wearing a very short, off-white skirt topped by a loose, sparkly, silver blouse that left most of her back exposed, Amanda was daring enough for the both of them. And with the spiky-heeled, silver sandals that completed the look, she was sure to tower over most of the club goers. Next to Amanda, there was little chance anyone would spare Syssi a glance.

"I'm glad you're wearing heels. They make you so tall, there is no chance I'll lose you. I'll be able to spot your head above the crowd."

"You'll only have to follow the line of drooling males to zero in on my location." Amanda smirked and sauntered to the makeup table. "Come, let's see what we can do about that innocent-looking face of yours." She patted the stool facing the mirror.

"Oh, boy. I think I'll close my eyes for this. Please don't make me look like a streetwalker," Syssi pleaded with a cringe.

"Trust me, you're gonna look amazing. Don't open your eyes until I say it's okay." Amanda commanded, brandishing the brush like a cudgel above Syssi's head.

"Yes, mistress," Syssi parroted Igor, Dracula's servant.

Amanda laughed, exposing her somewhat overlong canines. "I look the part, don't I? Black hair, fangs..." She made a hissing sound.

That she did.

"You should audition for it. You'd make a perfect vampire—beautiful, scary, bossy...," Syssi ribbed.

"Yeah, not in the cards, regrettably. Now close your eyes. I want it to be a surprise."

"You can look now," Amanda announced after fussing

endlessly with Syssi's hair and makeup. Looming over Syssi, hands on her shoulders, she smiled with satisfaction at both their reflections in the mirror.

Syssi gazed at herself in wide-eyed amazement. "Wow, who is that girl, and what have you done with plain old me?" The makeup made her look beautiful and sophisticated without being obvious.

Pushing up, she got closer to the mirror, then retreated, examining herself from different angles.

"Thank you. It's perfect!" She cheerfully hugged Amanda.

"Careful on the makeup! No kissing!" Amanda tilted her head backward, avoiding Syssi's enthusiastic, gloss-covered lips.

"I see the party started without me." A tall, muscular woman sauntered into the room and tossed her heavy leather jacket on the bed.

"Kri, this is Syssi. Syssi, meet Kri." Amanda made the short introduction.

Syssi offered her hand for a handshake only to be pulled into a crushing hug.

"Don't you dare ruin her makeup!" Amanda shrieked.

Letting go, Kri took a step back. "You two look awesome!" she said, admiring their outfits. "I feel underdressed... And don't even think about offering to dress me up," she forestalled Amanda, then turned to Syssi. "Did she torture you for hours?"

"Not for hours, but long enough." Syssi snorted.

Amanda wielded the brush like a weapon again. "Let me at least do something about your hair."

Taking Syssi's place in front of the mirror, Kri straddled the small stool. "Okay, give it a shot."

Watching Amanda unbraid Kri's long wavy hair, Syssi

observed that there was something both intimidating and vulnerable about the girl.

She was big. And even though not much taller than Amanda, she dwarfed her not so small older cousin.

Kri's outfit of black leather pants and heavy combat boots made her look like a serious kickass. But then the pink rhinestone heart on the front of her black muscle shirt, with Girl Power printed over it, seemed to say, "Hey, I might be tough, but I'm still a girl."

She looked to be about twenty. Powerfully built with wide shoulders and pronounced biceps that spoke of many hours spent at the gym. And yet, reflected in the mirror, the girl's face was surprisingly feminine— the loose waves of her waist-long tawny hair framing gentle blue eyes and clean, smooth skin.

"Okay, girl, what do you think?" Amanda fluffed Kri's hair, creating more bounce. "Is there any chance I could convince you to put on some lip gloss?" Looking at Kri in the mirror, Amanda waved the small tube above the girl's head.

"No way, I hate the way the stuff tastes." Pushing up to her feet, Kri flipped her long hair back and raised her chin as she examined her profile's reflection. "I'm hot enough without it. Just look at me. You think any guy could resist all this?" She ran her hands over her curves.

"I'm sure none would dare." Amanda smirked with a wink at Syssi.

"Are we ready, ladies?" Kri picked up her leather jacket and swung it over her shoulder.

"Let's go. I just want to stop by Kian's on our way out." Amanda grabbed her sequined clutch and headed out the door.

Syssi felt a flutter of excitement at the prospect of

seeing Kian again. Or rather, of him seeing her—all decked out and looking fab. Clutching the purse she borrowed from Amanda, she crossed the vestibule behind the two tall women.

"Wait here. I'll just let him know we're leaving." Amanda started down the hallway toward Kian's office.

"I heard you come in. Though next time, I would appreciate it if you knocked..." Kian intercepted her and together they returned to the living room.

He looked so good. An old pair of faded jeans hung low on his hips, and a thin, worn-out T-shirt stretched over his chest, showing off all those incredible muscles. Barefoot, even his feet looked sexy.

Who knew feet could be so enticing? Or was it the whole man she found irresistible. Every little bit of him.

It wasn't until Kri moved aside that Kian got an unobstructed view of Syssi. And when he did, his expression was priceless. With his eyes traveling the length of her body, he made her feel beautiful. Desired.

Rubbing his hand over his sternum, it took him a moment to compose himself before he approached her. "You look beautiful," he stated simply as he took both of her hands in his. "Where are you going?"

"We are heading to the Underground; just us girls." Amanda spoke to his back.

Kian ignored his sister—his sole focus on Syssi. "Give me a minute to change, and I'll join you."

"Hello? Girls. Night. Out. No boys invited... Sorry, bro." Amanda headed back to the vestibule.

"It's not safe. I should go with you," he tried, his eyes staring into Syssi's as he held on to her hands.

"Don't be silly, we have Kri with us. And don't wait up; we're gonna party until late... Ta-ta..." Amanda pressed the elevator button, turning around and motioning for the girls to hurry out.

Syssi pulled her hands out of Kian's grip. "Don't worry. We're going to be fine." She stretched up to place a quick kiss on his cheek.

"Be careful!" he called after them as they entered the elevator.

"Night, Kian." Amanda waved goodbye as the doors were closing.

On the way down to the parking level, Syssi thought back to the way Kian had looked at her and wondered; had jealousy been the reason he had wanted to join them? Had he been worried about her going to a club looking like that?

Would he show up there despite Amanda's veto?

Did she want him to?

SYSSI

*T*he Underground, as the name suggested, was a basement. From the outside, the only indication that there was a club in the building was the long line of people hoping to get in.

Roped off with a thick red cable, the line snaked all the way to the parking lot of the industrial complex.

Going straight for the door, Syssi felt like a red-carpet celebrity as the three of them bypassed the gawking, roped-off cattle.

Shocked by some of the outrageous outfits on the girls standing behind the rope, she did a little gawking herself—watching them shift from foot to foot in their uncomfortable sky-high heels and tiny, tight skirts.

It seemed Amanda had been right about Syssi's dress being a little too long. But then again, it wasn't as if Syssi cared to blend in with the rest of this crowd.

They were let right in, with the bouncer holding the door as he nodded respectfully at Amanda. Once inside, they got the same royal treatment from the guy in charge of the elevator.

Evidently, in this place, Amanda ruled.

It took no longer than a few seconds for them to reach the basement, and as soon as the elevator doors opened, Syssi was blasted with the club's deafening music and nauseating smells.

Sticking her fingers in her ears, she tried to block the onslaught. And yet, it still felt as if everything in her abdominal cavity was thumping to the pounding of the beat. She grimaced, wishing for two extra hands so she could shield her belly and protect her insides as well.

She should've remembered how loud and crowded clubs were, and brought earplugs... and a nose clip...

Breathing through her mouth to ward off the cloying smells of perfumes, sweat, booze, and God-knew-what-else, she didn't dare inhale through her nose until they cleared the crowd, climbing the stairs to the VIP balcony.

Up there, the music was just as loud, but at least the air was fresher and it wasn't as crowded.

Out of the five round granite-topped tables by the railing, only two were occupied, with most of the balcony's exclusive clientele preferring the privacy of the intimate, dark booths lining the back wall.

Sitting down at the table next to Amanda, Syssi peered over the railing at the packed dance floor below, watching the dancing crowd as it appeared and disappeared in between bursts of throbbing strobe lights.

She wondered if the couples and sometimes three-somes writhing against each other, touching and fondling, were aware of the fact that they were providing a peep show for those sitting above them on the balcony.

Most likely, though, as tightly packed as everyone was on the smoky and dim platform, they must've assumed they had some measure of privacy.

Or maybe they didn't care.

"Amanda, haven't seen you in here for a while. How're ya doing?"

"I'm doing great. How about you, Alex?" Amanda replied.

Shifting her attention away from her voyeuristic fascination with what was going on below, Syssi looked at the man pulling a chair from a nearby table and parking it at theirs.

The guy was so well put together, she wondered if he was gay. Very few of the straight men she knew paid that much attention to their looks.

His blond hair was perfectly styled, and although he wore nothing fancier than jeans and a white, button-down shirt, both looked like expensive designer items that had been custom tailored to his exact fit.

Still, she wouldn't have thought much of that getup if not for the row of three diamond studs in his right ear and the matching set of a diamond watch and bracelet.

The guy had more jewelry on him than she and Amanda combined. Kri wasn't even wearing a watch.

But then, the leering glance he sneaked Syssi's way was all heterosexual.

"Alex, sweetheart, meet my friend Syssi. It's her first time here, so be a doll and take good care of her." Amanda smiled at the guy.

"Syssi, this is my good friend Alex, the owner of this fab place."

"A pleasure to make your acquaintance." Smiling with the confidence of a man who was well aware of how handsome he was, Alex lifted her hand for a kiss.

As he held onto it way longer than was polite, his dark eyes bored into hers, sending strange shivers up her spine.

The guy was making her very uncomfortable—and not in a good way. And yet, she couldn't force herself to look away or pull her hand out of his grasp.

"Back off, Alex, she's Kian's. And I'm sure you would rather avoid tangling with him," Amanda warned with a wink.

As if suddenly burnt by it, Alex let go of Syssi's hand so fast it remained suspended in front of her face for a split second before she shook off the stupefied sensation and retracted it to her lap.

What was that? Syssi wondered at her peculiar reaction to him.

The shivers and the mesmerizing effect he had on her didn't make any sense, as she didn't find him attractive at all. There was a lascivious quality to his demeanor, and although handsome, he looked too slick and kind of sleazy; like a pushy salesman or a campaigning politician.

"What can I get you, ladies?" He pushed up from his chair, and his smile was so genuinely friendly that she thought for a moment that the whole thing had been a product of her imagination.

"The usual for me. Kri, the same?" When Kri nodded, Amanda turned to Syssi. "What would you like, darling?"

"Club soda for me, thank you." Syssi offered Alex a perfunctory smile.

"You sure?" Amanda cocked a brow.

"Absolutely, I had enough to drink for one day." Syssi grimaced. It took almost two hours before the vertigo sensation from earlier had dissipated, and there was no way she was subjecting herself to that kind of misery anytime soon.

After a quick kiss on Amanda's cheek, Alex left for the bar.

Her companions began to chitchat, and Syssi tried to join in, but gave up when her voice got hoarse from straining to be heard over the music. And yet, it deterred neither Amanda nor Kri. Oblivious to the noise, they kept at it as if they were sitting in Amanda's living room.

How they could hear each other was beyond her. Even trying to listen in on their conversation was proving too much of an effort. Which left her with nothing better to do than watch the sexually charged dancing scene below.

If not for the clothing that provided some small barrier between the writhing bodies, it would have looked like a mass orgy.

Had it always been like that?

She didn't remember it being so bad. Had things changed so much in only a few years? Or was it possible she just hadn't noticed it before?

Be that as it may, it was kind of depressing to think that she had gotten either too old for the club scene or had been too clueless to notice what had been going on around her before. Or both.

"Come on, Syssi. Let's go dancing." Amanda tapped her shoulder, diverting her attention from the pseudo porn show below.

"Go ahead. I'm going to stay here. It's way too crowded down there for me, not to mention stinky." Syssi strained her voice, trying to be heard without actually shouting.

"You sure?" Amanda asked, exchanging looks with Kri.

"I'll stay with you." Looking disappointed, Kri sat down.

"No way! Go have fun. I'll watch you guys from up here. Go!"

Amanda glanced at Kri and nodded, apparently deciding it was safe to leave Syssi on her own.

Heading down, Amanda stopped by the upstairs bar to

talk to Alex, and with a hand on his shoulder said something in his ear. When both of them briefly glanced Syssi's way, she waved and smiled, letting them know she was on to them.

Doubtless, Amanda had asked Alex to look out for her *little friend*.

35

KIAN

*O*nce the girls had left, Kian paced restlessly for about two minutes before pulling out his phone and calling Onegus.

"What's up, Boss?" His chief of Guardians answered after several rings.

"I know it's late, but I need you to grab Bhathian and go to the Underground. Amanda is heading there with Kri and Syssi, one of the potential targets for the Doomers. I want them guarded."

"Amanda will have our heads for following her. She doesn't like us snooping around her hunting grounds."

"I don't care. If she gives you any crap, tell her to take it up with me." Kian slowed his agitated pacing only to kick the couch, making the whole thing slide and hit the coffee table.

"Yes, Boss."

"Thank you, and try not to get in her face. I just need you to keep an eye on them."

The easing of pressure he had expected after ensuring the girls' safety never came.

As much as he hated to admit this even to himself, his motives hadn't been all that noble. The truth was, he loathed the idea of Syssi in a club teeming with lustful males—without him by her side to scare them off.

Just imagining the men leering at her made him see red.

Since when did he develop such a possessive streak?

Sending the guys to basically spy on Syssi was almost as bad as stalking her himself.

Damn, he wasn't that kind of guy... or was he?

The kind of man he wished to be would trust Syssi and give her all the space she needed without obsessing like a lunatic the moment she got out of his sight.

But this wasn't about him not trusting Syssi. This was about the men that would be lusting after her, their dirty thoughts touching her, somehow contaminating her.

He knew the sort of things men would be fantasizing about doing to her, not because he was a mind reader, but because he had been guilty of the same.

Men are pigs... each and every one of them.

Taking a deep breath, Kian ran his hands through his hair and tried to calm down. *Come on, buddy, every attractive woman would be the source of male fantasies, it's harmless... most of the time...*

Yeah, trouble was, he couldn't help feeling as if those supposedly harmless fantasies were sullying his Syssi.

36

SYSSI

*S*yssi watched Amanda and Kri weave across the dance floor, each dragging a hunky guy behind.

That didn't take long, she thought as they started undulating and rubbing against their partners in an overtly sexual way.

It was kind of shocking to see Amanda behave like that. Despite all of her prior proclamations of wantonness, Syssi couldn't believe her boss would get randy, with a stranger, on a dance floor, in a crowded club.

The distinguished professor, Dr. Amanda Dokani, was indeed a slut.

Syssi chuckled, admitting that she shouldn't be surprised. Amanda had made it abundantly clear—on numerous occasions—that she was ruled by a ferocious appetite for sex. The fact that Syssi had believed her boss had been greatly exaggerating for dramatic effect and had been proven wrong was her problem and not Amanda's.

And her young cousin was even worse.

By the way Kri was grabbing her partner's butt, grinding against him and shoving her tongue into his mouth, it was obvious the girl was cut from the same cloth as her cousin. Except, she was more aggressive about it. Not that the guy had a problem with her dominance. Judging by his stupefied expression, he was loving every moment of it.

Amanda and her guy were a step further. He had his hand under her loose blouse and was fondling her braless breast while she had her palm pressed between their bodies. And it didn't require X-ray vision to imagine what was going on down there.

Too embarrassed to watch, Syssi turned her back to the railing and reached for her soda glass. But it was empty.

Symbolic of her situation, that seemingly insignificant fact unnerved her more than it should have. With nothing to hold in her hands and no desire to keep watching what was going on below, there was nothing to distract her from the awkwardness of sitting alone in a club that was bursting at the seams with people.

Looking for the waitress, she spotted the young woman taking an order from one of the booths, and as soon as the girl turned, she waved her down.

Watching as she sauntered over in her high heels, Syssi pitied the poor girl's feet at the end of the shift. Not that she thought the waitress had a choice in the kind of footwear she wore on the job.

The black pumps, as well as the really short black shorts and tiny white halter top, seemed to be a uniform of sorts for all the hostesses serving drinks—with only slight variations in style and make.

With a boss like Alex, Syssi was willing to bet that the girls were required to buy their own version of the uniform. Not only would it be in line with his sleazy character, but it would also explain why the outfits were not identical.

"What can I get you?"

"I'd like a sangria, please. And some nuts or tortilla chips if you have them." Syssi wasn't hungry, but the snack would keep her hands busy while she waited for Amanda and Kri to come back.

This outing was turning out to be not as fun as she imagined it would when Amanda came up with the idea. Not by a long shot. Instead of sitting alone, nauseated by the noise, watching others making out, and feeling like she didn't belong, she would rather have been snuggling with Kian at his place. Or doing other things…

But then, the whole point of going out had been to get away from him, so she could think clearly and rationally without the hormonal haze of being around him clouding her head.

Which proved to be an exercise in futility.

Without something to distract her, she kept obsessing about him anyway.

Mercifully, it didn't take long for Amanda to come back. Syssi smiled at her friend and the guy she was dragging behind her; the same one she saw her getting busy with on the dance floor.

Except, instead of returning to the table, Amanda stopped at the bar, and after exchanging a few words with Alex and a little hand-wave in Syssi's direction, she and her partner disappeared through a door hidden behind a thick velvet curtain.

Forgetting the club was underground, Syssi had assumed that the thing was covering a window to the outside, not a doorway to God-knew-where or what. When a few moments later Kri pulled the same stunt, Syssi struggled to see what was behind the curtain. But it was too dark.

As if lying in wait for just the right opportunity, Alex showed up the moment the curtain had dropped behind Kri and parked his butt in the chair next to Syssi.

Sitting way too close to her, with his arm on the back of her chair, he was invading her personal space.

"It's hard to hear above the music," he explained, but the hunger in his eyes and his leering smirk made it clear he had more than talking on his mind. "So, how do you know Amanda?" he asked in her ear as he pretended to absent-mindedly play with a lock of her long hair, winding it around his finger.

Was this the special attention Amanda had asked him to show her? For some reason, Syssi didn't think so...

Shaking her head a little, she tried to free her hair without being too obvious about it. "We work together," she answered in the coolest tone she could muster, which was only a shade away from outright rude.

"Ah, the university... must be exciting," he continued in the same seductive tone.

"Where did Amanda and Kri go?" Syssi tried to divert his attention. And regretted it as soon as his expression turned from leering to pure lust.

Oh, boy... She'd diverted his attention all right... In the wrong direction...

"We have some private rooms in the back, reserved for... special guests... with special needs... Come, I'll show you." With each pause, he wound a little more of her hair on his finger until he reached her scalp. Not pulling on it or causing her pain, he was nonetheless holding her immo-bilized as he slowly closed the distance between their mouths.

With his smug face no more than an inch away from hers, she was about to tell him to stop, and if that didn't do the trick, to kick him where it would count, when he suddenly let go of her.

Following his gaze, she saw what or rather who had given him pause. Walking toward them were two very large men—the kind that made the bouncers up front look like accountants.

"Hello, Alex old man. Have you seen Amanda and Kri? They and another girl, Syssi, were supposed to be here. Kian sent us to check up on them." The guy seemed friendly enough, easygoing. And yet, judging by Alex's tensed body, he made him nervous.

"Bhathian, Onegus, always good to see you guys. I guess that you haven't met Syssi yet because she's right here. I'm keeping her company while Amanda and Kri are doing their thing in the back."

The men seemed oblivious to the implied activity that was taking place in the rooms behind the curtain, as well as to the way Alex had been all over her when they'd walked in.

Apparently, Kian hadn't specified the kind of checking up he had in mind.

"Syssi, nice to meet you. I'm Onegus." The pretty blond one offered his hand, smiling a smile that could melt ice.

"Bhathian." The tall, serious one shook what was offered.

"Nice to meet you too, would you care to join us? *Please, please say yes...* Syssi pleaded with her eyes, hoping their presence would keep Alex's tentacles at bay.

But apparently, being male meant that they sucked at reading facial cues. "We would love to, but Amanda is not going to be happy about us showing up on her turf. We'll just go and sit over there at the bar; give you gals your space." Onegus smiled politely.

"I'm sorry, but I can't stay either. After all, I have a club to run." Alex made it sound as if she had been keeping him there.

Whatever, she wasn't about to correct him. Syssi was just glad to be rid of him, and as far as she was concerned, he could keep his damn pride and shove it.

Alone at the table again, she glanced at the men. Sitting at the bar, the two were hard to ignore, drawing the attention of the few single females there, and even some covert wistful looks from those accompanied by a partner.

Onegus… Bhathian… What peculiar names. Come to think of it, so were Anandur, Brundar, and Kri. Even Kian was unusual. The only one with a common name was Amanda.

Maybe they were foreigners? But where were they from? They had no accents that she could discern. Except, sometimes their choice of words and some of their gestures seemed out of place, or rather from a different era.

The way Brundar lifted off the sofa when she came in, bowing a little… Come to think of it, both Bhathian and Onegus bowed slightly when shaking her hand. Maybe the bunch spent some time in Japan, absorbing the local penchant for bowing.

Still, that didn't explain the names. If she had her phone, she could have Googled it while waiting for the girls to come back. But Kian hadn't provided the replacement he had promised yet. She would have taken care of it herself if given a chance to get out. But as Kian and Amanda were determined to keep her prisoner, she was forced to rely on her jailer.

"Hey, you." Amanda plopped down next to her, looking spent and relaxed until she noticed Kian's men at the bar. "What are they doing here?" she hissed.

"They said Kian sent them to watch over us. Who are they? Do they work for Kian, or are they friends of yours?"

"More like family."

"More cousins? You must be kidding."

"What? I told you it's a family business. We are big on employing our own." Amanda waved the waitress over and ordered more drinks. Then went back to glaring angrily at her cousins. "But it pisses me off that they are here. Like they have nothing better to do than follow me around."

37

KIAN

*A*fter pacing around his living room like a caged animal for what seemed to him like hours, Kian pulled out his phone.

Update! he texted Onegus.

It took the guy forever to answer. *They are fine, nothing interesting going on, besides Alex pestering Amanda's friend.*

Fuck, that was it. He was going to that club whether Amanda liked it or not. And if Syssi accused him again of unwarranted jealousy, so be it.

Kian could barely tolerate the thought of all the other males in the club sniffing around Syssi, and Alex was a sleazeball bastard to top them all.

There was a limit to what Kian was willing to suffer in the name of gentlemanly conduct.

Even though Alex managed to run his club skirting around clan law by not breaking any clan specific rules, he was breaking plenty of the human ones.

The prostitutes Kian had to grudgingly accept as their services were needed for some of his men. But he abhorred the drugs. Alex claimed he didn't deal and just turned a blind eye to the stuff changing hands in his club, but Kian had his doubts.

The guy was living a lifestyle that even a successful club like the Underground couldn't support. To make that kind of money, Alex must've been doing something illegal.

Hell, he had just bought a new super-yacht; a luxury Bluewater beauty that must've cost over twenty-five million.

For some inexplicable reason, Amanda liked the guy and considered him a friend. A bad judgment on her part. But she was a big girl and he couldn't tell her who to be friends with.

Syssi, on the other hand, he would keep as far away from that scumbag as possible.

Without bothering to change, Kian slid into a pair of loafers, grabbed a jacket, and heading for the garage called for Okidu to drive him—in case he decided to stay and indulge in more than a couple of drinks. Not that drinking would be enough to impair his driving, but the last thing he needed was to be pulled over and fail the breathalyzer test.

38

SYSSI

*S*yssi couldn't help but notice that Kri's expression upon returning from her back room activities was very different from Amanda's. She looked irritated. Walking behind her, her partner looked kind of lost and confused. And as Kri took a seat at their table, the guy went downstairs without even waving goodbye.

Come to think of it, Amanda's partner hadn't joined them either. Strange. The club scene must've changed a lot in the six years Syssi hadn't been part of it; and not for the better.

"I feel like dancing some more. Anyone care to join me?" Kri said and finished her drink.

"I will!" Amanda chirped, shooting up from her chair.

The woman sure bounced back quickly.

"I'm good. You go ahead." Syssi shooed the two away.

They kept staring at her as if she was nuts.

"You didn't dance even once. What's the point of coming here if all you do is sit up here? You have to come with us... at least one song." Amanda reached for Syssi's arm.

Syssi leaned away. "No, really, I'm fine here. Watching you guys is enough entertainment for me," she said, failing to hide the slight note of sarcasm in her tone. Though with all the noise, she doubted the girls could've heard it.

Exchanging looks with Amanda, Kri shrugged and headed for the stairs. A moment later, Amanda shook her head at Syssi and followed Kri down.

Sorry to be the disappointing prude…

Syssi was angry with Amanda, for the head shaking, for dragging her here and then behaving the way she did.

It wasn't that Syssi condemned their promiscuity; they were big girls and could do as they pleased. She just wished they wouldn't do it while she waited awkwardly alone.

Sighing, she glanced at the bar. Maybe she could join the guys. But they were gone. Turning to look at the dance floor, she spotted them not far from Amanda and Kri, watching the girls dance.

Observing them, it struck her that there was a military flair to their demeanor. It manifested in the way they held their bodies and the alertness with which they were scanning the crowd. Come to think of it, Anandur and Brundar, and even Kri were the same.

Bodyguards. It was so obvious she wondered how she could've missed it before. For some reason she'd thought the brothers were Kian's assistants. It didn't make sense to have family as bodyguards. Yes, they could be trusted more than strangers, but who wanted to risk their own cousins' lives?

Apparently Kian had no such reservations.

The question begging to be asked was what kind of business were Kian and his family in that it produced so much competition and animosity and required that level of protection?

Mafia! It has to be.

Suddenly, she saw it all clearly; recent events creating a pattern and all the puzzle pieces fitting together to form one scary picture.

All that money.

The big family business…

It hadn't been a group of zealots that Amanda and Kian had been running from that evening at the lab. They'd been ambushed by a hostile competitor. And the goons after them had belonged to another mafia. Unable to strike at their targets, they had returned at night and ransacked the lab to send a message.

Probably turf wars…

Was Amanda dealing drugs? On campus? Here at the club?

The guards Kian had sent had mentioned she didn't like them showing up on her turf. Was that what she and Kri had been doing behind the curtain? Selling drugs to those guys? That would explain why their partners hadn't hung around, scurrying away quickly once the deed had been done.

Oh. My. God. I had sex with a mafia boss! Syssi inhaled sharply as panic threatened to cut off her air supply.

Pushing her chair back, she grabbed her purse and was about to flee when Alex stuck his sleazy face in front of her, blocking her escape.

"Where are you running off to, sweetheart?" He reached for her arm.

Twisting away, she clutched her purse with both hands. "Ladies' room? Can you point me toward one?"

"There is one behind that curtain. I'll take you there." His eyes gleaming dangerously, he grabbed her bicep, digging his fingers into her flesh.

"Let go of her! Before I rip off your goddamned arm!" came the hissed command from Kian.

Relief and panic warred for dominance in Syssi's frantic mind. The Lion King was rescuing her from the clutches of the hyena. Unfortunately, he just looked like Mufasa but was really Scar...

"Come dance with me." Kian clasped her hand as soon as Alex dropped it, ignoring the jerk's resentful glare as he sauntered off.

Afraid to say anything, Syssi let him pull her down the stairs and onto the dance floor. But at the same time, her mind was going a thousand miles per hour, calculating her options. If she could somehow get away, she could run to Andrew for protection. But then what? They knew where she lived, and she'd lose her job. Which was a big problem, as finding a decent one in this economy was next to impossible.

Oh, well, there was always the option of joining her parents in Africa, but she really didn't want to do that. And anyway, as well guarded as Kian had her, her chances of escape were nil.

She had to face facts. As long as Kian wanted her around, she was trapped. Like in the movies, the wife or mistress of the mafia boss was a captive—never allowed to leave... alive!

Oh! My! God! What a mess.

And yet, as he held her close she didn't resist—powerless against her need to cling to him. Burying her nose in the fabric of his shirt, she inhaled his unique scent, getting high on it like some junkie.

The pathetic truth was that, on some irrational level, she felt safe in his arms despite who she believed he was and needed him so badly that it hurt.

She was driving herself crazy; the feelings of trepidation and disappointment clashing with the intense longing, conflicting and augmenting each other and wreaking havoc on her mind.

39

KIAN

*H*olding Syssi close as they swayed to the music, Kian had no trouble reading her emotions, even without his enhanced senses. Though for the life of him, he couldn't fathom what caused her such distress. Or how the hell she could be so afraid of him and at the same time cling to him like he was her lifeline.

You'd think that he'd know a thing or two about women after almost two thousand years, but evidently he still had a lot to learn.

"Don't be upset, sweet girl, I meant what I said before. My jerky behavior had nothing to do with my opinion of you. I think you're a rare treasure, my sweet Syssi...," he whispered in her ear while rubbing gentle circles on her back.

Syssi didn't respond and remained tense and rigid in his arms. Then, as he waited for what seemed like forever for her to say something, anything, it dawned on him that with her limited mortal hearing, she couldn't have heard a word of what he had said over the excruciatingly loud music.

Taking her hand, he pulled her behind him up the short flight of stairs and led her out the back door, where Okidu was waiting with the limo.

Syssi didn't resist, but he was painfully aware that she followed him with the enthusiasm of a prisoner led to her own execution.

"I need to let Amanda know that I've left with you," Syssi whispered as Okidu pulled the limo out from the alley behind the club.

It hurt watching her sit glued to the limo's opposite side, as far away from him as she possibly could in the confined space. She was gazing out the window, clearly to avoid looking at him.

"Don't worry about it. I'm texting her right now." Kian was truly baffled by Syssi's emotional storm and the mixed signals he was getting from her.

Earlier, when he had made an ass of himself, she had been upset and disappointed. Now she was way worse.

If he didn't know better, he would've thought Syssi had just lost a loved one. Micah had projected a similar scent when he'd brought her the devastating news of her son's death.

Grief.

What a fucking mess.

Something else must be going on. It didn't make sense for her to be that distraught over his petty jealous tantrum.

But what did he know?

If she was anything like Amanda, she might've twisted the whole thing in her head, blowing it into monstrous proportions.

"I'm really sorry for hurting your feelings. If it's any excuse, I'm terribly inexperienced in dealing with these kinds of emotions. It's all new to me." He reached to take her hand but then reconsidered—afraid she'd pull away.

"It's okay. You don't have to explain. I understand. I'm sorry that I overreacted," Syssi said in a flat voice, looking out the window and pretending nonchalance.

Except, she kept playing with her purse, tugging the magnetic clasp open and letting it snap back into place—over and over again.

"You still look upset. Please tell me what I can do to make it better. I'm going out of my mind here." Kian wasn't exaggerating; he really was becoming desperate, hating the helpless feeling of not knowing what to say or do next.

Was it just him? Or were all males completely clueless about women and how to deal with their peculiar emotional states? It seemed a man had to tread carefully through the minefield of a female's psyche to avoid unwittingly stepping on a land mine. Kian would've paid good money for someone to draw him a map and help him navigate safely through these dangerous grounds.

"It's nothing."

Nothing? It was the worst kind of answer. He could've dealt with accusations, with anger, even with tears. But nothing gave him nothing to work with.

All he wanted was to pull her onto his lap and kiss her senseless, until she forgot all about whatever it was that was causing her to be so upset and so remote.

He didn't.

Sadly, he didn't think he'd be welcomed.

After what had felt like an endless silence, Syssi turned away from the window and looked straight into his eyes. "I need to ask you a question, and I need you to answer me honestly." She sounded dead serious.

"Anything, I'll answer any question you might have."

And he meant it. Even if she guessed what he was, he would admit it.

"Are you a mafioso? Is that what your family's business is all about—dealing drugs?"

"What? That's what you wanted to ask? Why would you think something so absurd?" Out of all the questions he had anticipated, this one completely threw him off.

"Not absurd at all. One, you guys seem to have shitloads of money." She lifted a second finger. "Two, everyone I meet is family. Three, the men and Kri are very obviously bodyguards. Four, the attacks on Amanda and then her lab stink of retaliation or a warning strike by another mafia. Most likely, one that is competing with you for drug territory. Five, Amanda asks me to keep your location secret. Did I miss anything?"

Unable to hold back, Kian burst out laughing. "Oh, baby, I'm sorry. You're right. I totally get it how you could reach the wrong conclusion putting it all together like that. That's not why I'm laughing." Holding his hand over his heart, he took a moment to calm himself. "I'm just so tremendously relieved that this is what got you upset. I was racking my brain, trying to figure out what landmine I had stepped on."

He made a move to pull her to him, but Syssi stopped him with a hand to his chest. "You still didn't answer my question. Are you, or are you not, a mafioso?"

"I swear on everything that's dear to me, neither I nor any other member of my family is in the mafia or has any connections to any kind of organized crime. As far as I know. Okay?"

Scrunching her forehead she looked at him with narrowed eyes, scrutinizing his face for any signs of deception, then frowned. "Not yet, you need to tell me more than that."

With a sigh, he acquiesced. "Our family owns a large international conglomerate of enterprises that I assure you is all perfectly legal and has nothing to do with organized crime. Actually, our main objective is to benefit humanity by encouraging scientific innovation in a variety of fields, cultural shifts toward more freedom and equal opportunity around the world, women's rights, eradication of prejudice and oppression, etc…"

"So why the bodyguards? The secrecy? And what about the attack? It all seems so clandestine," Syssi interrupted.

"I'm getting there. We have enemies, those who hate what we do and what we stand for. They're ruthless, hateful people who will stop at nothing until they annihilate my family and destroy all the amazing progress our work has accomplished."

"Why?"

"It's an old and complicated story. I don't want to go through all the long and sordid history of it. All I can say is that it's an ancient feud that started eons ago with a scorned suitor that didn't take the rejection well, to say the least. He swore himself and his descendants to an eternal vendetta. His progeny are very powerful and influential, and they pose an existential threat to us. Bottom line, we have to hide; operating under shadow corporations, always in a defensive mode. That's the reason behind the bodyguards, and why only family can be trusted in our inner circle."

Syssi seemed dumbfounded.

Did she believe his tale?

He had done his best, being very careful with how he phrased it, attempting to give her all the main points without divulging too much or twisting the truth. But was it enough? Were her instincts telling her he had been genuine despite being forced to omit the things he couldn't tell her? Searching her eyes, he was seeking reassurance that she was willing to accept what he had told her.

She looked at him for a long moment, her brows drawn together as if deliberating whether she should believe him or not. Then, taking a deep breath, she seemed to come to a conclusion. "I believe you. Though you're not telling me everything, but that's okay. I'm still a stranger to you, and you don't know if you can trust me, despite how close and intimate we got. It all just happened too fast. I understand that your family's safety must come first. I respect that."

Was this woman something else or what? One in a million... Scratch that. One in a billion!

Relieved that she'd believed him and grateful she hadn't pushed him to reveal more than he was comfortable with, Kian pulled her into his arms for a soulful kiss. She didn't resist, but even though her body had lost its stiffness, she was still far from truly participating.

Holding her close, luxuriating in the sensation of her soft body pressed against his, he felt buoyant. With the relief of finally touching her, knowing he had her back, the heaviness that had been weighing him down had lifted.

It didn't take long for the kiss to morph from something sweet and gentle into something hungry and wild. With his hand cradling the back of Syssi's head, he wedged the one on her back under her bottom and lifted her onto his lap.

As if a dam had burst inside her, Syssi's passive acquiescence turned into wild abandon. With her hands finding their way under his T-shirt, she caressed his pecs frantically, then clawed into his skin as if she couldn't get enough of him. Moaning into his mouth with what sounded like desperate longing, she undulated her hips, rubbing her soft behind against his shaft.

"God, I missed you." She groaned when they came up for air, grabbing at his shoulders and going for his neck, licking and sucking on his skin.

"You have no idea." He looked at her neck hungrily while snaking his hand under the hem of her short, loose-fitting dress. With his palm on the inside of her thigh, he kept caressing it, slowly going up to where it met its twin, taking his time.

He didn't want to overwhelm her—wasn't sure she was up to taking their passion further yet. But it seemed he had nothing to worry about.

Syssi welcomed his touch, and spreading her legs a little, let him in. He hissed as he pushed her panties aside and inserted a finger between her wet folds, finding her already drenched.

As another strangled moan escaped her throat, she glanced nervously at the half open partition, recalling they were not alone.

"Okidu," she whispered, gesturing with her head toward the driver.

Not willing to let go of his prize, Kian leaned with her still impaled on his finger, and with his other hand punched the button that raised the partition.

"Better?" he whispered.

"Yes," she slurred and closed her eyes.

In the limo's dim interior, her beautiful face was bathed in the lambent light cast by his glowing eyes. He kept pleasuring her, his finger going in and out, slowly, deliberately, carefully kindling her fire so it would burn steadily; getting gradually hotter before bursting into one big flame.

Feeling his glands swelling with venom, Kian dipped his head to suckle on her nipple through the thin fabrics of her dress and bra. Pulling on it carefully with his lips, he swirled his tongue around the turgid peak, creating a big wet spot on the silk.

Oh, how he loved the little tortured sounds she made when he turned her mindless with pleasure; they were sweet music to his ears. But even more, he loved the sounds she made when she climaxed. Adding another finger to his in-and-out motion, he pressed his thumb to her clitoris, and rubbing it gently, brought his masterpiece to its grand finale.

Syssi erupted, falling apart on his lap and making the loud keening moan he loved. Man, he would never tire of hearing that. Prolonging her pleasure, he kept his hand pumping and rubbing while his lips and tongue took care of her other nipple, producing another big wet spot.

It took momentous effort not to sink his fangs into the nipple he was working on. Dropping his forehead to her chest, he breathed in and out slowly, trying to regain control—commanding his throbbing erection and his fangs to let off.

Syssi lay so limply in his arms, he would have thought he had killed her with bliss, if not for her chest gently rising and falling with her shallow breaths.

Kian lifted his head, and as he looked at Syssi's blissful face—the long lashes fanning out of her closed lids, her flushed cheeks, her red and swollen lips—a tide of tenderness that he was afraid felt too much like love washed over him. Cradling her head, he brought her cheek to rest on his chest, and as he held her nestled against him, Kian suspected he would never be able to let her go.

Too soon, though, Okidu parked in the underground

garage and Kian had to reluctantly release his treasure. With a sigh, he helped her up to a sitting position and straightened her dress.

As Syssi glanced down at the two wet spots, her cheeks reddened in embarrassment. "I can't get out of the car like this," she whispered, smiling her shy little smile.

He shrugged out of his jacket and handed it to her. "Here, you can wear this over your dress."

After wiggling her arms inside the sleeves, she held the two halves clutched in her hand, waiting for Kian to exit and help her down.

"As you have my jacket, you'll have to walk in front of me to provide cover." He smirked, glancing down at himself.

Syssi giggled, positioning herself with her back to his front.

It was sly of him. He wasn't worried about Okidu noticing his bulge, and the chances of anyone else arriving right then were slim. But it was fun holding her in front of him as they made their way to the elevator.

Waving them off, Okidu began wiping dirt off the limo's windshield.

Good man. Kian smiled at the butler's unexpected subterfuge. Evidently, Okidu had learned a few things during his long existence. Though Kian had a strong suspicion that this newfound knowledge was gained mainly from watching shitloads of television.

With a wicked smirk, he followed Syssi inside the elevator, and the moment the doors closed, pressed her against the mirrored wall, his body enveloping hers from behind. She was wearing high heels, and her sweet little butt was perfectly aligned with his groin, providing delicious friction for his aching shaft.

Rubbing himself against her, he glanced at his reflection in the mirror and was alarmed by what he saw.

His eyes were glowing brightly even in the well-illuminated elevator, and with his lips pressed tightly over his elongated fangs, he wondered how was it possible for Syssi not to be terrified of him.

He didn't look human even to himself.

At that thought, something snapped inside him. Forgetting he'd been in the doghouse just moments ago, he was seized by an overwhelmingly savage impulse to make Syssi his, to possess her.

And he wanted her to watch him do it. Holding her eyes in the mirror, he grabbed her long hair and tilted her head to the side, exposing her neck as he bared his fangs.

Her eyes widened in fear, but he gave her no time to process what was happening. With a snakelike hiss, he struck, sinking them deep into her smooth, creamy neck.

As he pumped her full of his venom, he was all animal, the tremendous relief of it triggering his other long overdue release.

Spent, he sagged boneless against her back, braced his hands on the mirrored wall, and closed his eyes. Now that it was all over, he was mortified by his behavior; afraid to look at Syssi in the mirror and see the horror and disgust on her face.

40

SYSSI

Oh, my God! What is he?

Syssi had a moment of pure terror as Kian flashed a pair of monstrous fangs and sank them into her neck. The sharp burning pain of the twin penetrations had lasted no more than a few seconds before a euphoric pleasure swept through her, wiping away everything but its own mind-blowing effect.

Yes! Don't stop!

Her knees buckling, Kian's bruising grip on her hips was the only thing holding her up.

Dimly aware of Kian's fangs still embedded in her neck and his lips forming a tight seal on her skin, the pain failed to register.

She couldn't think. Just feel pleasure.

So good...

That too didn't last long, as a wave of powerful lust washed over her contented haze, contracting and focusing all of it into her sex.

Her already wet nipples tightened into two stone-hard

aching points, and her channel spasmed, creaming, begging to be filled.

Please…

She was about to do exactly that—beg Kian to impale her from behind—when the mere image of him doing so triggered an orgasm so powerful, her whole body shook with its aftershocks.

She blacked out.

The intense pleasure coming on the heels of such a terrifying experience must've been more than her body could take.

A moment later, as Kian's fangs retracted and his grip on her loosened, Syssi came to.

What had just happened?

Though still drugged and euphoric, she managed to crack her lids open and look at Kian's terrifying reflection. His intense blue eyes were glowing. The light wasn't coming from some outside source; the illumination came from inside. And those fangs, those monstrous long fangs of his, were tinted red from her blood. "What are you? What have you done to me?" she whispered.

Kian licked his fangs clean, his expression changing as they slowly shrank to an almost normal size. With guilt written all over his handsome face, he let go of her and took a step back.

Without him to hold her up, Syssi's knees buckled and she crumpled down to the elevator's floor.

41

KIAN

I'm despicable. Kian cursed as he picked Syssi up and carried her inside. *I should get whipped for what I've just done.* What was I thinking?

He wasn't... Succumbing to an instinct like a fucking animal...

Getting a thrill out of terrifying her? Coming in his pants? Where was all that self-control he prided himself on?

Shot to shit; that's where.

With Syssi, he was starting to think he had none.

Laying her gently on his bed, he was about to rectify the situation and thrall the memory away when her lids fluttered open.

Syssi looked at him and smiled seductively, her expression languid and satisfied from the euphoric effect of the venom. "You didn't answer me," she said with a purr, sounding as if she was talking about something carnal.

"I'm still Kian, the ass who momentarily lost his mind but is going to fix it right now." Kian focused on her eyes, attempting the thrall again.

Shifting her eyes away, she leveled them at the wet spot on his pants and giggled, breaking his concentration.

"Did I do this to you?" Shifting back to his face, she sighed contentedly. "Holy shit, that was amazing. I never knew I could actually black out from an orgasm." She giggled again. "But what kind of a vampire are you? Aren't you supposed to suck my blood out or something? Not pump me with some aphrodisiac... Oh, God, I still feel so loopy... But soooo gooood..."

She must be still high on the venom, that's why she is not panicking. Yet...

It was so tempting to just tell her the truth. What was the point of repeatedly thralling her anyway? He could always do it at the end of it, if and when she turned out not to be compatible. The best time to tell her was now when she was too hazy to freak out.

"I'm not a vampire." He sighed. "Vampires don't exist. At least as far as I know, although the stories about them most likely originated with my kind."

"Your kind?" Syssi's eyes seemed to get a bit clearer and more focused as she studied him closely.

"We are immortals—a more accurate definition would be near-immortals. We age extremely slowly, we don't get sick, and we heal very quickly if injured. But we can still be killed, it's just harder to do." Kian observed her reaction, waiting for either disbelief or alarm, but there was none.

Instead, she frowned. "What about the fangs, the biting, what's the story with that? Not that I'm complaining, mind you..." She fluttered her long-lashed eyelids.

Kian smiled and sat down on the bed beside her, then hesitated for a moment before taking her hand—afraid she'd pull away.

Amazingly, she tightened the grip reassuringly as if sensing his apprehension.

"The males of my kind produce venom when aroused sexually or provoked to aggression by other males. During sex, it's a powerful aphrodisiac for the female, as you have experienced yourself, and a euphoric. In a violent struggle, it serves to incapacitate an opponent, the drugging effect weakening his ability and resolve to fight, paralyzing him. In large dosages, the venom can be lethal, stopping the heart."

Syssi took a moment to mull over what he had told her. Then sounding more curious than worried, she asked, "How do you make sure you don't accidentally overdose your partner... You know, get carried away in the throes of passion and all that..."

"It cannot happen unintentionally. I'm not sure if it's biology controlling the amount and the potency of the venom produced, or if it's driven by intent. I've never heard of any male harming a female this way. But I'm not qualified to say if it's physically impossible or not. Although it makes sense that different emotions trigger the production of different hormones, which in turn deter-mine the appropriate quantity and composition of the venom required for the particular situation. In any case, you're safe with me. Despite what just happened in the elevator, and I'm so sorry for losing it and frightening you, I'd never harm you... you must know that." He caressed her cheek, flabbergasted by how calmly she was accepting all of this.

Turning her face into the caress, she kissed the inside of his palm, the sweetness of the gesture sending a wave of tenderness through him.

"I know," she said. And yet, she didn't sound as if she truly believed that.

"At first, when I saw your fangs, I was terrified. And when you bit me, it hurt like hell, but only for a few seconds, and then the pain got washed away by what I assume was the aphrodisiac in the venom. What I felt after that... is just indescribable... A girl could get addicted to that." She smiled sheepishly.

You have no idea... It was eerie the way her random shots hit home.

"Was it the first time you bit me?" She frowned, her tone suggesting she suspected it wasn't.

"It was the second time," he admitted, feeling like a scumbag. Second bite, third thrall. But he wouldn't mention it if she didn't ask.

"How come I don't remember it? And how come there are no marks on my neck? I can't feel anything different there." She touched the smooth skin where he'd bitten her, running her fingertips over the area and searching for the puncture holes that should have been there.

"You won't find anything. My saliva carries healing properties. The wounds close in a matter of seconds." He hoped she'd be satisfied at that and let go of the other part of her question.

"And the memory?"

No such luck.

Kian sighed. "I thralled you to forget it. I'm sorry. I know it's unconscionable, but I had no choice. We can't allow the knowledge of our existence to leak to the world. And to answer your next question, refraining from biting is like trying to hold back ejaculation. Eventually, the need becomes impossible to suppress."

Syssi frowned. "What a strange biology... I wonder what the evolutionary benefits were for it to evolve this way." Lifting her arm with marked effort, she caressed his cheek as if to let him know it was okay, and she wasn't mad. But she couldn't hold it up for long and let it plop back down. "I feel so woozy... Am I still drugged?"

"It takes time for the effect of the venom to dissipate, not to mention that it's past two in the morning and you had a long and eventful day. Go to sleep, sweet girl. I'll answer the rest of your questions tomorrow." He brushed back her tangled hair and kissed her forehead.

Syssi struggled to keep her eyes open. "I have so many questions swirling in my head..." But exhaustion and wooziness from the venom were winning. "Promise you will not make me forget...," she whispered.

"I promise." Kian squeezed her hand.

Satisfied, she sighed and let her lids drop.

Kian held on to her hand as he watched her sleep, absentmindedly caressing her palm with his thumb.

Strange biology indeed, he grimaced. And he hadn't gotten to the punch line yet—that there was a chance she was a Dormant carrier of the same biology, or that she was right about the venom being addictive, and she might get hooked and come to crave it like any other junkie their drug of choice.

He had always suspected that their kind was not the product of evolution but the work of genetic manipulation. Some brilliantly deranged ancestor of theirs must have sought to bind their precious females to their mates, counterbalancing the females' stronghold on the race's unique genetics.

Or maybe he had thought to create an antidote to infidelity. Except, if that had been his goal, he had failed miserably. His people had found a way to circumvent it by methodically doing exactly the thing he had been trying to prevent.

Served the loon right, to witness what a joke his tampering with nature had turned out to be.

KRI

*K*ri was doing her best to ignore the sounds coming from the backseat of the SUV. Sitting up front with Onidu, she gazed out the window and tried to keep her focus on the deserted streets they were passing by on their way home from the club.

Amanda had decided that one more round was in order and took her dessert to go; snaring another schlump to take home with her and starting on the fun in the car.

Hell, Kian wouldn't be happy with his sister bringing the guy up to her place and ignoring the SOP that no one but clan members was allowed on the top floors.

Never mind that he'd broken the rules himself with Syssi. But then again, the girl was a potential Dormant, and it looked like Kian had claimed her for himself. So in her case an exemption made sense.

But the same could not be said about the random dude Amanda had picked up. However, trying to persuade Amanda to take her guy to one of the timeshare apartments on the lower level would probably be a waste of energy.

Kri sighed and began braiding her hair.

It was her duty to at least give it a try, and once they got to the building, she would. But at the same time, she knew from experience it would be impossible to reason with the stubborn woman.

Let Kian deal with his obstinate sister.

And good luck with that.

Smirking, Kri snapped the elastic on the bottom of her completed braid.

Man, she could just imagine the tantrum he'd throw if he found out. But whatever, it wasn't her problem. She had no authority over the princess. Being a Guardian didn't mean she could just slap handcuffs on Annani's daughter and drag her to a holding cell in the basement.

All she could do was to flap her gums at the female. Uselessly.

In contrast, Kri never broke the rules and never brought her partners home. Not that there had been anyone at that club she had felt like screwing tonight. At home or anywhere else…

She grimaced, thinking about what had happened, or rather had not happened in the back room.

It wasn't that the guy hadn't been good-looking enough or sexed up enough, it was just that she'd kept comparing him to Michael and he'd kept coming up short.

Weird, she'd never used to compare the ones she'd picked up with Kian.

Maybe being so high up on the pedestal she had erected for him, he'd been in a completely different category, making the comparison irrelevant.

Not to mention the small detail of the taboo.

But Michael, well…

She kept seeing his smiling eyes admiring her in that

sweet boyish way of his. He hadn't leered like some guys or tried to front some macho bullshit to impress her. The boy was man enough to admit that he really liked her. Straight out. No bull. And how sexy was that?

In the end, she hadn't done anything with the guy in the club. Couldn't. After some heavy necking that had done nothing for her, she had thralled him and sent him on his way.

Except now, sitting in the car, she debated the wisdom of that move. Still needy and antsy, the backseat activity not helping, she seriously contemplated waking Michael up.

It was such a bad idea, though.

Unless she had some feelings for the kid, it wouldn't be fair to him. He wasn't one of her kind, and with his mortal sensibilities about sex, she would in all likelihood crush his young, vulnerable ego.

Oh, he would love to have her any way he could get her —of that she had no doubt. But how would he feel the morning after when he'd realize he was just a one-night stand? Still having to face her day after day?

Some guys would have no problem with that, but she had a strong feeling Michael was different. He was a one woman man, and once he found his one, he would look no further.

Unless she planned on being exclusive with him, at least until it was determined that he wouldn't turn and they sent him away clueless, she couldn't do it to him.

But wait... what if he really was a Dormant? If she had a relationship with him prior to his turning, then most likely he would remain hers to keep.

Sweet.

Smiling like the cat that ate the canary, Kri wondered

how come it hadn't occurred to her before. She was in a unique position to call dibs on the first potential near-immortal male not of her clan.

What a coup.

And yet, as she had no frame of reference for a long-term relationship, she had a hard time imagining what it could be like having a man of her own.

Feeling a little out of sorts, Kri leaned back in her seat and gazed out the window again. The streets of downtown LA were deserted this late, and tonight, the familiar sight of the occasional homeless vagabond disturbed her for some reason.

Curled sleeping on a street bench, with a shopping cart containing all of his or her earthly belongings within reach, these homeless were completely alone in the world.

With no roots and no one to take care of them in their time of need, they were adrift in a sea of indifferent humanity. Abandoned.

If one died tonight, there would be no one to mourn the loss.

Their misfortune made her feel both guilty and lucky for having a large family at her back. If she ever lost her mind and didn't know who or where she was, there would always be someone to make sure she was all right and take responsibility for her.

Her kind wasn't susceptive to mortal diseases, but that immunity didn't extend to some afflictions of the mind, and there were a few cases of insanity among them.

Some had been the result of post-traumatic stress disorder, others due to God knew what.

Her own mother suffered from a mild case of obsessive compulsive disorder, compelled to keep everything in her house in precise groups of three.

It wasn't a big deal to just go with it and oblige her, but the hysterics when someone forgot and moved things out of their groupings were trying.

Yeah, it was good to be part of a clan; to belong to a community that gave a damn. But how much better would having a mate of her own be?

Someone she could come back to at the end of the day, share her nights with, her thoughts, her memories.

Well, putting it this way, a roommate could provide similar companionship. But the benefits of having one were not worth the compromises she'd have to make.

And in any case, it wasn't the same as someone sharing her bed. Permanently.

All of a sudden she craved it, which was strange because she'd never given it much thought before. But now, she longed for a partner with surprising intensity.

And the one she wanted was Michael. With his cute smile and his big shoulders and sincere face.

Except, he was so damn young.

SYSSI

*S*yssi cracked one eye open, not sure what had woken her up. It was either the sound of running water coming from the adjacent bathroom or the sun rays filtering through the parted curtains and shining brightly on her face.

Squinting against the glare, she looked around the unfamiliar bedroom, and it took her a moment until she remembered where she was. Or why...

With the cobwebs of sleep clearing, what had happened last night still seemed like a surreal dream or a drug-induced hallucination.

Yet, she knew it had been neither.

As out of it as she'd been while the whole thing happened, the memory of that bite and the things Kian had told her were too vivid to be a dream. And he'd brought her here last night—to his bedroom.

Well, at least he wasn't a mobster, she chuckled. And he claimed he wasn't a vampire... Though, considering the fangs and the biting, she still had her doubts.

Funny, that this was what was troubling her in light of

the bigger picture she was starting to put together from all the bits and pieces he had told her.

The tale was pretty fantastic, but it was hard to argue with the sharp, pointy evidence of Kian's fangs. Apparently, some kind of immortal beings were living hidden among mortals, secretly helping humanity and manipulating global affairs with no one any the wiser. Except, it seemed a faction of them wasn't on board for the humanitarian effort and posed a serious threat to Kian's family.

She was only guessing that other immortals and not humans were the powerful enemies Kian's family was hiding from. But it made more sense than the scenario favored by fiction of some secret order devoted to the elimination of supernatural creatures.

Oh, well, whatever the full story was, the fang thing was strange and scary.

But oh, boy... was it hot.

The way Kian had made her feel, she didn't care if he was a vampire or something else. He was welcome to bite her anytime.

Surrounded by his scent, she snuggled in Kian's incredibly soft bedding, luxuriating at the way it felt on her bare skin...

Bare skin? Syssi realized she was completely naked beneath the duvet.

But for the life of her, she couldn't remember if she had undressed herself or had it been Kian who had taken everything off? Probably Kian... because she would have left her underwear on...

Unless it was wet...

Which it probably was.

Whatever.

Stretching her toes, Syssi felt happy. Which implied

that she must be either out of her mind or still affected by the venom.

In light of the bombshell Kian had dropped at her feet, she should've been alarmed, disbelieving, panicking, running for her life; as any normal person would. Instead, all she felt was good.

No way would she let any negative thoughts intrude on her feelings of serenity and wellbeing. She felt healthy, strong, sexy... and pampered.

Kian's bedroom was fit for a king... or a queen... The king-sized bed sat on a raised platform, facing a fireplace with a large screen television hanging above it and a pair of overstuffed bookcases flanking it.

She couldn't see the titles from this far, but judging by their messy and uncoordinated arrangement, the books had gotten a lot of actual use.

Kian must've spent most of his time in here reading, unless he liked watching TV from bed, because instead of facing the screen, the sitting area was oriented toward the wall of sliding glass doors and the terrace beyond.

Syssi loved it. If it were hers, she would've never left this room. She could see herself spending a lot of lazy afternoons here, sitting in one of the comfy chairs, reading a book and drinking a latte as the curtains fluttered in the breeze that blew in through the open patio doors.

Or, she could be lounging lazily in this heavenly bed, preferably with Kian in it...

Naked...

Or almost naked...

Walking in with only a towel wrapped around his hips, and his hair dripping droplets of water down his sculpted chest, Kian took her breath away. There was no doubt in her mind that she would never get tired of seeing him like this, and that each and every time she did, she would be awed anew by his perfection.

Now that she knew what he was, her first impression of him made perfect sense. She was right to think that no mere mortal could look so good because Kian wasn't human. And neither was Amanda.

Oh, boy! Did she have questions for him.

"Good morning, sunshine," he greeted her, smiling a big toothy smile—one she realized she had never seen on him before. His fangs were clearly visible now, but they were nothing compared to the scary things he flashed her in the mirror last night and could easily pass for slightly larger than normal canines.

Did they elongate in response to the triggers he had mentioned? Retracting when of no further use?

"We need to talk," she said, thinking that from here on out, these words that were dreaded by males everywhere would hold a whole new meaning for her.

"I know, and I promise we will. But first... we have some unfinished business from last night..." Growling, Kian let the towel drop as he advanced on her, looking like a mighty jungle cat ready to pounce on his prey.

The effect of seeing his powerful, naked body moving sinuously toward her was like flipping on a switch, igniting a lust so powerful that it had her body trembling with need.

Yeah, talking can definitely wait.

Suddenly, the comforter felt scratchy and too warm on her naked, oversensitized skin, and she threw it off. Framing her aching breasts with her hands, she arched her hips—offering herself like a feline in heat.

44

KIAN

"So fucking beautiful..." Crawling on the bed to straddle Syssi, Kian felt feral. And yet, looking down at her flushed body, the few neurons still functioning in his blood-deprived brain managed to process the fact that her level of arousal was alarming.

Syssi's normally pink nipples were red and turgid, and as she spread her knees to welcome him in between them, he found her already wet and swollen. Urging him on, she rolled her hips and cupped her breasts as a needy moan left her parted lips.

Was it even possible for the addiction to take hold after only two bites? He hoped this wasn't the case, and that her wildness could be attributed to plain old lust.

But regardless of the impetus, her explicit carnality effectively slammed down all of his buttons, driving reason and his good intentions away.

Mindless with lust, he was all animal as he drove into her, burying himself to the hilt in one powerful thrust.

Syssi climaxed instantly. And as her convulsing inner

muscles gripped him tightly, Kian groaned, straining against the pressure building up in his shaft.

It was too soon.

Slowing down, he was able to hold off for no more than a few strokes before need overpowered his resolve, and he began pounding into her mercilessly, going fast and hard, grunting and groaning like the beast he was.

Somewhere in the back of his mind, a thought was trying to filter through and warn him that he might be hurting her. But its voice was drowned by the turmoil of the blood boiling in his veins.

Growing impossibly hard, he was on the brink of the inevitable eruption, when Syssi turned her head—submitting her exposed neck for his bite.

That was it for him. With the iron links of his self-imposed manacles not so much snapping as crumbling to dust, he bared his fangs and bit her, pumping her full of his venom along with his seed.

Syssi went over again. With her sheath gripping onto him on the inside and her arms holding on tight, she kept his chest pressed against hers as their bodies shook from the exertion and the force of their climaxes.

Long moments passed with them entwined in each other, dazed in a mindless stupor, unable to move, or talk, or even think coherently.

They must've fallen asleep, because when Kian opened his eyes next, the light in the room had changed, indicating that the sun had moved across the sky, changing the angle of its rays.

With his mind clear, Kian felt like scum. He had no doubt some form of addiction had already taken root, and not only in Syssi.

He had never experienced sex like that before, not even

close. And looking back at almost two thousand years of it, he could think of only one logical explanation. The one he dreaded most.

"I'm so sorry, baby," he whispered into Syssi's neck, thinking she was still sleeping.

"What the heck for?"

He heard her barely audible whisper, as her hand started a lazy trek up and down his back.

"You make me so wild, cats in heat have nothing on me." She chuckled. "Or you...," she added, nuzzling his neck. "Do you turn all your women into mindless sex maniacs? Or is it just me?" she whispered, blowing hot air in his ear.

Did he imagine it? Or was she attempting to hide her possessiveness and jealousy by pretending to tease? Not that he minded, he kind of liked that she did. And it had nothing to do with satisfaction over the shoe being on the other foot. Nothing at all...

"I'm not sure who made whom more wild. Though I doubt that having the dubious honor of being the only one I've ever rutted on like a crazed animal was good for you. I'm sorry if I hurt you."

"No, you didn't hurt me, you sweet boy. I wanted you exactly like that: mindless with passion, crazed... I'm happy you were just as out of control as I was. I would be dying of shame at my own sluttishness otherwise." Syssi kissed his neck, running her hands over his sweat-slicked body. "I think you need another shower, lover boy." A smirk curled her lips. "We can have one together..."

Later, when the joined shower didn't evolve into another mindless carnal attack, Kian reevaluated his earlier conviction that the addiction was responsible for their crazed sex.

They both seemed comfortably satiated, enjoying some lazy caressing and kissing but not taking it any further than that.

And what a relief that was.

"Oh, damn, I have nothing to wear. All my things are at Amanda's, and I'm afraid the dress I was wearing last night is ruined." Syssi frowned. Sitting on the bed wrapped in a bath towel, she looked at the dress in her hands. "Could you send it to be dry-cleaned? I can't return it to Amanda in this condition."

"Don't worry about it. I'll take care of the incriminating evidence." He chuckled and stepped out from inside his closet with one of his T-shirts. "You can use this in the meantime."

Wearing his plain white shirt, Syssi looked absolutely adorable and sexy as hell—the thing reaching below her knees and providing a semi-decent cover to her otherwise naked body.

The *semi* being the operative word.

With her sweet ass clearly visible through the thin fabric, he kept glancing behind her and ogling it as they walked into the kitchen, holding hands.

"Good morning!" Okidu beamed at them and immediately got busy serving them breakfast.

Once he was done, Kian shooed him away, knowing Syssi would prefer their conversation to be private.

Sitting at the kitchen counter and drinking her coffee, Syssi kept quiet until Okidu left. Then, with her cheeks growing red, she giggled before slanting a quick glance at Kian. "I don't know what came over me. I've never been so out of control before… wouldn't have believed I even had it in me." She lowered her eyes, focusing on the mug she was holding. "Do you think it had something to do with your venom? Did any of the other women react to it like this?"

And here it was again, that jealous note in her tone…

"It might have been the venom. Though I must admit, your reaction was surprising. Don't get me wrong, I loved it. Most intense sexual experience I've ever had. And if you're embarrassed by it, please don't be. I don't think you can top my coming in my pants… twice… That never happened to me with anyone but you either." Kian chuckled nervously. "It seems we're having lots of firsts together, don't you think?"

"I guess… it's just that my experience is very limited. I had only one lover before you. We were together for four years. He and I… we never got that intense. It was kind of lackluster… And since we broke up two years ago, there wasn't anyone I wanted to be with… before you, that is."

Syssi sighed, playing with her mug and looking into her coffee as if the right things to say could be found inside. "I thought I wasn't into the whole thing, the sex thing I mean, couldn't understand what all the hubbub was about. And then you show up. And I burn for you, go wild for you… I never imagined it could be like that." She slanted a tentative glance at him.

Kian pulled her into his arms and hugged her tightly. "Your ex was a moron. His inadequacy, or his confused sexual orientation, influenced the way you thought of yourself because you had nothing to compare it to. Believe me, you're the hottest, most passionate, perfect woman I have ever known. And coming from me it says a lot… I've been around the block… way more times than I care to admit." Tilting up her chin with his finger, he looked into her beautiful eyes. "You believe me, right?" he said in a tone that brooked no argument.

"So, what are you saying? That you're old? Or that you're a slut?" Syssi chuckled, teasing. Still, she looked pleased, her eyes glowing from his compliments.

"Both." He smiled back and kissed her cute little nose. "You got yourself a dirty, dirty old man."

"How old is old? And how dirty?"

Kian took a deep breath, not looking forward to her reaction to what he was about to tell her. "I'm almost two thousand years old, and since reaching puberty, I've been with a different woman almost every night. I'm not proud of it. In fact, I resent my physiology. My kind is driven by a very strong sex drive, probably as a way to counteract our extremely low fertility rate... So yeah, I've been a major slut. I hope that doesn't disgust you..." He searched her eyes, hoping she'd understand and accept.

Syssi was quiet for a moment, mulling over that ditty. "You're two thousand years old, you're serious?"

"In four years I'll be... yeah." If that was the only part that bothered her, he was good.

Well, maybe...

He didn't mind the age difference, but she might have a different take on a disparity measured in centuries as opposed to years or even decades.

"Okay, I think you'd better start at the beginning and tell me the whole story. I'd rather hear it all at once and get over the shock than get flummoxed with every new bombshell." Syssi got loose from his embrace and leaned back, getting comfortable on her barstool.

"There are quite a few more explosive details coming your way, so you better brace yourself." Kian sighed.

Learning the truth, she might decide to leave, wanting nothing more to do with him. But he had no choice. It was the right thing to do.

"My kind had lived among mortals for thousands of years. We don't know if we were a divergent species, remnants of a previous advanced society that suffered some kind of cataclysm, or a group of refugees from somewhere else in the universe.

"In the ancient world, we were the gods of old, worshiped and loved by the mortal societies we were helping to evolve. Besides our remarkable regeneration abilities, we could also control mortal minds quite easily; creating realistic illusions, planting thoughts, thralling... as you had experienced.

"The original number of gods was very small. The limited gene pool, combined with an extremely low conception rate, prompted the gods to seek partners among the mortals. It worked, and many near-immortal children were born. But when those children took human mates, their children were born mortal.

"They discovered a way to activate the dormant godly genes, but only for the children of the female immortals, it didn't work for the children of the males." Kian took a sip of his coffee, giving Syssi the opportunity to ask questions. But she said nothing, looking curious and waiting for him to continue.

"My mother, Annani, a full blooded goddess, was supposed to marry her cousin Mortdh, but fell in love with another. According to their code of law or maybe just custom, mating had to be consensual. So she was free to marry her love.

"Mortdh felt betrayed and humiliated and being insane murdered Annani's love. He then declared war on the other gods. That war ended in a nuclear disaster that wiped out the gods as well as a huge portion of the mortal population.

"My mother, alone out of all the gods, escaped the cataclysm, taking with her the advanced knowledge of her people. She made it her mission to continue their work and trickle this knowledge to humanity, guiding it to become a better society.

"Mortdh was killed by the shockwaves of his own bomb, but some of his descendants survived. They carried on his rabid hatred of females, influencing the societies they controlled to eliminate the human rights women had previously enjoyed, plunging that part of the world further into darkness. They took on his vow to eliminate Annani, her progeny, and any progress humanity achieved with her help.

"We, as her children, are helping her with her mission. Unfortunately, there are not many of us, and as we all share the same matrilineal descent, we are forbidden to mate with each other. Annani mated with mortals to have us, and my sisters continued doing the same, as did their daughters, and so on.

"We believe, though, that there are Dormant mortals in the general population, people who carry our genetic code, descendants of the survivors of other lines who we can activate. Potential mates for us.

"We've been searching for them since the beginning, and not finding any, all of us were basically doomed to one-night stands. The females at least can have children that are like us. The males can produce only mortal children. Can you imagine how hard it is to watch your children grow old and die while you remain unchanged?"

Kian sighed a heavy sigh. Sensing his sadness, Syssi clasped his hand and held it in silent encouragement.

"Amanda thinks that paranormal abilities could in some cases lead to Dormants. As you know, out of all her subjects, you and Michael are her top candidates. That's why the Doomers want you; the Devout Order of Mortdh Brotherhood, or Doom Brotherhood for short. Our enemies of old."

"So if I'm a potential Dormant, how would you know for sure? How do you activate your Dormants?"

"The venom. Our boys get activated at thirteen, and usually one injection is enough, three at most. The girls change much younger. For them, being nurtured by Annani and exposed to her daily is the only catalyst needed. But we don't know how many injections it takes to activate the dormant genes in an adult. It was never done before."

Syssi frowned. "So when were you going to tell me? Don't you think you should have asked me if I was okay with it?" Syssi's voice quivered. "After all, it is my life you're playing God with. I would think the decent thing to do was to at least warn me before dousing me with your venom." She glared at him, her back straight and her arms crossed protectively over her chest.

"Guilty as charged. You're absolutely right. The thing is, I'm still sure Amanda is grasping at straws, and you're not a Dormant and neither is Michael. Who, by the way, is down in our basement and on board with giving it a shot."

"Oh, this is just getting better and better... So it was fine to inform Michael but not me?"

"We just told him yesterday, and I was planning to tell you as well. It just took me some time to gather the nerve to do it. In some ways, Michael has it worse, but his situation is less complicated."

"Why?"

Kian sighed. "To attempt his activation, he needs to fight one of us just well enough to trigger the aggression needed for venom production. Not a big problem, him being a young, strong guy. The worst that he'll suffer is some pounding—not that much different from other forms of combat training. A young man his age would probably find it an invigorating challenge."

Syssi snorted. "It would seem I have the better deal. I actually find it pleasurable when you pound into me."

"I'm glad you can still find it humorous." Kian raked his fingers through his hair, trying to think of a way to deliver the bad news as gently as possible.

"If Michael doesn't turn, we'll have to thrall away his memory of us, and of him being here, and plant some other plausible scenario in his mind. He might get a little confused from time to time, remembering bits and pieces of things, not sure if he dreamt them or experienced them. Hopefully, this would be the extent of it, and he wouldn't suffer any lasting brain damage." Looking into her eyes, he took her hands in his, waiting for the implications to sink in.

45

SYSSI

*S*yssi's eyes widened as the meaning of what Kian was trying to communicate hit home. "Oh, my God, you're planning to erase my memory and send me off, clueless, same as Michael. I can't believe it! And to think I was actually falling for you. Talk about naive."

Pulling away from him, she jumped out of her seat and almost toppled the thing as she stormed into the bedroom she had occupied before—remembering too late that her things weren't there anymore.

Exasperated, she slammed the door behind her, hoping Kian would at least have the decency to stay out.

Not a chance.

A second later, the door banged open and he stormed in. "What would you have me do? What would you have done in my place, huh? I'm listening... Any bright ideas? No? I didn't think so."

The nerve of the guy, venting his frustration and acting as if he was the injured party here. She was the one that would be cast off like yesterday's news. Not him.

It was just too much, and as traitorous tears began

sliding down her cheeks, she couldn't stop her chin from quivering. God, why couldn't she be tougher, or at least hold off with the girly emotional display until he was gone. But as there was no chance in hell of him leaving anytime soon, she lashed out. "You're the two-thousand-year-old immortal who should be smart enough to figure something out." Sitting on the bed, Syssi plopped back and grabbed a pillow to hold it over her tear-streaked face.

Kian sat down beside her and tugged on the pillow. "Hiding will not solve anything." Yanking harder, he took it away.

With her temporary shelter gone, she covered her face with her hands—determined not to look at him. "I don't want to talk to you. Go away!" She managed to suppress the quiver in her voice.

Pulling at her arms, he uncovered her teary face. "Please don't cry, you're killing me." Kian leaned to kiss her tears away, planting little pecks all over her face.

Which made it even worse.

"You're such a phony, pretending to care when you knew all along you'd be getting rid of me soon." Syssi turned her face sideways in an attempt to escape his kisses.

"I do care, a lot. It's just such an impossible situation. I'm screwed whatever I do. If you don't turn, and I want to keep you, I'd either have to thrall you repeatedly, which will mess with your brain and might cause long-term damage, or keep you locked up in here unable to leave or get in touch with your family, and you'd grow to hate me either way. The only decent thing I could have done was to let you go. And believe me, I tried. But I couldn't do it, and not only because I couldn't help how much I wanted you. I'm selfish, but not that selfish. This is bigger than just me and what I want, or how unfair it is to you. The slim chance that you might be a Dormant is too important for the future of my clan." Stroking her hair, he leaned into her and waited for her to turn and look at him.

Instead, she grabbed another pillow to hide under.

"Look, let us enjoy the time we have together and see what happens. You wouldn't want me to make promises I couldn't keep, would you? I'm trying to come clean and be completely honest with you. Please don't shut me out."

His pleading tone touched her. And besides, as much as she hated to accept the grim reality, she had to admit he was right.

Discarding the pillow, Syssi shifted her teary eyes to his sad face and opened her arms, inviting him in.

With a relieved sigh, Kian leaned into her embrace and held her tightly to his chest, completely unconcerned with his T-shirt getting wet from her tears. "I'm so sorry. I wish there were more I could offer you." He kissed her forehead.

Syssi sniffled, burying her face in his shirt. "I hate the fact that I need you so much. Just feeling your body against mine calms me down. It's as if I'm addicted to you, craving you even though I know you're no good for me."

Kian's body stiffened and he sat back. "Now that you mention it, there is one last screwed-up detail I haven't told you yet... The venom is addictive. The more your body gets, the more you will crave it, suffering unpleasant withdrawal if denied it."

"What kind of withdrawal?"

"You'll crave only me and get repulsed by any other man trying to be intimate with you. Until it leaves your system, you will not be able to have sex with anyone but me. And that might take a while."

Syssi frowned. She wouldn't want any other man after Kian, regardless of the addiction. No one could take his place, and she wondered if she would ever be able to stop comparing every guy to him and find each and every one wanting.

Still, that wasn't what had gotten her upset. "How about you, will you develop an addiction to me?"

"Eventually, but supposedly it takes longer for males to get hooked. As your body's scent gradually changes, bearing my particular mark, it will both attract me and serve as a repellent to other males of my kind." For some reason, what he had just told her made him frown.

Looking at his hard face, Syssi couldn't decide if he frowned because explaining the compulsory nature of his kind irritated him, or was he secretly yearning for the addiction to shackle her to him... Was his possessive nature once again raising its ugly, primitive head? Except, if it did, she was guilty of the same thing, clinging to what he had said in a desperate hope that he'd get hooked on her... and fast.

Sighing, Kian clasped her hand. "Don't worry, it normally takes a very long time for the addiction to set, probably months. We'll know one way or the other long before it happens," he added, evidently misreading her expression and attempting to assuage her fears.

Syssi wanted to tell him that she wasn't worried, she was disappointed.

Kian had just destroyed the last glimmer of her irrational hope that he would soon come to crave her so much that he would never be able to let her go regardless of whether she turned or not.

Then, the obtuse man misinterpreted her dejected expression again and made it worse by trying to make it better. "If a miracle happens and you turn, you'll have your pick of clan males before you're compelled to choose one because of the addiction."

Not getting the relieved reaction he had anticipated, he continued to make it worse. "You don't have to commit to one man right from the start. The way to prevent getting addicted to a specific venom is to vary partners and get several different types of it in your system. You can take your time and choose someone that is right for you with the confidence that you aren't compelled to rush into it."

What the hell? Yesterday he was ready to punch Anandur for flirting with her, and today he was okay with her choosing someone else?

Again, she wanted to scream at him to make up his mind. Come to think of it, throwing something heavy at his head would have been way more satisfying.

Men were so frustrating.

Who could understand the twisted way their minds worked… And to think they accused women of making no sense and being irrational. Ha!

Nonetheless, it hurt like hell.

The only way she could make sense of his bizarre behavior was to accept that as long as he considered her his, he didn't want any other males sniffing around her. But evidently, he wasn't planning on anything long-term. He knew he'd eventually tire of her and then pass her on to someone else.

She must've meant so little to him. Just a convenient lay. Another notch on his belt… A very, very, long belt.

Unless she turned…

Then she would be important alright… to the clan. Not him personally, but to all the other males in his family.

Syssi felt so stupid. She had no one to blame for the pain she was feeling but herself. What did she expect? A man like him falling in love with her? Wanting her to be his forever? Forever taking a whole new meaning in his case. He was the freaking son of a goddess, for heaven's sake. Gorgeous, successful...

Syssi wanted to scream in frustration.

She couldn't let him know how deeply he had cut her, though, and regretted even the small glimpses of feelings she had already allowed him to see.

If he could treat their time together as a temporary fling, so could she. Pretending to be just as casual about it, she'd treat him as nothing but a hookup and try to be just as cynical as everyone else.

Too bad, though, that fronting as if it was nothing to her would be hard to pull off. She wasn't that good of an actress.

Pulling her hand from his clasp, she pushed up to her feet. "I need to go to Amanda's place to get dressed."

Kian reached for her as she turned to leave. "Are you okay?" Pulling her in between his thighs, he wrapped his arms around her waist.

"Yeah, sure... I can't spend the day wearing your T-shirt, can I? I have to go." Syssi tugged at his arms until he let go of her. "I also need to put in some work with Amanda, or I'll lose my pay." She tried to smile reassuringly but failed miserably.

Kian seemed reluctant to let her go, catching her hand as she once again turned to leave. "Okay, but I'll come to see you later. Maybe in the afternoon?"

"Yeah, sure, whatever..." She pulled until he let go and walked out.

46

SYSSI

*S*tanding outside Amanda's door in her ridiculous getup of platforms and Kian's flimsy T-shirt and nothing underneath, yesterday's underwear bunched in her hand, Syssi knocked, then waited a few moments before knocking again, louder this time.

"Let yourself in!" She heard Amanda call.

Syssi opened the door just a crack and peeked in. "Hello? It's me. Can I come in?"

Amanda couldn't answer since her mouth was busy kissing a bare-chested guy. And it wasn't the one Syssi remembered from the club…

The woman was simply unbelievable…

"Here you go, sweetheart." Amanda handed him his shirt and shoes. Without giving him a chance to put them on, she pushed him toward the door.

"Onidu! Where are you? Sam is ready to go. Please drive him back to the club."

Poor Sam looked completely out of it, stupefied. And judging by his unfocused eyes and gaping mouth the guy was probably thralled within an inch of his life.

But what really caught Syssi's attention were the small bite marks on the side of his neck and both of his smooth pecs.

Amanda kissed Sam's cheek, then shoved him out the door with a pat on his butt. As she turned her full attention to Syssi, there was a knowing smirk on her face. "Good morning, stranger, I see you ended up having some fun after all." She tugged her own long T-shirt down from where it rode up her thighs.

Syssi decided giving being blunt a shot. "How come your guy had visible bite marks, and I don't?"

"I see that Kian has finally spilled... So what exactly did he tell you?" Amanda walked over to the couch and sat down. Tucking her bare legs under her butt, she covered her knees with the long shirt. "Come tell mommy everything." She patted the spot next to her.

"I guess the main points... Who and what you guys are, your enemies, how I might be a potential immortal, and how crucially important it is to the clan if I am, and so on." Syssi stuffed her underwear in her purse, leaving it on the table before settling next to Amanda. Tucking her legs under Kian's long shirt, she mirrored her boss's pose.

In the quiet that followed, Amanda's stare was unnerving. Turning away from those knowing eyes, Syssi grabbed one of the throw pillows strewn on the couch and hugged it to herself, pretending to admire the colorful pattern.

"He did something to hurt you, didn't he... Tell me, so I can go and pummel the fool to the ground." Amanda held her fists up, then chuckled as Syssi arched a brow. "Okay, I'll hire some muscle to do it for me."

"He didn't hurt me. I had like two seconds of panic when he flashed those monstrous fangs of his, but after that, well... it was amazing... It's just that I'm kind of shell-shocked. All of this is a lot to wrap my mind around—to absorb. I need time to think it through—formulate my questions... And speaking of questions; you didn't answer me about the bite marks." For some reason, talking about it helped Syssi get some perspective and organize it in her head, and she felt some of the turmoil inside her subside.

"He told you about the venom, right?" When Syssi nodded, Amanda continued. "Females don't have any. Our small, wee fangs, if you can even call them that, are for decoration only. They don't elongate like the males' do either. I guess it's like the difference between a penis and a clitoris." Amanda snorted. "I bite because I like it and it feels good, not because it can do anything interesting, like activate a Dormant or incapacitate an opponent. Without the venom, it takes longer for the marks to heal... on mortals anyway. An immortal male's body would have healed those in no time, and maybe it's a big turn-on for them. Who knows? I never had one." Amanda looked down at her hands.

"You never had a lover of your own kind?"

"I don't know any immortal men that I'm not related to. So only plain mortals for me. Yay!" Amanda looked up at Syssi with sad eyes.

That's right, Kian had said that they couldn't mate with members of the same matrilineal descent.

Suddenly, the full weight of their plight dawned on her. The lonely existence they were doomed to endure. Being confined to mortal lovers, they had no chance of having lifelong partners, spending their extremely long existence alone.

How sad...

"Have you ever fallen in love? With a mortal?" Syssi probed.

"No, I hardly ever have sex with the same guy twice. None of us do. Even for an idiot, it wouldn't take long to figure out something is not kosher. Eventually, someone that you're close to is bound to notice that you never get sick, heal in seconds from accidental cuts and nicks, that you're stronger and faster than normal and your senses are sharper. The males have it even worse; kind of hard to explain the fangs away. And there is the addiction factor. Did Kian share that little morsel with you?"

"He did." Syssi grimaced.

"It's funny, but we forgot all about it. Mother told Kian a long time ago, but as it wasn't relevant to our situation, one-night stands and all, he forgot. He was reminded because of you."

Syssi rubbed at her chest, the subject sharpening the knife's barely dulled edge and bringing back the pain. "Yeah, not very convenient for a fling... Still, I bet your ancestors had very stable marriages—being forced to be faithful to each other like that."

"Not necessarily, we are a lustful race, as you are surely aware of by now. The way our mother explained it to Kian, mated couples that didn't want to limit themselves were having sex with other partners from the get-go, mixing up the different venoms to prevent being addicted to a particular one. More so in the upper class, where most marriages were arranged and not the result of any great love. Besides, sleeping around was not frowned on. It was an acceptable behavior for both males and females. What do you think the myths of the gods frolicking with one another and with mortals are based on? That's the way they really were."

"So what's the point of having this system if it's so easily circumvented?"

"Kian and I talked about it. We guess, but it's speculation only, that our race was genetically manipulated to have the peculiar traits we have. The scientist responsible for it might have been a romantic at heart, or loved an unfaithful mate. Who knows?" Amanda smiled.

"Kian thinks he was a deranged lunatic, but I think it was sweet. Imagine falling in love, getting married, and during the honeymoon—when everything is still wonderfully exciting and love is fresh—an addiction forms. Voila! Lifelong fidelity. No nasty surprises, no divorces... and an amazing sex life to boot. It could have been a wonderful thing for a true love mating."

"Ha! What if after the honeymoon period—as you call it —they started to annoy each other so much that they grew to hate one another, but were stuck together because of the addiction? What then?" Syssi crossed her arms over her chest and switched to sitting with her legs crossed at the knee.

"Well, if it got so bad that they were willing to suffer through withdrawal and abstain from sex for a few months, then they could've gone their separate ways. But it gave them one hell of an incentive to just get along." Amanda laughed, giving Syssi a quick hug.

"I don't know... Relationships are complicated, people are complicated, feelings change, people change, shit happens... You cannot hope to solve all possible problems with good sex." Syssi thought her situation with Kian was a perfect example of that.

Amanda's face turned serious. "Look, I don't know what exactly Kian told you, or how he presented it. I know he can be overbearing and insensitive, and expressing his feelings is not something he is good at. Not much of a diplomat, my brother. That's why we have someone else to do the smooth talking for him at business negotiations. But his intentions are good. He hardly ever thinks about what's good for himself. His life is all about the survival of our clan and ensuring that our work continues to help humanity thrive and evolve. It's such a huge burden to carry. You have no idea how much I admire and respect both Kian and Sari for shouldering that huge responsibility. And how grateful I am for being spared from having to shoulder it myself. I don't think I could've done it."

"Your work is important too. You're trying to find compatible mates for your family. I'm sure they appreciate it, especially if you actually succeed." Syssi sensed that Amanda felt overshadowed by her older siblings and wasn't used to getting praise.

"Yeah, after two centuries of being a selfish party girl, I'm finally trying to make a contribution."

Yep, Amanda definitely wasn't used to praise… And she was two hundred years old? Wow!

"So, does that mean you don't party anymore?" Syssi asked, thinking Amanda partied plenty.

"Of course I do, silly. I just put some work in as well."

47

KIAN

*K*ian stared at the small box sitting on his desk, fighting the urge to grab it and use it as an excuse to go see Syssi.

Almost an hour had passed since she left for Amanda's, and during all that time he kept churning over their conversation in his mind, ignoring the paperwork stacked on his desk.

All along, he had been afraid that once she realized what was in store for her, she would react exactly the way she had. Grow cold and distant and push him away.

But then again, he couldn't really blame her, could he?

It was exactly as she had said. He was a jerk. He had lied to her, hadn't asked her if she wanted to be changed, and in the end, he would be forced to send her away.

And that wasn't even the worst of it. The truth was, he hadn't been thinking about changing her when he had sunk his fangs into her lovely neck. During those intense moments, he had thought of nothing but the sex.

It had been all about his need and his craving...

He wondered what Syssi would've thought of him if she

had known that the supposedly noble intentions he'd been fronting were nothing but a cover for him being a beast. Or that the little speech about letting her choose whoever she wanted had been total crap.

In fact, even though he'd lied through his teeth about giving her a choice, the mere act of verbalizing the lie had him almost popping a vein. He had a feeling he would not hesitate to annihilate any male who dared to try to take her away from him.

Family not excluded.

Snatching the box with Syssi's new phone, Kian pushed out of his swivel chair, shoving it so hard that the thing hit the bookcase behind him and rolled sideways as it bounced off.

In several determined strides, he crossed the short distance between the apartments, but then as he stood in front of Amanda's door, he hesitated.

Given the laughter percolating from the other side, it sounded as if Syssi and Amanda were having a good time, and he wondered if he hadn't blown things out of proportion.

There was only one way to find out, and he sure as hell wasn't going to do it by standing outside and eavesdropping like a coward.

He rapped on the door and walked in without waiting for an invitation. "I brought you your new phone as soon as it was delivered," he said, smiling at the domestic scene of Syssi and his sister sharing a couch in their oversized T-shirts. "You can call anyone you want and give them your new phone number. The phone uses our own satellite, and the line is untraceable and secure."

With a quick look at Amanda, he searched his sister's

expression for a clue as to Syssi's mood. But her impassive face gave nothing away.

"Thank you, I was feeling lost without a phone." Syssi took the white box and tore at the wrapping, eager to get to her new toy.

Using her momentary distraction, Kian looked at Amanda again, this time gesticulating his question.

"Jury still out," she mouthed, shrugging her shoulders, then made a shooing motion urging him to leave.

"I'd better go. See you later, ladies." He excused himself but remained glued to his spot, waiting for Syssi to look up; hoping she'd smile at him or, at least glance his way. But to his chagrin, her head remained bowed over the phone's instructions as if he wasn't even there.

Swallowing a bitter sense of disappointment, he said, "Goodbye then," and beat feet to the door.

"Goodbye," Syssi called after him.

He whipped around, hoping to catch her looking his way. But she didn't—killing his small spark of hope.

Standing outside Amanda's apartment, Kian ran his hands through his hair and sighed. It would be a waste of time to go back to the office. He was too agitated to be able to concentrate on anything.

Instead, he took the elevator down to the basement.

At the gym, Kian found Brundar and Michael training, with Kri watching them from the sidelines. It seemed Michael's training session had been going on for a while. The kid was tired and frustrated. Not that Kian could blame him, Brundar had Michael practicing the same three moves over and over again.

Detect, block, deflect... detect, block, deflect.

"Again!" Brundar ordered and launched another mock knife attack. With a rubber stick in each hand, he kept slashing relentlessly at Michael, cutting through his ineffective defense and hitting him time and again.

Bundled as he was in protective suiting, Michael no doubt felt the blows, but besides his ego, he wasn't really getting hurt. Nonetheless, he was sweaty and exhausted and looked ready to call it quits.

Except, Kri was watching him from her spot next to the punching bag. Jabbing perfunctorily at it, she seemed more interested in Michael's training session than her own. And given the quick glances he was sneaking her way, it was obvious that as long as she kept watching him, the kid would keep pushing until he dropped.

Kian smirked, turning away quickly before Kri caught him observing her, then went back to watching Michael.

The kid was inexperienced and somewhat clumsy, but Kian had to admit that there was raw potential there. What he lacked in endurance and discipline, he made up in brute strength and youthful enthusiasm.

Brundar was driving him hard, but then again, no one got good by watching how it was done from the couch. At his current level of skill, Michael wouldn't stand a chance against a trained opponent, and the sooner he got the basics, the sooner he'd be able to defend himself.

"Okay, kid, take a break. You did well." Brundar clapped Michael on the shoulder.

"Thanks. But when are we going to move to something else?"

"When those moves become second nature, when no matter when, or from what angle, I come at you—you'll execute them perfectly. Then... we can move on, and not before." Brundar walked over to the fridge and took out a water bottle.

Kri abandoned her post next to the boxing bag and

sauntered to stand next to Michael. "You better listen to him. Brundar is our weapons master and there is no one in the world that's better. Consider yourself lucky he is training you." She patted his cheek, but the pat sounded more like a slap.

"Yeah, I feel very lucky..." Michael groaned, wiping the sweat from his face with a towel. "Any luckier, and I'll be dead... He is killing me!"

"Wuss." Kri snorted. "He is teaching you how to stay alive. And just between you and me..." She leaned to whisper in his ear conspiratorially, "I'm surprised he volunteered to train you. He is not exactly the friendly, giving type if you catch my drift. And he only trains experienced fighters. Taking on a newbie... Damn! He must really believe in you." She punched Michael's shoulder. "Go get yourself some water. It's important to stay hydrated during training." She smiled and sauntered away, swaying her hips.

Kian rubbed his hand over his chin. There was definitely something going on between Kri and Michael.

Good, it was about time for her to shed the immature fascination she had with him and move toward something more appropriate. For Kri's sake, as much as for the good of the clan, Kian hoped Michael would turn.

Which raised the issue of choosing an initiator for the boy. The honor of accepting the role carried with it some serious responsibility. The male Michael would challenge to a fight would not only be the one to induce his transformation but also assume the role of a lifelong honorary big brother.

The coming of age ceremony usually involved two boys: a thirteen-year-old Dormant and a transitioned boy —if possible no more than a year or two older. The friendship encouraged by the ritual benefited both boys, as it created between them a brotherly bond similar to the one between real brothers.

Siblings were a rarity in their community, and even if one was lucky enough to have a brother, chances were that they were separated by hundreds of years in age. Having an adopted one certainly beat growing up alone.

Kian walked over to the center of the gym and stood on top of the rubber mats delineating the wrestling area. "Listen up. I want you all in the small conference room in half an hour. Go shower and change. We'll be choosing Michael's initiator."

"What? Now? I'm completely beat!"

"At least you got a good warm-up." Kian clapped Michael's shoulder. "Don't worry about it. You've got about an hour to recuperate, and then you only need to provide some kind of a challenge. No one is expecting you to remain standing for more than a couple of minutes. You'll be fine."

"In that case, I'd better hurry and shower... Phew!" Michael grimaced as he began stripping off his protective suiting and smelled the nasty coming out of it. "I would rather not show up for my own ceremony smelling like dirty socks."

Later, once everyone made it to the conference room, Kian stood at the head of the table and motioned for Okidu to serve the ceremonial wine.

"I'll have to change the traditional wording a little to allow for Michael's age, so don't try to correct me when I cut out the whole thing about a boy becoming a man." Kian nodded at Michael.

Looking nervous and excited, the kid stood at the other end of the table, presenting himself to the assembled group as required by custom.

Kian cleared his throat. "We are gathered here to present this fine young man to his elders. Michael is ready to attempt his transformation. Vouching for him are Guardian Yamanu and Guardian Arwel. Who volunteers to take on the burden of initiating Michael into his immortality?"

"I do." Yamanu stood up.

Kian nodded his approval.

"Michael, do you accept Guardian Yamanu as your initiator? As your mentor and protector, to honor him with your friendship, your respect, and your loyalty from now on?"

Michael had sneaked a quick glance at Kri before he answered. "I do."

The ritual demanded that Kian, as the leader of this group, verify that everyone agreed it was a good pairing—regardless of it being unnecessary in this case. "Does anyone have any objections to Michael becoming Yamanu's protégé?" When no one did, Kian raised his wine glass. "As everyone here agrees it's a good match, let's seal it with a toast. To Michael and Yamanu."

Once the Guardians were done with the cheers, Yamanu pulled Michael into a crushing bear hug. "Always wanted me a little brother." He rubbed his knuckles against Michael's skull.

"Ouch! And I always wanted a big brother, but now I'm not so sure." Michael laughed and twisted free from Yamanu, only to get caught by Kri.

Now, that hug he didn't seem to mind at all. And as he lifted her off the ground and twirled her around, the mighty Kri squeaked a very girly squeak.

As he held her plastered against him, it might have been the squeak or the Guardian's brouhaha, or maybe both that had given Michael the courage to plant a sloppy kiss smack on her lips.

Kri, on the other hand, didn't need any encouragement, and not being shy by any stretch of the imagination, kissed him back for all she was worth without the slightest regard for her cheering comrades.

Kian felt his face stretch into a wide grin.

Like a proud father, he was glad to see his people excited and happy. It had been a long time since anything new and positive had happened in their stronghold.

It was about bloody time.

48

SYSSI

"*I*'m in the mood for a run, but as you guys will not let me out…" Syssi cast a look askance at Amanda. "Do you have a treadmill I could use?"

"Do we have a treadmill? We have the mother of all gyms down in the basement. Go get changed. We'll go together and I'll give you a tour."

"Good… By the way, when are we going to do some work? Not that I mind lazing around all day, but I do need to earn my keep."

"First, I'm going to introduce you to William, our computer guy, so you'll know who to turn to in case you run into programming problems. In fact, we can stop by his lab on our way to the gym."

"I hope he won't mind dealing with someone as techno-logically challenged as I am."

"Don't worry about it, William is a sweetheart, you're going to like him, you'll see."

And she did. Later, when they reached his cluttered domain, Syssi was surprised to find William looking nothing like the rest of his hunky cousins. He was chubby and bespectacled, and boy did he love to talk...

"Will—" was all Amanda managed to say before he interrupted.

"Hi, you must be Syssi, I'm William." Leaving Amanda with her mouth open, he took Syssi's hand and shook it vigorously. "Don't ask me how I know. I know everything that's going on around here, and not because anyone bothers to tell me anything." He cast Amanda an accusing glance. "Sorry, I tend to blabber. Which might explain why no one comes to visit me."

The poor guy was out of breath, either from excitement over the unexpected visit, or talking at the speed of a firing machine gun. With an awkward glance at Syssi, he took off his glasses and wiped them on his billowy Hawaiian shirt.

"And now you know why we nicknamed him Uzi, after the machine gun." Amanda chuckled. "William, darling, you know we all love you." She patted his shoulder. "I brought Syssi over so she'll know you're the go-to guy with everything concerning tech stuff."

Syssi offered him a bright smile. "It's really nice to meet you, William. My programming skills are nonexistent. I would be grateful for any help you'd be willing to offer."

"Whenever you need me, I'm at your service. And if you want, I would be more than happy to teach you all you need to know. Amanda's research might be complicated as far as the tests she runs, but it requires only basic programming skills."

"That would be wonderful. Are you sure you can spare the time?"

"Of course, I have the time. And when you come," he whispered conspiringly, "I'll show you the underbelly of this monster. Even for a non-techie, the technology I've implemented in this building is fascinating. I showed some of it to Ingrid the other day when she came for help with her interior design software. She was very impressed. Did you meet Ingrid? Everything that looks nice was designed by her, and—" William stopped mid-sentence as Amanda raised her palm.

"I'm sure Syssi would love to hear all about it later, but we need to go."

"Yeah, sure, see you later, Syssi." William's shoulders sagged.

"Wow, he certainly talks fast," Syssi said once they were out of his earshot. "I like him, though. Is he working all by himself down here? The way he is hungry for someone to talk to, I guess he must be lonely."

"Yeah, I guess he must be. Though on Tuesdays and Thursdays, he teaches programming to a group of our kids."

Walking the rest of the way in silence, Syssi observed that the belly of the beast, as William had called the underground levels, had more of a utilitarian look to it than the public areas above. Wide, well-illuminated corridors with plain office-style carpeting and unadorned white walls, lacked even the motivational posters or reproductions of famous art one would find in most office buildings.

Evidently, Ingrid the interior designer hadn't gotten to wield her magic here. Syssi wondered if it was intentional, or if the designer just didn't get to it yet because she was busy elsewhere; the building looked to be relatively new.

"I would like to meet Ingrid," she told Amanda as they stopped in front of the bank of elevators. "I love the way she furnished your place and Kian's, and I'm curious to see some of her other work."

With a ping, the elevator doors opened, the opulent

interior a sharp contrast to the drab corridor they were leaving.

"Ingrid has her hands full at the moment. She is helping settle the evacuees from the Bay Area and needs to prepare apartments for clan members trickling in from all over Southern California. It'll be a while until she has any free time."

Exiting the elevator at the gym's level, Syssi noted it was just as plain as the one they'd left.

"Did you say, evacuees?"

"Yeah. Tragically, a few days ago, the Doomers murdered one of our top programmers in that area. Kian ordered everybody out of there. Having a small force of Guardians, we can only protect our people in here. They are not happy about it. It's hard to just get up and go, and Ingrid's job is to make them as comfortable here as we can."

"I'm so sorry for your loss... I don't know what to say." Syssi dropped her eyes. Amanda looked so pained it was clear she knew the victim and mourned his loss.

"There is nothing to say. Mark was one more casualty in this endless war of good versus evil. He wasn't the first and won't be the last. That's just the way it is." Amanda's strides got faster and longer, betraying her anger and determination.

It was a sad reality. No matter how strongly you wished for a peaceful existence, if your enemies were the kind that would not rest until they killed each and every one of you, you had to go on fighting, and make damn sure you were smart enough and strong enough to prevail.

Syssi sighed and followed Amanda into the gym.

The woman had been right; this was the mother of all

gyms, with rows of top-notch equipment of every imaginable kind lining the walls of the cavernous room.

At its center, standing on top of an arena of blue matting, Michael and a stunning dark man were embracing in a brotherly hug. Surrounding its perimeter stood a group of who she now knew were the Guardians.

Syssi recognized most of them: Kri, Onegus, Bhathian and the brothers, Anandur and Brundar. The only new faces belonged to the tall guy on the mat with Michael, and a pleasant-looking blond standing next to Kian.

For some reason, there was a palpable air of excitement in the gym. And even though it looked like nothing more than two guys in simple gym clothes about to engage in a training exercise, she had a strong feeling that a monumental event was about to take place.

"What's going on?" she whispered in Amanda's ear.

"Michael is about to fight Yamanu, who I assume was chosen to be the one to initiate him. By accepting this role, Yamanu promises to be Michael's guide and protector, becoming his surrogate big brother. Embracing before they begin the fight symbolizes their new bond of friendship."

Nice way to give a caring twist to a brutal coming-of-age ritual, Syssi reflected. "The sentiment is beautiful, but that guy is huge. He's going to pulverize the poor kid." The man looked formidable. Yamanu had several inches on Michael, and although slim, he was all sinewy muscle.

"If you don't have the stomach for it, maybe you shouldn't be here. Even a friendly match may seem rough to someone that didn't see one before. We could go and come later when it's over and done with." Amanda grasped Syssi's elbow with the intent of turning her around.

Syssi crossed her arms over her chest and planted her

feet firmly on the concrete floor. Someone had to look out for Michael, and as the only other mortal around, she felt it was up to her. "No, I want to stay and make sure he's okay. I know he is strong, but compared to these guys he looks like the little kid who got caught in the big boys' playground."

Amanda sent her a measuring look. "As you wish. And anyway, if I pull you out, you're probably going to imagine things being way worse than they actually are." She shrugged, crossing her arms over her chest as well. "Just promise not to scream or faint on me."

Syssi slanted her an affronted look. "Don't hold your breath..."

"Are you ready for some ass whupping, little brother?" Yamanu smiled, flashing a gorgeous set of gleaming white teeth.

Michael grinned, his eyes sweeping over the faces of his witnesses as he crouched in a fighting stance. "Bring it on, big brother."

Watching the Guardians' expressions as they stood around the blue mat, Syssi was moved by the unexpected fondness and encouragement they showed Michael. It dawned on her then that taking part in this ritual, this coming of age ceremony, symbolized more than Michael's transition from one state of being to another.

These people were welcoming him into their club—into their family.

Someone sounded a whistle and the match began. Trading kicks and punches, Michael used his bulk to topple the taller man to the mat and even managed to get out of Yamanu's choke holds a few times. But he was seriously outclassed, and a minute into the fight the poor kid was sporting a bruised eye and a bleeding lip.

On the sidelines, Kri was making a fool of herself shouting and cheering Michael on. "Yeah! Go Michael go!" She jumped up and down excitedly, ignoring her fellow Guardians' amused expressions.

At first, it was obvious that Yamanu was going easy on Michael, but as it became evident that he was not as easy to subdue as Yamanu had expected him to be, the guy got serious and in short order had the boy pinned face down on the mat.

With a knee between Michael's shoulder blades, Yamanu twisted the boy's arms painfully behind him, keeping Michael's struggling body immobilized as he bared his venom-dripping fangs. With a loud hiss, Yamanu sank them deep into Michael's neck.

Michael's body tensed and arched off the mat before going lax as the venom hit his system. Slowly, as his grimace morphed into a euphoric smile, his eyelids slid shut and he passed out.

"Is he all right? Should we call for help?" Syssi made a move to run for the mat.

Amanda caught her arm. "Easy, girl, everything is all right. He'll shake it off in a few moments."

"Are you sure? Is this normal?"

"Yes, darling, this is a perfectly normal reaction for males. You have nothing to worry about. I've seen my thirteen-year-old nephews and grandnephews go through this ceremony. The boys get knocked out, black out and shake it off in no time. Our big guy is in no danger."

Coming back from the adjacent facilities with several wet washcloths in her hands, Kri knelt beside Michael's prone body. "I'll take care of him," she said, and turning him a little, began wiping away the blood from his busted lip and bruised knuckles.

With a wicked smirk curling the side of her mouth, Amanda leaned into Syssi and pretended to whisper. "It's usually the mother that does the aftercare, and although technically, Kri could be his mother, I don't think she's acting from a motherly place right now."

Kri flipped Amanda the bird and sat down on the mat. Cradling Michael's head in her lap, she wiped his sweaty forehead with a clean washcloth. "Jealous?" she taunted.

"Already fighting over the prize, ladies?" Anandur teased them over the catty exchange, then looking to his comrades for support, he chuckled as the guys attempted nonchalance.

Evidently fearing Amanda's wrath, they tried to hide their amused faces and pretended like they'd heard nothing. Standing at the edge of the mat and huddling close, they did their best to avoid looking at either Amanda or Kri.

Instead, they began discussing the match.

"The kid did well," Brundar stated, his austere face showing the slightest nuance of pride.

"He's a natural fighter," Anandur agreed with a quick glance at Kri, making sure she had heard him, apparently trying to get back in her good graces.

"Yeah, Yamanu, you didn't expect him to get away that first time, did you?"

Arwel's comment made Yamanu grimace. "He surprised me, that's all. I didn't know he had any wrestling training, otherwise, I would have held on properly." Yamanu crossed his arms over his chest with an affronted expression on his handsome face. "Didn't want to hurt him unnecessarily, you know."

"Yeah, suddenly you're a fucking Mother Teresa. Give the kid some credit, you arrogant ass." Arwel punched

Yamanu's shoulder. "Like we don't know you're a merciless bastard."

"All right, I have no problem admitting he has potential, but today he just got lucky. Maybe if I spent some time training him, he could become a decent fighter. At least against mortals."

"He'll do better with my weapons training. Until he turns, he'll need the advantage they provide," Brundar said.

With an amused grin, Kian interjected, "No need to fight over the bone, boys, you could both train him. Think how well he'll do, getting two great teachers instead of one." He glanced at Syssi, and smiled with a slight nod.

Syssi smiled back before averting her eyes. Kian wasn't the only one uncomfortable with acknowledging the thing that was going on between them. Except, right now she wasn't sure there was even anything to acknowledge.

From the corner of her eye, she saw him look at her for a brief moment before turning to Onegus. "That's actually not a bad idea. The men are on to something."

"What do you mean?"

"The two fighting over who should train Michael gave me an idea. We could bring more young men to be trained by the Guardians. And young women..." Kian seemed to remind himself that times had changed. "With this new threat looming, the clan needs more Guardians, and the men seem hungry for some new blood in their ranks. I never gave it much thought before, but it makes sense that they would like to impart the knowledge and skills they've accumulated throughout the centuries to a new genera-tion. With no sons or daughters of their own, I can under-stand their need to validate the importance of what they know how to do best."

"You're awfully philosophical today." Onegus chuckled.

"You have a point, though. And I think something along the lines of a basic self-defense course for all members of the clan would be even better. It wouldn't hurt if everyone had some skill at defending themselves. And from the ranks of trainees, we could choose the best for more advanced training and eventually the Guardian force. What do you think?"

"I like it. We should do it, and the sooner, the better," Kian said, then glanced at Michael. "I think our boy is coming around."

Michael's eyes fluttered open, a huge grin spreading across his battered face as he saw Kri smiling down at him. Except, with his head and shoulders cradled in her lap, her heavy breasts were hovering barely an inch away from his nose, and it seemed he was having a hard time focusing on her pretty face.

As his tongue darted to his lips, Syssi smirked, imagining what must've been going through his head. And if she needed additional proof, the loose gym pants he was wearing were not much in the way of hiding what was going on down below.

Face gone red, Michael sneaked a quick glance at his audience. Realizing they were all watching him, he jerked up to a sitting position and bent at the waist in an attempt to hide the evidence. "That wasn't so bad... Ouch!" He winced in pain as he tried to get up.

Kri offered her arm. "Take it easy, big boy. Slow down... I'm going to help you up."

"I'm good, thanks." Michael made another go at standing on his own, but swayed, having to hold on to Kri's shoulder to regain his balance.

"Hey, Yamanu! Next time I won't go so easy on you!" Michael attempted some bravado.

Yamanu grinned. "Yeah, I want to see you try… Come here." He pulled Michael into a hug and clapped his back. "Not bad. Not bad at all, kid."

"Let's go, tiger. I'll take you to your room." Kri wrapped her arm around Michael and helped him limp out of the gym.

49

DALHU

*A*bout thirteen miles away, in a rented Beverly Hills mansion, Dalhu woke up to the sound of light snoring. Turning to look at the call girl sleeping beside him, he braced on his elbow and traced his finger over her puffy red lips.

Allowing a hooker to stay the night wasn't like him, except, after what he had put her through, the girl had been in no shape to go anywhere.

Not that she had voiced any complaints.

She sure hadn't expected to enjoy what he'd done to her so much. After he had sunk his fangs into her neck, the girl had orgasmed so hard her voice had become hoarse from her screams. And then he had her again... and she'd screamed some more.

He smiled. She sure looked like a woman well satisfied; her pretty face flushed and her bleached-blond hair tangled and sticking wetly to her rosy cheeks. What a shame he couldn't allow her to remember any of it.

Still, even though she was a pro, she had passed out way

before he'd been ready to be done with her. Unfortunately, there was a limit to what a mortal female could take.

Not for the first time, Dalhu wondered what sex with an immortal female would be like. For all he knew, she might be able not only to match his stamina but tire him out...

Or even bite him back...

Dalhu closed his eyes as the image sent a shiver of lust through his body. His palm found his growing erection and he began stroking it in leisurely up and down strokes, building on that image. She would go wild for the pleasure he would bring her, remember every wickedly sensual thing he would do to her, and beg for more.

Nice fantasy... But it was not to be.

The only immortal females he knew of were Annani's descendants—his sworn enemies—and even though he had no problem overlooking that small detail, he didn't know where to find one.

Deflated, Dalhu lost his good mood along with his erection.

Pushing off the bed, he trudged to the master suite's luxurious bathroom, stepped into the waterfall shower and turned all of the jets on. With his arms braced on the marble wall, he closed his eyes and tilted his head back. The water sluicing down his hair, he once again allowed his mind to conjure the elusive phantasm of an immortal female of his own.

As pointless as it was, it felt incredibly good to indulge in the fantasy, and as he tried to envision his perfect female, the face he saw belonged to the beautiful woman in the framed picture he kept by his bed.

The professor...

He would hold onto a woman like that forever. There would be no more whores for him to share with his brothers; he'd never soil himself like that again. It would be just her for him, and needless to state the obvious, only him for her.

She'd bear him a son, maybe more than one. Or even a daughter…

With her, he could have the kind of life he only caught a glimpse of in the mortal world. The only thing he ever envied humans in their wretched existence was having a family.

Smiling, he imagined himself a proud patriarch; admired, respected, surrounded by his children and grandchildren. The head of his own clan. He would be a good leader, providing for and protecting his own.

Honorable. Appreciated…

Yeah, right.

With a heavy sigh, he leaned his forehead on the wet shower wall, his hold on the illusion crumbling—the beautiful picture he had created dissolving into the mist.

He was old.

And his over eight hundred years of life felt pointless. The endless and senseless wars he had fought in. The meaningless sex with meaningless women he had shared with his fellow soldiers. Even the hating got old.

Lately, he couldn't summon the energy to loathe his enemy with the same passion he had used to.

He didn't really care about anything anymore.

If Annani continued to corrupt the West with her immoral and loose ways, so be it, they could all go to hell as far as he was concerned.

Let someone else take up the hating.

He was tired.

If he could only find an immortal mate, he wouldn't give a rat's ass if she belonged to the enemy's clan. He'd grab the woman and run. Hide somewhere, where no one would ever find them—neither her people nor his.

He needed to fulfill his own godforsaken dream—a family of his own.

With no money and no source of income, he'd have to start from scratch. But he'd manage, selling his collection of valuable jewelry to hold him over until he found another job. Killers for hire were always in high demand and the pay was good. Dalhu doubted there could be more than a handful of professionals who could match or surpass his level of skill. He was very good at what he did.

Indeed...

A fucking wonderful role model he would be for his hypothetical progeny.

Chilled from the inside by the ugly reality of who and what he was, the cold spread from the center of his chest to his extremities, and he shivered despite the shower's humid heat.

Who was he kidding? A doting patriarch? A loving mate and father? These kinds of fantasies befitted a naive, young boy with hopes for the future still fresh in his heart; not an ancient soldier hardened by life's cruel reality.

A killer for hire.

Turning the water off, Dalhu stepped out of the shower, wrapped a towel around his hips, and reached for another to dry off his beard and the rivulets of water streaming from it down his chest.

With the wadded towel in hand, he moved over to the vanity and wiped the vapor off the mirror, then took a good look at his face. He looked hard and old—more so with that dark beard and mustache covering most of his suntanned skin.

It had to go.

The few young men that he had seen on the streets with his kind of full-on beard were mostly the unattractive ones. The better-looking males had been either clean-shaven or sported a couple of days worth of growth but no more, and they had it stylishly trimmed.

Rummaging through the vanity's drawers, Dalhu found the scissors he was looking for and proceeded to snip away the bulk of the hair.

Once he was done, he examined his face again.

At first, he had planned to leave a short stubble. But now, as he stared at his reflection in the mirror, he had the urge to just get it all off.

When he was done, he felt as if a weight had been lifted off of him. For the first time in ages, he felt a cool breeze on his newly exposed skin, and even though it was only the recirculated air blowing through the air-conditioning vent, it felt damn good.

Dalhu hadn't seen his own face without a beard since he had been fifteen. When it had finally gotten dense enough for him to feel like a man, he'd been so proud of the damn thing. But now, looking at himself clean-shaven, he decided he looked much better without it. Quite hand-some, in fact, younger, if one didn't look too closely at his deadened, dark eyes.

Splashing water on his face, he removed the last of the shaving cream and bits of hair still clinging to his skin, then dried it off with the towel.

When he got back to his bedroom, the hooker was still

sleeping. He moved to stand near the bed and shook her shoulder. "Wake up. It's time to go!"

As her eyes flew open, he gripped her chin firmly, forcing her to look into his. She had a brief moment of fear and confusion before he entered her mind and thralled her to forget him, the sex, the mansion. Instead, he gave her new memories; of a plain-looking middle-aged man, in a plain-looking hotel room, and plain, boring sex.

Exchanging the extraordinary and unusual for the normal and mundane. Except, he regretted erasing the memory of her incredible orgasms and gave them back.

Even a whore deserves to have some pleasure in her miserable life, he reasoned his uncharacteristic kindness.

Rubbing his neck, Dalhu wondered if his mother and sister had ever been granted any, but suspected they had gotten none. No one cared for a whore's pleasure or any of her feelings for that matter. They were treated as objects, not as human beings. As if they deserved being despised and mistreated for choosing to be what they were. Except, most of the wretched women didn't have that choice.

Come to think of it, the attitude toward women in general in his part of the world wasn't much better. They were at the mercy of the men in their lives, be it fathers or husbands.

Even here in the West, where women were free to make their own choices for the last eighty years or so, he suspected very few sold their bodies voluntarily.

A wrong turn somewhere, an abusive boyfriend, drugs, poverty… Most probably thought it was only temporary— just until things got a little better. But things seldom did.

They usually got worse.

Blurry-eyed and stupefied, the woman got dressed clumsily and brushed her hair with her fingers. Dalhu gave her a few moments to clean up in the bathroom before leading her to the mansion's grand vestibule.

Still hazy, she stared myopically into space as she sat on the dainty chaise by the massive entry door, waiting for the taxi that would take her home.

50

SYSSI

*H*eading for the row of treadmills, Amanda winked at Syssi. "Aren't you glad the process is so much more pleasurable for females?"

"Yeah, I don't think I could've gotten Yamanu even slightly worked up with my fighting skills."

"Oh, I'm sure you could get him worked up all right." Amanda chuckled. "Just not with your fists... Well, maybe you could do something with them..." She laughed a deep throaty laugh.

"Amanda!"

"What? I'm just saying... It's true!"

Syssi rolled her eyes and decided to change the subject before Amanda embarrassed her even more. "By the way, I was wondering about how different it is for the girls. Kian said that being around your mother was enough to facilitate the change in them. What about the boys? Why doesn't it work the same for them? Was it tested?"

"Of course it was tested. It doesn't work for the boys. My guess is that it's easier to turn the girls because they are the ones that can actually transmit our specific traits to their offspring; they might have a stronger predisposition. But I can't say for sure that's the reason. It just works this way.

"Our children are born and raised at my mother's place, with the expectant mothers traveling to be with her as their time grows near. It's beneficial for the boys as well as the girls to spend their early years with Annani. And besides, she loves having them there. It's not like there are that many, and sometimes decades pass with no children at all, even centuries. So when they arrive, her greatest joy is spending time with the little ones, hugging and kissing the babies, taking care of the mothers.

"Her place is amazing, a real heaven—like a miniature Hawaii. The same perfect temperature year round. Pools and streams of warm water, waterfalls with slides... It's beautiful. The kids have a wonderful time with her and they are safe, protected." Amanda paused, a sad shadow crossing her beautiful face.

"The boys are mortal until they reach puberty and are able to put up a decent fight against a transitioned boy. Until they are turned, they're just as vulnerable to injury and disease as any other mortal. In order to keep them safe, most mothers choose to stay at Annani's place until their sons are old enough to transition. We've lost several of our precious little boys to accidents and illness over the generations. It's always tragic to lose a child, and we have so few." Amanda whispered the last sentence, struggling to breathe as tears glistened in her eyes.

Oh, God! No! The anguish in her friend's eyes could mean only one thing. Syssi felt her chest tighten, Amanda's pain cutting straight to her soul. "I'm so sorry," she whispered.

"He was such a beautiful boy." Amanda's lip trembled as

tears trickled down her cheeks. "I don't want to talk about it. I can't. It happened over a century ago, but it still hurts like hell... as if it had been only yesterday." Wiping her face with her hand, Amanda turned the treadmill on, and without bothering to warm up began running as if the hounds of hell were on her tail.

Turning her own machine on, Syssi began with a brisk walk. She knew how it felt. She didn't lose a child, which must've been even more devastating than losing her brother had been, but four years after the tragedy she still couldn't think about his death without a choking sensation constricting her throat and her eyes burning with tears.

After about fifteen minutes of running at a breakneck speed, Amanda finally slowed down, gradually coming to a stop. Fighting to bring air into her lungs, she bent at the waist, supporting her upper body with her hands on her thighs. "Hard to run when you're choking," she huffed.

Syssi understood all too well. Slowing, she brought her machine to a halt and stepped down. With a ragged sigh, she touched her hand to Amanda's shoulder, and choking on her own emotions, she whispered, "We carry our pain buried deep within our hearts, hidden away and securely locked, and when these raw emotions escape the prison we've built for them, it feels like acid is eating us from the inside. It burns... burns so bad."

There was nothing more she could say, no magic words that could ease Amanda's pain. Instead, she pulled the taller woman into her arms and ran her hands soothingly up and down her back. Sharing her body's warmth with her shivering friend was really all she had to offer.

Mortal or near-immortal, it didn't make a difference. The pain of loss was the same, and physical contact provided the only comfort to be had.

For a few moments, they commiserated in silence, holding on to each other, with Amanda leaning into Syssi and resting her head on her shoulder. Then, heaving a shaky sigh, she disentangled from the embrace and drew in a calming breath.

Looking up into Amanda's eyes, Syssi saw in their depths the dark shadows of the woman's grief and her valiant effort to push against the pain. Tragically, Syssi often saw the same miserable expression staring back at her from the mirror.

And even though the loss they had shared had brought them closer than ever, it was a pity that what had helped strike this new kind of communion between them had been the result of anguish and grief.

Nevertheless, given the fact that she still had a hard time dealing with her own loss, Syssi was glad Amanda hadn't wanted to talk about it. So maybe she was being selfish and wasn't such a good friend after all, or maybe she was weak, or cowardly. But she just didn't have the strength to take that on; couldn't handle the added dose of grief.

"I'm okay now, I can breathe again..." Amanda shot Syssi a sad, thankful smile. "Let's run." She climbed back on the treadmill and resumed her breakneck speed.

Syssi maintained an easier pace on her own machine while going over the conversation in her head.

She wasn't thinking about what had made them both sad. Since her own tragedy had struck and changed her forever, keeping her mind off the depressing subject became a mental exercise she was getting better and better at as the years went by.

Instead, her head was buzzing with all the questions

she was dying to ask Amanda, mainly about her mother—the Goddess.

What did she look like? What kind of a person was she? How powerful and in what way? What was their relationship like? And where was that heaven Amanda had described?

Except, now was not the time for it. With Amanda pounding away on the treadmill, trying to outrun her demons, Syssi figured she'd better save her questions for later.

51

DALHU

*D*alhu left the hooker sitting on the bench and headed for the mansion's dining room, which served as their makeshift headquarters. His six remaining warriors were waiting for him there.

As he entered the room, he glanced at the large street map of downtown Los Angeles and its adjoining neighborhoods, which he'd tacked last night onto the tapestry covering the room's east wall. The thing was covered with colorful pins, marking the locations of the numerous nightclubs and popular bars he planned on scoping once the reinforcements he had asked for arrived.

Tonight, he'd start with what remained of his original team. The same bunch that was now staring at him as if he had sprouted horns. At first, he didn't understand their dumbfounded expressions, but as he ran his fingers over his smooth chin and realized what had caused their moronic reaction, his face pinched in anger.

What a bunch of mediocre simpletons. But what could he expect? A full beard was considered a sign of potency and virility, and it was expected from fearsome warriors to sport one. These guys knew nothing other than what had been drilled into their heads. They were incapable of thinking independently or observing their environment and then adapting accordingly.

They knew only what they had been told, and questioned nothing. Brainwashed since birth by Navuh's propaganda, their deeply ingrained hate made them into the well-sharpened weapons with which he delivered death and vengeance to those he considered his enemies.

In the way of true zealots, they were ready to die fighting for Navuh's cause without really understanding what they were willing to sacrifice their lives for.

Not that Dalhu could really blame the morons. It had taken him long enough before he had begun questioning what he had been told, and even longer for the supposedly holy cause to lose its luster in his eyes.

But then, he was smarter than most, and with how easy it was to obtain information in this new, Internet-connected world, he was better informed.

It all boiled down to the quest for power and wealth. Who had it, and who did not. Dalhu preferred to be on the side that had it—regardless of its moral underpinnings.

It was all crap anyway.

The whole world was corrupted, and those who believed differently were stupid and naive and deserved being led like cattle to the slaughter.

Dalhu was as far from naive as it got.

For real, though? What he needed from his men were their muscle, fear, and blind obedience. The thinking and strategizing he could manage himself.

In the cutthroat world of the Brotherhood, having idiots for foot soldiers was a necessary evil; a smart ass, capable underling was liable to challenge your position, take you out, and seize leadership of your unit.

Dalhu should know. Realizing early on that he didn't want to spend his long life as a foot soldier, he had cunningly disposed of his first immediate commander. Though in his defense, he had believed he had no choice; as no one ever retired willingly or left to vacate a spot, it had been the only way to advance in the Brotherhood's ranks.

To become a leader, he had to oust his predecessor.

The men were still shooting quick glances at his face when the elderly cook and her rolling cart, loaded with their breakfast, granted them a short reprieve.

For a few blissful moments, they gave their undivided attention to wolfing down the huge stacks of eggs, toast, and hash browns on their plates. Once they were done, and the cook cleared the table, Dalhu pushed up from his chair.

"I have a plan," he began. "The colored tacks on the map mark the locations of nightclubs. Each night, you will go out and scope for immortal males in the clubs you'll be assigned to. For now, it will be one man per club. When reinforcements arrive, we'll scope a larger area, and you'll be working in teams of two. But even with the reinforcements, we'll be stretched thin covering such a large city."

Given the guys' clueless expressions, it was obvious they had no idea where he was going with this, and he explained. "In the past, we managed to snag a few of the clan's males in whorehouses. Their biology being the same as ours, they need a constant supply of mortal females. Except they are not as lucky as we are, with a built in brothel at our disposal courtesy of our exalted and brilliant leader, Lord Navuh."

He paused for them to finish their chuckling and

saluting. "They are forced to constantly prowl for females. As we all know, given the rampant corruption of the West, willing women come to the clubs and bars looking for males to fuck them. Therefore, it stands to reason that we'll find what we are looking for in those places."

Dalhu waited, giving the men a moment to process what he had told them, then assuming his most severe expression, delivered the instruction that would trouble them most. "Your beards have to go; they are not popular here in the West, and you need to call as little attention to yourselves as possible. Consider it a sacrifice for our holy cause."

"But, sir, we'll get ridiculed upon our return," one of the men protested.

The panicked expressions of his comrades should have warned him that he had made a huge mistake; questioning your superior was not something a subordinate Doomer dared to do. Their lives belonged to their leader to do with as he pleased and to question his orders was to court dangerous retribution.

"Come here!" Dalhu called the soldier to him. "You worthless dog! You do not think! You do not question! You obey!" he hollered and sent his fist flying, at the last moment aiming lower and instead of the guy's jaw, punching his middle. The powerful punch had the guy double over on the floor, retching his food. Still, the man had been lucky; Dalhu needed his face to remain pretty for tonight.

Taking a steadying breath and then another, Dalhu tried to rein in his rage. It was becoming harder to do lately—the anger would rise at the slightest provocation and linger, poisoning his mood and impairing his thought process. But at least he retained enough self-control to change the trajectory of that punch...

Thank Mortdh...

The bastard had a point, though. The few unlucky men born without the ability to grow facial hair were ridiculed and humiliated for not being real men. And to add insult to injury, the poor bastards were not allowed to join the warrior ranks, becoming servants in the barracks or the brothel—a truly disgraceful existence.

Cowering in their chairs, his men were trying to ignore the sight of their comrade wiping his vomit off the rug, but their troubled expressions spoke of all the unanswered questions they still had.

"I know what you're thinking, but don't worry, I've thought of everything. You're asking yourselves how are you going to catch and extract the males, without getting close enough for them to realize what you are. Right?" Dalhu pulled a small plastic bag with white powder out of his trouser pocket. "You'll thrall the bartender or the waitress to slip this powder into the male's drink. The drug will make an average-sized immortal male sleepy, but although he'll be too fuzzy to talk or offer resistance, he'll still be able to walk with your assistance. To the mortals, the male will appear drunk while you'll look like the good friend taking him home. With the thing being tasteless and odorless, the male will not suspect he is being drugged until it's too late. Good plan, huh?" Dalhu smiled smugly. The drug connection the Brotherhood had in Los Angeles was proving once again to be a most valuable resource.

"You'll bring them here for me to interrogate. If you value your own lives, they'd better be alive and well enough to talk when they get here. So make sure you don't accidentally overdose any. Even if your intention is to knock the male out, don't use more than two packets." Dalhu looked around, making sure they got it. "We go out tonight. I'll text each one of you the address of the club you'll be scoping. Before you leave, check the map to orient yourself. Make sure to get all clean and scrubbed by eight this evening and dress appropriately. Jeans are okay, a dress shirt, and don't forget the cologne. No playing with the females until it's closing time, and then only the willing ones. No thralling until after the deed. Am I clear?"

"Yes sir!" the men acknowledged.

There was really no way for him to ascertain if the thralling occurred before or after the sex, but hopefully, the men feared him enough to follow his orders.

2

AMANDA

*O*ut of breath and drenched in sweat, Amanda stepped off the treadmill and glanced at Syssi. "I'm done. Are you ready to go up and put in some desk work?"

After an hour-long run at a speed that could've put an Olympic athlete to shame, Amanda at last felt as if she was done exorcising her demons. For the time being at least... Walking over to the paper-towel dispenser, she pulled one and used it to wipe the sweat off her face.

"Thank God! I thought you'd never stop. I'm exhausted from just trying to keep up at a fast walk," Syssi said, following behind her.

Being the last two at the gym, the sound of their voices echoed off the walls, making the place feel like a crypt. Hurrying out and stepping into the elevator's welcoming interior, Amanda was relieved to leave behind the empty gym and the bad memories that had surfaced there.

Syssi was quiet and somber all through the ride up to the penthouse, and Amanda wasn't in the mood for small talk either. Which was okay. The silence didn't bother her,

282

and at this point she hoped that Syssi was comfortable enough in their friendship for the quiet to feel companionable as opposed to oppressing.

Be that as it may, it was time to do something about Syssi's bad mood and to fix the mess Kian had made.

At the penthouse, Amanda showered, changed, and then spent a good ten minutes applying her makeup. Feeling like herself again, she walked into her office and smiled as she saw her best girl already at the desk. "Ready, sweetie?"

"Show me." Syssi rolled her chair sideways and pulled another one for Amanda.

It didn't take her long to introduce Syssi to the proprietary software that was developed by none other than William. The thing was years ahead of what they had in the lab, which, of course, meant that any significant trend they'd discover could not be used in the official research papers. But it would save them time by identifying, quickly and efficiently, which of their assumptions were correct and which were not. That way, they could focus their efforts and use the official program, which was a slow and inefficient monster, on what was more likely to work.

"I have to leave for a little bit. Are you okay here on your own?" Amanda asked once Syssi got the gist of the new program and began uploading the research data they had accumulated over the past several weeks.

"Yeah, I'm good. With this software, I'll probably be done in a couple of hours. If you're not back by then, I'll text you when I have the results so you can decide what you want to do next."

"Good deal. I'll check on you later."

Letting a few minutes go by, Amanda peeked into the

office to make sure Syssi was immersed in her work, then snuck out her front door, closing it soundlessly behind her.

In several strides of her long legs, Amanda crossed the vestibule and entered Kian's place without knocking.

Too much was at stake, and she wasn't going to let Kian blow it.

53

KIAN

"We need to talk," Amanda said as soon as she entered Kian's office.

Lifting his head, Kian's lips twisted in an involuntary grimace. An angry expression marring her pretty face, she looked ready for battle. Bracing for the attack that was sure to follow, he eased back in his chair and folded his arms across his chest.

Amanda halted in front of his desk and placed her hands on her hips, tapping her shoe on the hardwood floor. "What did you do to her this time?" she accused.

He really didn't have the patience for the scene she was making, and her offensive behavior was getting on his nerves. And what's more, once it dawned on him that he was the one assuming a defensive posture, his temper flared hot. The little hellcat was the one who was supposed to bow to his authority and answer to him. Not the other way around. He was cutting her way too much slack and forgiving her impudence out of love. But enough was enough.

Uncrossing his arms, he placed his palms on the glossy

surface of his desk and pinned her with a hard stare. "What do you want, Amanda?" he barked back, letting some of his anger leak into his voice.

Amanda winced. Plopping down on the chair facing him, she continued in a softer tone. "Syssi is upset and unhappy. You must've either done something or said something to hurt her."

"I know. But I'll be damned if I know what it was. I hoped she would tell you." Kian ran his fingers through his hair. Now that Amanda had abandoned her combative attitude, his anger gave way to frustration.

She frowned and straightened in her chair. "Syssi told me she was overwhelmed with all the stuff she had to wrap her mind around, but I know there is more to it. The way she was holding her arms around her middle she seemed almost in physical pain." She was watching him carefully, and Kian knew Amanda was searching his face for signs of guilt.

What the hell was she thinking? That he had gotten too rough with Syssi? Except, what if he had? What if Syssi had only pretended to be okay? Kian winced uncomfortably.

It didn't escape Amanda's notice. Suspecting the worst, her intense blue eyes began glowing from under her clenched brows.

The hellcat looked ready to tear him a new one.

But then he shook his head. "No, she was fine after we… after we made love… It was only after I told her our story that she clamped down."

"Tell me everything exactly as it happened. You may not know what you've done wrong, but I might."

"Everything?" Kian cocked his brow with a little smile tugging at his lips.

Amanda waved a hand in front of her face. "Ugh! I don't

need the steamy details! Too much information. Just the sequence of events, and what you said to her, or rather how you said it. We both know you tend to be somewhat uncouth."

Kian sighed. Maybe she had a point. As a female, Amanda might have the insight he was apparently lacking. Except, he had a feeling that as a near-immortal, her way of thinking would be very different from Syssi's. But be that as it may, it was worth a shot, even if talking with his sister about his relationship with Syssi felt uncomfortable. But what choice did he have?

There was no one else.

"Okay. So last night, after we came back from the club, I didn't thrall her after the sex. She was spacey from the bite, and I figured it was the perfect time to tell her what was going on, while she was still in a receptive mood and wouldn't freak out. It just didn't feel right to keep thralling her and lying to her. I decided to come clean the way we did with Michael. I told her some of it last night and the rest this morning. She didn't freak out, didn't panic, but she got upset. Mainly because she figured out that I would have to erase her memory if she didn't turn. But then it looked as if she understood why it was necessary and seemed better, then got upset again and wouldn't tell me why."

"Tell me exactly how you explained it to her."

"Why?"

"Just humor me. I have a feeling your presentation lacked finesse. And since I wasn't there, the only way I can figure it out is to hear it word for word." Amanda tapped her long fingers on her biceps, nailing him with her blue stare.

"I told her everything, pretty much the same way we

explained it to Michael. Our history, the unique biology, how important both Michael and she might be to the future of our clan. Then I elaborated a little more about the venom and how it works. The first time she really got upset was when she realized she'd be sent away if she didn't turn. The second was when I explained about the possibility of her getting addicted to the venom. Instead of alleviating her concerns, the more I explained how it could be circumvented by having several different partners, the more cold and distant she became. I think I did the best I could to make it clear that she wasn't trapped in a relationship with me because of it, and would be free to choose anyone she wanted." Kian felt his face twist with rage. Just imagining Syssi being approached by another male made him want to shred the hypothetical bastard to pieces. "And believe me, it cost me to get the words out of my mouth," he growled the last sentence.

"Suave, Kian... really suave, almost two thousand years old and clueless." Amanda shook her head. "I'm amazed that an intelligent and experienced man like you can be so blind."

Blind? Who was she calling blind?

She was the one who, oblivious to his state of mind, was fueling his rage with her insolence, instead of offering to calm him down. Breathing hard, he fisted his hands until his knuckles turned white; feeling like anytime now smoke would start coming out of his nostrils and horns would poke out from his forehead, making him look like one of his demonic illusions. "That's enough, Amanda! I will not tolerate this tone of voice from you. You're my sister and I love you, but that doesn't mean I'll allow you to talk to me with disrespect."

True to form, instead of cowering before him, Amanda

bowed her head with mock penitence. "My apologies, Regent, you're right of course. This era is not very respectful toward its elders." She smirked.

And just like that she had him disarmed.

"You're forgiven. Now talk... respectfully..." Kian looked at her sternly, but a smile was tugging at his lips. She'd gotten him there. Was he really too old and rigid? Clinging to some outdated notion of propriety? He didn't think so.

Kian considered himself an easygoing ruler, far more forgiving and lax than his mother ever was. Amanda would have never dared to use this tone of voice around Annani, even when not addressing her directly.

Amanda straightened her back and clasped her hands before her on his desk, looking like a chastened schoolgirl in the principal's office. All that was missing were pigtails and a naughty schoolgirl uniform to make her performance good enough for a comedy skit.

It was a shame, really, that she couldn't pursue an acting career... With her looks, natural talent, and predisposition for drama, she would have made it big. Despite himself, Kian shook his head and chuckled.

Except, Amanda had no intention of being funny. Using her teacher's voice, she asked, "How do you feel about Syssi? Think about it for a moment before you answer. I want you to get a clear picture in your head."

Looking at Amanda's beautiful face wearing an expression that was composed and serious for a change, Kian was startled by the resemblance she bore to their mother. Most of the time it was masked by the marked differences between them. Amanda was tall as opposed to the diminutive but formidable Annani, and her mischievous and lively demeanor was very different from their mother's regal composure. Except, right now, the similarity of their features was striking. And for some reason it made it easier for him to open up to his sister.

Still, long seconds passed as he tried to come up with an honest answer. "She is sweet. I like how unassuming she is. She is definitely smart, and not prone to dramatics or exaggerations like some people I know…" Kian looked at Amanda pointedly as she rolled her eyes. "Syssi is beautiful, lush, sensual… lustful… I can't get enough of her, and she responds in kind… We are definitely in serious lust with each other." Kian smiled before taking in a hissed breath as memories of their wild lovemaking assaulted his body.

"Are you sure it's only lust?" Amanda probed gently.

No he wasn't, but he wasn't ready to admit it either. To himself or to Amanda. "What else could it be? We've known each other for less than a week." Kian avoided Amanda's smiling eyes. He was a lousy liar and she knew him too well. Hiding the truth from her wasn't easy.

"So you didn't become a jealous monster when another male was sniffing around her, or turn practically demonic just at the thought of her with another guy?" Amanda sounded smug.

Bracing his elbows on the desk, Kian dropped his head on his fists. "I did. Big time." He sighed. "I was ready to pound Anandur to a pulp, and barely held myself from breaking Alex's arm when the scumbag touched her. I don't know what came over me. I've never been the jealous type, not even with Lavena, whom I loved… had a child with… I don't understand what's happening to me."

Kian felt guilty.

Why the hell had he never gotten jealous over Lavena? Was it possible he hadn't loved her enough? For some reason, questioning what he believed he had with her brought on a despondent feeling.

Over the years, he had cherished the memory of the short time he had with Lavena as a precious nugget of good. A taste of normal—knowing that he would never have that again. But with what he was now feeling for Syssi, he was forced to question the authenticity of those memories.

Amanda watched him with pitying eyes—as if he was slow-minded. "Yet, you've told Syssi that she is important *to the clan*, that she should not fear addiction because she can choose *some other male* for her mate."

Kian's anger flared anew. "So? It's true! I wanted her to know she is important to us, and I didn't want her to feel trapped or forced. She has the right to know what her options are."

Amanda palmed his tightly fisted hand and held it in both of hers with an expression so somber, he was afraid she was slipping into her dramatics again. "You lied, Kian; lied to yourself, lied to Syssi, and by doing so you hurt both of you."

Yup, she did... Delivering her statement in a perfectly modulated tone to maximize the dramatic effect.

Kian tried to pull away from her, but she held on. "Listen to me! She is important to you, and you want her to choose you because you want her for yourself, not for the clan. That's what she wanted to hear, needed you to say, and it also happens to be the truth."

When he didn't try to refute her claims, she continued. "Syssi is not like us. She is not someone who has casual sex. This thing with you means the world to her. The poor girl had just one lover until now and went without for two years for goodness' sake... And the way you explained things made her feel like she is nothing to you. Way to go, Kian." With a last disapproving look Amanda finally let go of his hand.

"I'm an ass..." Kian dropped his head and rubbed at his temples. It was so obvious when Amanda had put it like that. How come he hadn't realized that before?

"I'm such a moron..."

"No, my dear sweet brother, you're not a moron, just inexperienced—shagging   thousands   of   women notwithstanding. You don't know how to deal with your own emotions, let alone someone else's. You've never had to woo a female, so you don't know how to go about it. But all is not lost. I'll help you romance her back." Amanda squared her shoulders and pushed her chin up.

Kian chuckled. "You, Amanda? What do you know about wooing or romance? What do any of us know? We use and discard partners like dirty underwear or used condoms."

"Okay, Kian, now you're being crude. As regent, you're not allowed."

He dismissed her with a wave of his hand. "In here, I'm just your brother."

"Could have fooled me... Watch your tone, I demand respect, Amanda..." She emulated his haughty tone, crossing her arms over her chest and jutting out her chin.

"Cut the crap. What do you suggest I do, Miss-Know-It-All?"

"I do have some human female friends, and I've read a few romance novels, so I do have some idea of what mortal females want—besides the shagging, or in addition to it, that is. You should take her out on a date, make it several dates, to some classy, romantic restaurant, or a show, or the theater. Take her dancing. And gifts—I think mortal females expect that from their suitors. Shower her with attention, but it has to be outside the bed... or the wall... or the closet... or the shower..." Amanda couldn't help herself and was trying to make him squirm a little. But he just smirked. "Make her feel she is the most important person in the world to you. Tell her how you feel, show her; give yourself to her and make her yours." Amanda sighed, her little speech evidently making her wistful.

"But what if she is not compatible, and I'll have to let her go, erase her memories? It's going to hurt like hell..."

"Letting her go is going to hurt like hell regardless of what you do. You're already head over heels with her. But, at least this way, giving it all, letting this thing between you bloom, you'll get to sample a little bit of wonderful. The consequences of not admitting the truth and following your heart would bring a whole new world of hurt—much worse than just letting her go." She shivered. "I hate to think what that would do to you."

"What do you mean? What could be worse?"

"What could be worse? Think of it this way; she turns immortal, but wants nothing to do with you, chooses another male... one you cannot kill because they are all your nephews."

"You're right, this is worse..." His eyes flashed dangerously as his imagination ran rampant with disturbing possibilities. Unbidden, an image of Anandur smirking at him while holding Syssi with his arm wrapped around her shoulders made Kian see red. Tamping down his fury, he pushed out of his chair and began pacing the length of his office.

"Take a risk, Kian. I have a really good feeling about Syssi. Michael too." Amanda's eyes followed him as he paced back and forth the thirty feet or so.

"You've had good feelings before," he said sarcastically as he stopped to glare down at her.

"This time it's different. You've never acted like that with anyone. And besides, I was just reminded of a talk I had with Mother a couple of months back. She said something I didn't pay attention to at the time, but I think you'll find it intriguing. You know how she sometimes makes those cryptic remarks that do not make any sense at the time, but then are crystal clear in hindsight?"

"What did she say?"

"She called me. We talked about my research, and she said, 'Finally you have found what the soul eternally craves.' I thought she just misused the language—you know, the way she sometimes translates from her native tongue and it comes out weird. I thought what she meant was that I'd found my heart's desire—something I like to do. But thinking back, she didn't say 'your soul,' she said 'the soul,' meaning that I'd found something not for me personally, but in general. What do all of our souls eternally crave, Kian?" Amanda gazed up into his eyes.

"A mate—an immortal, true love mate," he said quietly.

"Bingo!"

54

AMANDA

*A*s she gazed at her brother's stunned expression, Amanda struggled to keep a big grin from splitting her face.

Another milestone had just been achieved, and it had happened much faster than she'd hoped. Which in her opinion indicated that the third and final milestone was going to be achieved as well.

Kian had admitted he was falling in love with Syssi, and for this to happen that fast must mean that they were indeed true love mates. Which in turn must mean that Syssi was a Dormant and that she would turn.

True love pairing couldn't happen with a human.

Of course, none of it was guaranteed, but with each passing day, Amanda felt more and more certain that she was right. Everything was progressing in the right direction and at an amazing speed.

Still, a little prayer couldn't hurt.

Lifting her eyes to the ceiling, she beseeched the merciful Fates to bestow on Kian this ultimate reward for his many sacrifices. The man was selfless to a fault, dedicating his life to his family and to humanity at large. If there was anyone who deserved his happy ending it was her brother.

Please, I'm not asking for myself this time, and therefore my prayer should be heard. Please let Syssi turn, not only to reward Kian for his sacrifices, but to bring new hope to our clan.

TO FIND OUT WHAT HAPPENS NEXT!
CLICK HERE

BOOK 3 IN THE CHILDREN OF THE GODS SERIES
DARK STRANGER IMMORTAL
IS AVAILABLE ON AMAZON

TURN THE PAGE FOR AN EXCERPT
FROM DARK STRANGER IMMORTAL

When Kian confesses his true nature, Syssi is not as much shocked by the revelation as she is wounded by what she perceives as his callous plans for her.

If she doesn't turn, he'd be forced to erase her memories and let her go. His family's safety demands secrecy— no one in the mortal world is allowed to know that immortals exist.

Resigned to the cruel reality that even if she stays on to never again leave the keep, she'll get old while Kian wouldn't, Syssi is determined to enjoy what little time she has with him, one day at a time.

Could Kian let go of the mortal woman he loves? Would Syssi turn? And if she does, would she survive the dangerous transition?

EXCERPT

The silence that followed was interrupted by Okidu's light knock on the door. "Master, Dr. Bridget is here to see you."

Tearing his gaze away from his sister's hopeful face, Kian frowned. Amanda was so excited, her deep blue eyes were glowing. Unfortunately, she was reading too much into their mother's words, grasping for meaning where there was none.

In his opinion, false hope was more dangerous than the baser emotions people scorned. A cruel and powerful mistress, hope obscured common sense and made random occurrences appear as meaningful signs, prompting those who followed its misleading trail to take questionable actions. Mindlessly disregarding the wellbeing of others and their own sense of self-preservation for hope's illusive promise, more often than not, they were rewarded by nothing but chaos and pain.

"Show her in," he told Okidu. "On second thought, never mind. I'll go to her."

In the living room, Bridget was pacing the small distance between the front door and the edge of the rug, looking agitated.

Great. His lips pulled into a tight line. Another female ready to tear into him over something he had supposedly done wrong.

Take a number and stand in line.

"Good afternoon, Bridget, what a nice surprise." Kian wondered if she heard the thinly veiled sarcasm in his tone.

The doctor wrung her hands nervously. "Good afternoon, Kian, sorry to come up here without calling ahead, but this is urgent."

"Think nothing of it, everyone else does..." He placed his hand on her shoulder, conveying the reassurance his tone didn't. "What can I do for you, Bridget?"

"I've just learned that you have two potential Dormants here, and frankly, I was appalled I had to hear it from William. How come you didn't check with me before initiating the process? I need blood samples before and after each venom injection. It's the first time I have adult Dormants whom I could test as we are attempting to activate them, and there might be a chance that their blood will provide the clues I need. You know how important this is." By the time she finished her rant, her temper had painted her cheeks red to match the color of her hair.

"You're right. With everything that was going on, it

didn't even cross my mind. But my oversight aside, I don't want you to get your hopes up. I don't believe they are really what we are looking for, but just in case..."

"Yeah, just in case... Hi, Bridget." Amanda gave the petite woman a hug. "Don't listen to him, he of little faith. They. Are. It," she whispered in the doctor's ear, making sure it was loud enough for Kian to hear.

He rolled his eyes. "I'll make sure they'll be at your lab shortly."

"Thank you." Bridget smiled a tight, nervous smile and hurried out.

Closing the door behind her, Kian turned to Amanda. "I assume Syssi is at your place?"

"She is in my office. I've sat her down to do some work."

"Good, I'll get her. Call for someone to escort Michael to the lab, unless you want to do it yourself?"

They walked out together.

"Remember! Be nice... Woo her!" Amanda slapped his back before punching the button for the elevator.

Woo her, right.

What the hell did it mean? Kian racked his brain trying to come up with something that would qualify as wooing. Should he quote poetry? He chuckled. He didn't know any. Didn't like it, and in his opinion, it was a lot of pretentious crap. If one wanted to convey an idea, one ought to do it in a way that would be clearly understood and not mask it in vague wording. Whatever. His opinion on poetry notwithstanding, he needed something more concrete than that word.

Woo.

Being serious and pragmatic wasn't going to help him woo anyone, besides business associates, that is, not that he was any good at that either. Kian thought of himself as courteous and polite, and he was... most of the time... unless his temper got the better of him. Other than that, the extent of his social skills was limited to business dealings and seducing women in bars and clubs.

It wasn't much to work with. In comparison, even bloody Anandur seemed like a witty charmer.

I'm so screwed...

With his footfalls making almost no sound on the hallway's soft rug, Sissy didn't hear his approach. She didn't even lift her head when he peered into Amanda's office.

For a moment, he observed her unawares. She looked adorable; scrunching her little nose in concentration, her wild multicolor hair all over the place—cascading down her back and front, covering her left breast while leaving the other outlined perfectly against her white, low-necked T-shirt.

She was so damn sexy it hurt.

Did she wear those T-shirts on purpose to taunt him? How was he supposed to get his head out of the gutter when she looked so tempting? Kian heaved a sigh. It would be next to impossible to follow Amanda's advice and interact with Syssi in a nonsexual way.

She looked up from her work. "Hi, Kian... What was the heavy sigh for?"

For a moment there, he was tempted to yank her out of her chair and show her. Instead, he raked his itchy fingers through his hair. "Bridget, our in-house doctor, wants to take some blood samples from you and Michael. She needs to run tests before and after each venom infusion..."

On the wooing scale of one to ten, that was probably a minus two.

With an inward curse, Kian's brows drew tight. "Come, she is waiting for us in her lab." He offered his hand.

Yep, I'm Mr. Fucking Debonair.

BOOK 3 IN THE CHILDREN OF THE GODS SERIES
DARK STRANGER IMMORTAL
IS AVAILABLE ON AMAZON

THE CHILDREN OF THE GODS SERIES

THE CHILDREN OF THE GODS ORIGINS

1: GODDESS'S CHOICE

When gods and immortals still ruled the ancient world, one young goddess risked everything for love.

2: GODDESS'S HOPE

Hungry for power and infatuated with the beautiful Areana, Navuh plots his father's demise. After all, by getting rid of the insane god he would be doing the world a favor. Except, when gods and immortals conspire against each other, humanity pays the price.

But things are not what they seem, and prophecies should not to be trusted...

THE CHILDREN OF THE GODS

1: DARK STRANGER THE DREAM

Syssi's paranormal foresight lands her a job at Dr. Amanda Dokani's neuroscience lab, but it fails to predict the thrilling yet terrifying turn her life will take. Syssi has no clue that her boss is an immortal who'll drag her into a secret, millennia-old battle over humanity's future. Nor does she realize that the professor's imposing brother is the mysterious stranger who's been starring in her dreams.

Since the dawn of human civilization, two warring factions of immortals—the descendants of the gods of old—have been secretly shaping its destiny. Leading the clandestine battle from his luxurious Los Angeles high-rise, Kian is surrounded by his clan, yet alone. Descending from a single goddess, clan members are forbidden to each other. And as the only other immortals are their hated enemies, Kian and his kin have been long resigned to a lonely existence of fleeting trysts with human partners. That is, until his sister makes a game-changing discovery—a mortal seeress who she believes is a dormant carrier of their genes. Ever the realist, Kian is skeptical and refuses Amanda's plea to attempt Syssi's activation. But when his enemies learn of the Dormant's existence, he's forced to rush her to the safety of his keep. Inexorably drawn to Syssi, Kian wrestles with his conscience as he is tempted to explore her budding interest in the darker shades of sensuality.

2: DARK STRANGER REVEALED

While sheltered in the clan's stronghold, Syssi is unaware that Kian and Amanda are not human, and neither are the supposedly religious fanatics that are after her. She feels a powerful connection to Kian, and as he introduces her to a world of pleasure she never dared imagine, his dominant sexuality is a revelation. Considering that she's completely out of her element, Syssi feels comfortable and safe letting go with him. That is, until she begins to suspect that all is not as it seems. Piecing the puzzle together, she draws a scary, yet wrong conclusion...

3: DARK STRANGER IMMORTAL

When Kian confesses his true nature, Syssi is not as much shocked by the revelation as she is wounded by what she perceives as his callous plans for her.

If she doesn't turn, he'll be forced to erase her memories and let her go. His family's safety demands secrecy – no one in the mortal world is allowed to know that immortals exist.

Resigned to the cruel reality that even if she stays on to never again leave the keep, she'll get old while Kian won't, Syssi is determined to enjoy what little time she has with him, one day at a time.

Can Kian let go of the mortal woman he loves? Will Syssi turn? And if she does, will she survive the dangerous transition?

4: DARK ENEMY TAKEN

Dalhu can't believe his luck when he stumbles upon the beautiful immortal professor. Presented with a once in a lifetime opportunity to grab an immortal female for himself, he kidnaps her and runs. If he ever gets caught, either by her people or his, his life is forfeit. But for a chance of a loving mate and a family of his own, Dalhu is prepared to do everything in his power to win Amanda's heart, and that includes leaving the Doom brotherhood and his old life behind.

Amanda soon discovers that there is more to the handsome Doomer than his dark past and a hulking, sexy body. But succumbing to her enemy's seduction, or worse, developing feelings for a ruthless killer is out of the question. No man is worth life on the run, not even the one and only immortal male she could claim as her own...

Her clan and her research must come first...

5: Dark Enemy Captive

When the rescue team returns with Amanda and the chained Dalhu to the keep, Amanda is not as thrilled to be back as she thought she'd be. Between Kian's contempt for her and Dalhu's imprisonment, Amanda's budding relationship with Dalhu seems doomed. Things start to look up when Annani offers her help, and together with Syssi they resolve to find a way for Amanda to be with Dalhu. But will she still want him when she realizes that he is responsible for her nephew's murder? Could she? Will she take the easy way out and choose Andrew instead?

6: Dark Enemy Redeemed

Amanda suspects that something fishy is going on onboard the Anna. But when her investigation of the peculiar all-female Russian crew fails to uncover anything other than more speculation, she decides it's time to stop playing detective and face her real problem—a man she shouldn't want but can't live without.

6.5: My Dark Amazon

When Michael and Kri fight off a gang of humans, Michael gets stabbed. The injury to his immortal body recovers fast, but the one to his ego takes longer, putting a strain on his relationship with Kri.

7: Dark Warrior Mine

When Andrew is forced to retire from active duty, he believes that all he has to look forward to is a boring desk job. His glory days in special ops are over. But as it turns out, his thrill ride has just begun. Andrew discovers not only that immortals exist and have been manipulating global affairs since antiquity, but that he and his sister are rare possessors of the immortal genes.

Problem is, Andrew might be too old to attempt the activation process. His sister, who is fourteen years his junior, barely made it through the transition, so the odds of him coming out of it alive, let alone immortal, are slim.

But fate may force his hand.

Helping a friend find his long-lost daughter, Andrew finds a woman who's worth taking the risk for. Nathalie might be a Dormant, but the only way to find out for sure requires fangs and venom.

8: Dark Warrior's Promise

Andrew and Nathalie's love flourishes, but the secrets they keep from each other taint their relationship with doubts and suspicions. In the meantime, Sebastian and his men are getting bolder, and the storm that's brewing will shift the balance of power in the millennia-old conflict between Annani's clan and its enemies.

9: Dark Warrior's Destiny

The new ghost in Nathalie's head remembers who he was in life, providing Andrew and her with indisputable proof that he is real and not a figment of her imagination.

Convinced that she is a Dormant, Andrew decides to go forward with his transition immediately after the rescue mission at the Doomers' HQ.

Fearing for his life, Nathalie pleads with him to reconsider. She'd rather spend the rest of her mortal days with Andrew than risk what they have for the fickle promise of immortality.

While the clan gets ready for battle, Carol gets help from an unlikely ally. Sebastian's second-in-command can no longer ignore the torment she suffers at the hands of his commander and offers to help her, but only if she agrees to his terms.

10: Dark Warrior's Legacy

Andrew's acclimation to his post-transition body isn't easy. His senses are sharper, he's bigger, stronger, and hungrier. Nathalie fears that the changes in the man she loves are more than physical. Measuring up to this new version of him is going to be a challenge.

Carol and Robert are disillusioned with each other. They are not destined mates, and love is not on the horizon. When Robert's three months are up, he might be left with nothing to show for his sacrifice.

Lana contacts Anandur with disturbing news; the yacht and its human cargo are in Mexico. Kian must find a way to apprehend Alex and rescue the women on board without causing an international incident.

11: Dark Guardian Found

What would you do if you stopped aging?

Eva runs. The ex-DEA agent doesn't know what caused her strange mutation, only that if discovered, she'll be dissected like a lab rat. What Eva doesn't know, though, is that she's a descendant of the gods, and that she is not alone. The man who rocked her world in one life-changing encounter over thirty years ago is an immortal as well.

To keep his people's existence secret, Bhathian was forced to turn his back on the only woman who ever captured his heart, but he's never forgotten and never stopped looking for her.

12: Dark Guardian Craved

Cautious after a lifetime of disappointments, Eva is mistrustful of

Bhathian's professed feelings of love. She accepts him as a lover and a confidant but not as a life partner.

Jackson suspects that Tessa is his true love mate, but unless she overcomes her fears, he might never find out.

Carol gets an offer she can't refuse—a chance to prove that there is more to her than meets the eye. Robert believes she's about to commit a deadly mistake, but when he tries to dissuade her, she tells him to leave.

13: DARK GUARDIAN'S MATE

Prepare for the heart-warming culmination of Eva and Bhathian's story!

14: DARK ANGEL'S OBSESSION

The cold and stoic warrior is an enigma even to those closest to him. His secrets are about to unravel...

15: DARK ANGEL'S SEDUCTION

Brundar is fighting a losing battle. Calypso is slowly chipping away his icy armor from the outside, while his need for her is melting it from the inside.

He can't allow it to happen. Calypso is a human with none of the Dormant indicators. There is no way he can keep her for more than a few weeks.

16: DARK ANGEL'S SURRENDER

Get ready for the heart pounding conclusion to Brundar and Calypso's story.

Callie still couldn't wrap her head around it, nor could she summon even a smidgen of sorrow or regret. After all, she had some memories with him that weren't horrible. She should've felt something. But there was nothing, not even shock. Not even horror at what had transpired over the last couple of hours.

Maybe it was a typical response for survivors--feeling euphoric for the simple reason that they were alive. Especially when that survival was nothing short of miraculous.

Brundar's cold hand closed around hers, reminding her that they weren't out of the woods yet. Her injuries were superficial, and the most she had to worry about was some scarring. But, despite his and Anandur's reassurances, Brundar might never walk again.

If he ended up crippled because of her, she would never forgive herself for getting him involved in her crap.

"Are you okay, sweetling? Are you in pain?" Brundar asked.

Her injuries were nothing compared to his, and yet he was concerned about her. God, she loved this man. The thing was, if she told him that, he would run off, or crawl away as was the case.

Hey, maybe this was the perfect opportunity to spring it on him.

17: DARK OPERATIVE: A SHADOW OF DEATH

As a brilliant strategist and the only human entrusted with the secret of immortals' existence, Turner is both an asset and a liability to the clan. His request to attempt transition into immortality as an alternative to cancer treatments cannot be denied without risking the clan's exposure. On the other hand, approving it means risking his premature death. In both scenarios, the clan will lose a valuable ally.

When the decision is left to the clan's physician, Turner makes plans to manipulate her by taking advantage of her interest in him.

Will Bridget fall for the cold, calculated operative? Or will Turner fall into his own trap?

18: DARK OPERATIVE: A GLIMMER OF HOPE

As Turner and Bridget's relationship deepens, living together seems like the right move, but to make it work both need to make concessions.

Bridget is realistic and keeps her expectations low. Turner could never be the truelove mate she yearns for, but he is as good as she's going to get. Other than his emotional limitations, he's perfect in every way.

Turner's hard shell is starting to show cracks. He wants

immortality, he wants to be part of the clan, and he wants Bridget, but he doesn't want to cause her pain.

His options are either abandon his quest for immortality and give Bridget his few remaining decades, or abandon Bridget by going for the transition and most likely dying. His rational mind dictates that he chooses the former, but his gut pulls him toward the latter. Which one is he going to trust?

19: Dark Operative: The Dawn of Love

Get ready for the exciting finale of Bridget and Turner's story!

20: Dark Survivor Awakened

This was a strange new world she had awakened to.

Her memory loss must have been catastrophic because almost nothing was familiar. The language was foreign to her, with only a few words bearing some similarity to the language she thought in. Still, a full moon cycle had passed since her awakening, and little by little she was gaining basic understanding of it--only a few words and phrases, but she was learning more each day.

A week or so ago, a little girl on the street had tugged on her mother's sleeve and pointed at her. "Look, Mama, Wonder Woman!"

The mother smiled apologetically, saying something in the language these people spoke, then scurried away with the child looking behind her shoulder and grinning.

When it happened again with another child on the same day, it was settled.

Wonder Woman must have been the name of someone important in this strange world she had awoken to, and since both times it had been said with a smile it must have been a good one.

Wonder had a nice ring to it.

She just wished she knew what it meant.

21: Dark Survivor Echoes of Love

Wonder's journey continues in *Dark Survivor Echoes of Love*.

22: Dark Survivor Reunited

The exciting finale of Wonder and Anandur's story.

23: Dark Widow's Secret

Vivian and her daughter share a powerful telepathic connection, so when Ella can't be reached by conventional or psychic means, her mother fears the worst.

Help arrives from an unexpected source when Vivian gets a call from the young doctor she met at a psychic convention. Turns out Julian belongs to a private organization specializing in retrieving missing girls.

As Julian's clan mobilizes its considerable resources to rescue the daughter, Magnus is charged with keeping the gorgeous young mother safe.

Worry for Ella and the secrets Vivian and Magnus keep from each other should be enough to prevent the sparks of attraction from kindling a blaze of desire. Except, these pesky sparks have a mind of their own.

24: Dark Widow's Curse

A simple rescue operation turns into mission impossible when the Russian mafia gets involved. Bad things are supposed to come in threes, but in Vivian's case, it seems like there is no limit to bad luck. Her family and everyone who gets close to her is affected by her curse.

Will Magnus and his people prove her wrong?

25: Dark Widow's Blessing

The thrilling finale of the Dark Widow trilogy!

26: Dark Dream's Temptation

Julian has known Ella is the one for him from the moment he saw her picture, but when he finally frees her from captivity, she seems indifferent to him. Could he have been mistaken?

Ella's rescue should've ended that chapter in her life, but it seems like the road back to normalcy has just begun and it's full of obstacles. Between the pitying looks she gets and her mother's attempts to get her into therapy, Ella feels like she's typecast as a victim, when nothing could be further from the truth. She's a tough survivor, and she's going to prove it.

Strangely, the only one who seems to understand is Logan, who keeps popping up in her dreams. But then, he's a figment of her imagination—or is he?

27: Dark Dream's Unraveling

While trying to figure out a way around Logan's silencing compulsion, Ella concocts an ambitious plan. What if instead of trying to keep him out of her dreams, she could pretend to like him and lure him into a trap?

Catching Navuh's son would be a major boon for the clan, as well as for Ella. She will have her revenge, turning the tables on another scumbag out to get her.

28: Dark Dream's Trap

The trap is set, but who is the hunter and who is the prey? Find out in this heart-pounding conclusion to the *Dark Dream* trilogy.

29: Dark Prince's Enigma

As the son of the most dangerous male on the planet, Lokan lives by three rules:

Don't trust a soul.

Don't show emotions.

And don't get attached.

Will one extraordinary woman make him break all three?

30: Dark Prince's Dilemma

Will Kian decide that the benefits of trusting Lokan outweigh the risks?

Will Lokan betray his father and brothers for the greater good of his people?

Are Carol and Lokan true-love mates, or is one of them playing the other?

So many questions, the path ahead is anything but clear.

31: Dark Prince's Agenda

While Turner and Kian work out the details of Areana's rescue plan, Carol and Lokan's tumultuous relationship hits another snag. Is it a sign of things to come?

32 : Dark Queen's Quest

A former beauty queen, a retired undercover agent, and a successful model, Mey is not the typical damsel in distress. But when her sister drops off the radar and then someone starts following her around, she panics.

Following a vague clue that Kalugal might be in New York, Kian sends a team headed by Yamanu to search for him.

As Mey and Yamanu's paths cross, he offers her his help and protection, but will that be all?

33: Dark Queen's Knight

As the only member of his clan with a godlike power over human minds, Yamanu has been shielding his people for centuries, but that power comes at a steep price. When Mey enters his life, he's faced with the most difficult choice.

The safety of his clan or a future with his fated mate.

34: Dark Queen's Army

As Mey anxiously waits for her transition to begin and for Yamanu to test whether his godlike powers are gone, the clan sets out to solve two mysteries:

Where is Jin, and is she there voluntarily?

Where is Kalugal, and what is he up to?

35: Dark Spy Conscripted

Jin possesses a unique paranormal ability. Just by touching someone, she can insert a mental hook into their psyche and tie a string of her consciousness to it, creating a tether. That doesn't make her a spy, though, not unless her talent is discovered by those seeking to exploit it.

36: Dark Spy's Mission

Jin's first spying mission is supposed to be easy. Walk into the club, touch Kalugal to tether her consciousness to him, and walk out.

Except, they should have known better.

37: Dark Spy's Resolution

The best-laid plans often go awry...

38: Dark Overlord New Horizon

Jacki has two talents that set her apart from the rest of the human race.

She has unpredictable glimpses of other people's futures, and she is immune to mind manipulation.

Unfortunately, both talents are pretty useless for finding a job other than the one she had in the government's paranormal division.

It seemed like a sweet deal, until she found out that the director planned on producing super babies by compelling the recruits into pairing up. When an opportunity to escape the program presented itself, she took it, only to find out that humans are not at the top of the food chain.

Immortals are real, and at the very top of the hierarchy is Kalugal, the most powerful, arrogant, and sexiest male she has ever met.

With one look, he sets her blood on fire, but Jacki is not a fool. A man like him will never think of her as anything more than a tasty snack, while she will never settle for anything less than his heart.

39: Dark Overlord's Wife

Jacki is still clinging to her all-or-nothing policy, but Kalugal is chipping away at her resistance. Perhaps it's time to ease up on her convictions. A little less than all is still much better than nothing, and a couple of decades with a demigod is probably worth more than a lifetime with a mere mortal.

THE PERFECT MATCH SERIES

PERFECT MATCH 1: VAMPIRE'S CONSORT

When Gabriel's company is ready to start beta testing, he invites his old crush to inspect its medical safety protocol.

Curious about the revolutionary technology of the *Perfect Match Virtual Fantasy-Fulfillment studios*, Brenna agrees.

Neither expects to end up partnering for its first fully immersive test run.

PERFECT MATCH 2: KING'S CHOSEN

When Lisa's nutty friends get her a gift certificate to *Perfect Match Virtual Fantasy Studios*, she has no intentions of using it. But since the only way to get a refund is if no partner can be found for her, she makes sure to request a fantasy so girly and over the top that no sane guy will pick it up.

Except, someone does.

Warning: This fantasy contains a hot, domineering

crown prince, sweet insta-love, steamy love scenes painted with light shades of gray, a wedding, and a HEA in both the virtual and real worlds.

Intended for mature audience.

PERFECT MATCH 3: CAPTAIN'S CONQUEST

Working as a Starbucks barista, Alicia fends off flirting all day long, but none of the guys are as charming and sexy as Gregg. His frequent visits are the highlight of her day, but since he's never asked her out, she assumes he's taken. Besides, between a day job and a budding music career, she has no time to start a new relationship.

That is until Gregg makes her an offer she can't refuse —a gift certificate to the virtual fantasy fulfillment service everyone is talking about. As a huge Star Trek fan, Alicia has a perfect match in mind—the captain of the Starship Enterprise.

FOR EXCLUSIVE PEEKS AT UPCOMING RELEASES & A FREE COMPANION BOOK

Made in the USA
Coppell, TX
11 May 2020

25138856R00184